HOLLER WHISPERS

A Joe Turner Mystery

T.L. BEQUETTE

Black Rose Writing | Texas

This is a work of fiction. Names, characters, businesses, places, events, and incidents are either the products of the author's imagination or used in a fictitious manner. Any resemblance to actual persons, living or dead, or actual events is purely coincidental.

ISBN: 978-1-68513-725-0
LIBRARY OF CONGRESS CONTROL NUMBER: 2025946231
PUBLISHED BY BLACK ROSE WRITING
www.blackrosewriting.com

Printed in the United States of America
Suggested Retail Price (SRP) $21.95

Holler Whispers is printed in Baskerville

*As a planet-friendly publisher, Black Rose Writing does its best to eliminate unnecessary waste to reduce paper usage and energy costs, while never compromising the reading experience. As a result, the final word count vs. page count may not meet common expectations.

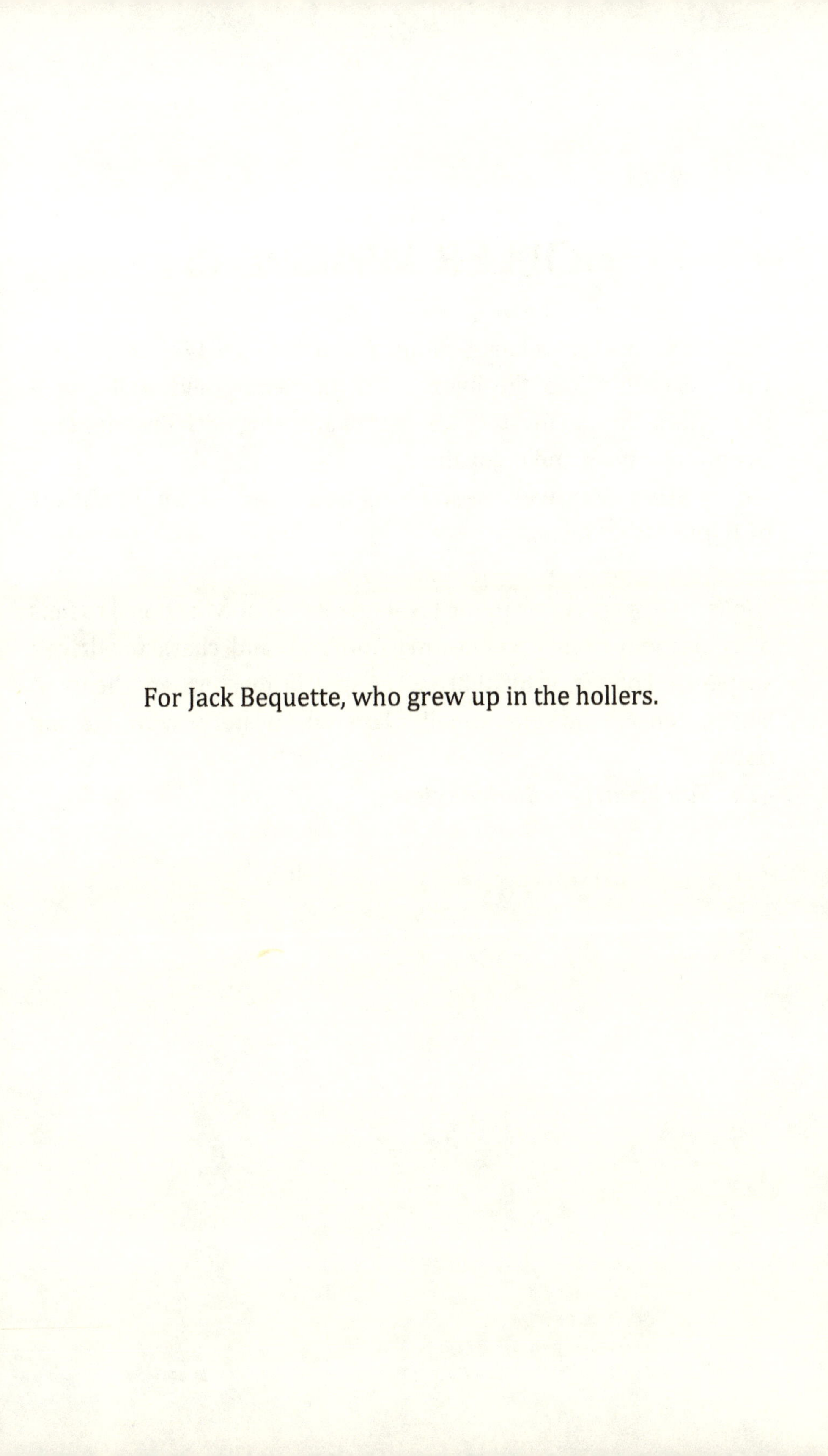For Jack Bequette, who grew up in the hollers.

Praise for
HOLLER WHISPERS

"A legal drama that's part Southern fiction, *Holler Whispers* draws you inexorably into the lives of its interesting and well-drawn characters. But the mystery keeps you guessing until the very end. Deeply satisfying and enjoyable."
–Mary Ellen Bramwell, bestselling and award-winning author of *When I Was Seven.*

"*Holler Whispers* is a gripping legal mystery that will appeal to fans of courtroom drama, small-town intrigue, and character-driven suspense. For me, it hit that sweet spot of mystery and heart. A smart, tense, and emotionally layered mystery with staying power."
–*The San Francisco Book Review*

HOLLER WHISPERS

CHAPTER 1

I have a session later, and I'm dreading it.

The worst thing is when they want me to talk about what I'm feeling. A doctor enters the room, smiling for no reason. If they're new, they switch on a blinding light and speak to me very loudly then wonder why I squint and cover my ears.

Their questions are always the same. "How are you, Carl? How do you feel, Carl? Are you doing okay, Carl?" Or my favorite, "You good, Carl?" Am I good? Good at what? I suppose they mean to inquire if I am well. And what is it with the adult obsession with repeating my first name? Who else could they be talking to? Only two of us are in the room.

But their overriding obsession is knowing precisely what I am feeling, which isn't easy to describe, by the way. If I'm not sick or cold or hot, what am I expected to say? That I feel the cool metal chair on the back of my legs or the smooth glass of the coffee table in front of me? Why in the world do they need to know any of that?

Eventually, they ask about the Cubs, my favorite baseball team. Either that or I'd just begin talking about them, intentionally unresponsive to their questions.

Since they seem intent on hearing from me, I might as well talk about something I like.

The Chicago Cubs. Founded in 1876 as a charter member of the National League. Of course, their original name was the White Stockings. If you're a true fan of the team, you know this. My brother James knew this, but he is deceased. At first, they told me he passed on, but then later I was told he was dead. I wish people would say what they mean. It would be much more helpful.

Anyway, at least when I'm talking, their voices aren't knifing at my ears, and I'm not expected to squint through the bright lights at their faces. Those faces, contorted with smiles for no reason, emitting impossible-to-answer, ear-splitting questions about my feelings.

Until then, though, I can relax alone in the dim light and be calmed by thoughts about the Cubs. They're playing the Reds today. Reynolds is pitching, which would normally be good, but he struggles in day games against teams with left-handed power. Of course, if you're a true fan of the team, you know this.

CHAPTER 2

Joe Turner sipped his coffee from the brown ceramic cup and looked up from the local paper, scanning the diner from under the bill of his Red Sox cap. Unlike the retro diners that were popping up all over San Francisco, this one in Barton, Georgia, was the real thing, complete with round bar stools aligned entirely too close together.

He sat at the blue vinyl booth, forearms resting on cool Formica, on the advice of his colorful investigator, Chuck Argenal. "If you want to know Barton," he'd said, "sit a spell with the *Herald* at Nadine's."

More specifically, Joe was in the small town—somewhere he'd never been—to defend Chuck's nephew, one Stanley Carl Ledbetter, who was accused of murder.

Chuck had told him that Stanley, who went by Carl, was autistic. The eighteen-year-old, who held an honorary title as the Barton High School football team's equipment manager, was accused of shooting a team member. According to Chuck, who spoke in a mix of Southern idioms and movie lines, Carl's defense would be funded by his father, Chuck's brother, who had "made more money than you can shake a stick at." Carl was currently out of custody pending trial, his family having posted the one-million-dollar cash bond.

So far, Chuck had been right about one thing. In his brief time in the diner, he'd learned a lot. Mainly that Chuck had left out some important facts. Half of the entire front page of the *Herald* was dedicated to a story about the murder, or more accurately, how the high school football team—the town's beloved Steelers—would survive without their star quarterback, the victim of the murder.

The decor in Nadine's was also instructive. The interior was painted blue and gray, the team's colors. A mural of the town's old steel mill, the origin of the team's mascot, dominated one wall. "High Bar," presumably the team's slogan, was emblazoned on the wall behind the counter, and a Steelers football helmet rested atop an elaborate pie display.

Joe grabbed his phone and texted Chuck. —*Really, Chuck, the high school quarterback????*

"More coffee, hon?" Joe hadn't noticed the server with the beehive hairdo approach.

"No, thank you." The server paused before walking away, as if contemplating a question for her customer.

—*Oops. Guess I failed to mention that.*

At the counter across from his booth, where two men had been talking football, the word "trial" caught Joe's attention.

"Word is the Ledbetter's are hiring some fancy-ass attorney from New York or San Francisco."

His friend snorted. "Typical Ledbetter. Just throw money at the problem. Tall cotton can't save 'em this time. I heard that loopy kid confessed."

"I heard that too. Hey, how do you reckon the defense is going to be this year? That Kirby kid is a helluva linebacker…"

CHAPTER 3

The statuesque woman in the stylish sun dress and hat stood in the doorway across from Joe, flared nostrils betraying her disgust as she surveyed the small office.

Joe stood to greet his guest. "You must be Aubrey Ledbetter," he said, for a moment picturing himself in a Mickey Spillane novel.

"Hello," the woman said pleasantly, extending a hand across the desk.

"I'm Joe. Please sit down."

Ms. Ledbetter removed a frilly handkerchief from a designer shoulder bag and unfolded it. "Mr. Turner," she began in a soft Southern drawl, "I really must apologize for the condition of this office. My cousin is our family attorney, and he's semi-retired. Apparently, he's not here much. This dust is appalling," she added as she spread the cloth across the seat of a leather armchair before gingerly sitting down.

"Please, call me Joe. And the office is fine. Thank you for providing it. And the lovely Victorian. I'll probably work there most of the time."

Ms. Ledbetter produced a thick manila envelope from her bag. "Thanks for meeting me. I just thought I'd get this in your hands as soon as possible," she said, handing it to Joe. "They're the police reports in Carl's case."

Joe looked confused. "Police reports?" With the homicide less than a week old, the police would never release the reports to the public at this stage. "How did you…" he asked, his voice trailing off as he opened the envelope.

"Oh, we've always been strong supporters of the police department here in town. Ironically, I suppose. Anyway, I hope you find them helpful."

"Thank you," Joe said, feeling vaguely sleazy. "I didn't expect to have these until I went to court."

"Also, I wanted to tell you a few things about my son. I know you're aware of his diagnosis, but before you sit down with him, I wanted to prepare you a bit."

"Sure," Joe said, subconsciously smoothing the wrinkles from his T-shirt. "That would be helpful. By the way, please pardon my appearance."

"Don't be silly," his guest said, her eyes quickly moving over Joe's clothing. "You're working on a Sunday. Of course, you're going to be comfortable. I've just come from church. Are you a Christian, dear?" she asked. "I shouldn't pry, but you're certainly welcome to attend when you're here."

"Oh, I'll probably be working most weekends," Joe said. "Trials can sort of take over your life. That," he added after a pause, "and I'm an atheist," having decided to answer her question after all.

Aubrey was silent for several seconds, her face frozen in a smile. "So, before I forget," she said, after a deep breath to refocus, "I have some questions about the jury selection process. Is the jury pool entirely local?"

"Oh, we'll both have to find out about that," Joe said, thinking it an odd question. "Every jurisdiction has different rules. So, about Carl?"

"My son is on the autistic spectrum, but he is high-functioning. For him, that means he doesn't relate well to people socially. Often, Carl doesn't express appropriate emotions. Ironically, he is extremely empathetic. So empathetic that tracking other people's emotions is just too intense, too overwhelming for him. So he avoids eye contact, social cues, and buries himself in his own thoughts."

"That must be challenging."

"It is. Carl has emotions just like everyone else but has no outlet for them. He has therapy sessions twice a week. He despises them, but all his doctors say the more he talks, the better, no matter what the topic. Apparently, it helps with his anxiety.

"Of course, one benefit is you never have to guess what Carl is thinking. He is blatantly honest. He says exactly what he thinks with no filter. Sounds like you might appreciate that," she said, and the two exchanged smiles. "Also, Carl is very literal. Most humor is lost on him. He's not unintelligent—he's a whiz at figures—but sarcasm just doesn't register."

"Got it," Joe said, nodding. "I've read up on autism, but this is very helpful."

She forced a smile, acknowledging his effort with a slight nod. "Just be aware that the saying goes, 'If you know one person with autism, you know one person with autism,' meaning each person is different in how their autism is manifest, much like you and I are different."

"Yes, of course," Joe said, feeling put in his place.

Her eyes gave away the faintest hint of victory before she continued. "Carl is a lot, as they say. Sometimes his mind gets stuck in a loop. It's hard to explain. Like the other day, I asked him what flavor of ice cream he liked the best. He began to concentrate, and I could see him imagining every possible flavor. I left the room and came back to call him for dinner a full hour later, and there he was, deep in thought. He told me he hadn't decided on a favorite flavor yet."

"I'm guessing he's often misunderstood?"

Ms. Ledbetter closed her eyes and nodded. "I can't tell you how many apologies I've had to make for a perceived slight or flat-out insult. Once the preacher made the mistake of asking Carl how he liked the sermon. Carl told him he didn't know because he had his earbuds in, listening to the Cubs game." Joe laughed. "And, by the way, in case you want to get him talking, Carl has two passions in his life, and not much else matters to him. The Chicago Cubs is one."

"Really?"

"Oh, my Lord. Carl's first name is Stanley, but he goes by his middle name because the most famous player on the Cubs' rival team, the St. Louis Cardinals, was Stan Musial."

"Wow, that is a commitment."

"Anyway, his other passion is the Barton High football team."

"So, I take it he loved being a team manager."

"Absolutely loved it. I don't think he actually did a whole lot. He was almost like more of a mascot. To his dad, of course, being a former Steeler, it was tough to watch him be sort of a gimmick. But the players were mostly good to him, and it was just the best thing for him.

"You'll also notice that Carl speaks very formally. That's very common with autism. And he rocks his torso back and forth when he's nervous. You'll see other little habits, some charming, some not."

"You mentioned Carl's seizures when we spoke on the phone. How often do they occur?"

"A couple times a month, I'd say. He had a seizure just a day before that party when…when the shooting happened," Ms. Ledbetter said awkwardly. "Carl was home alone when he had his seizure, so we met him at the hospital. All he could think of was whether I was going to let him attend that party." She paused and sighed. "I should have kept him home," she said quietly, dabbing her eyes with a tissue.

"I'm sure the decision made sense at the time," Joe said, offering another tissue from a box on the desk. He hated this part of his job.

"Well," Ms. Ledbetter said, managing a smile, "I've taken up entirely too much of your time, but we'd love to have you out to Bellcrest. That's our estate just north of here. You can meet Carl and get a good southern meal in you."

"I'd like that. Thanks." She stood and walked to the door then paused.

"Was there something else, Ms. Ledbetter?"

She sighed. "Mr. Turner, we lost our first son to cancer. Carl is all we have left."

Joe nodded. "I'll do my best," he said solemnly.

"And I'll leave you with this, Joe Turner. I'm sure you've heard this a lot, but I know my Carl. He couldn't have done this. He wouldn't have taken a life."

They exchanged goodbyes, and Joe collapsed in his chair. Reaching behind his desk where he'd been happy to find a small refrigerator, he grabbed a beer and cracked it with the opener on his keychain. "Yeah," he said to himself after a long drink, "I do get that a lot."

CHAPTER 4

After his meeting with Aubrey Ledbetter, Joe headed for his temporary home, the Victorian provided by his client's family. He walked north on Maple Street, the main drag in the town of four thousand that appeared to be stuck in the nineteen fifties. A barber pole spun outside the descriptively named Barton Barbershop, and an American flag flapped in the soft breeze outside Breymer's Hardware.

Most businesses displayed navy and gray placards proclaiming "Steeler Pride" and "High Bar," the latter also painted on the water tower in the town square. Joe had also thought he'd heard locals saying, "High bar," to one another as a greeting.

Joe crossed First Street and happened upon a small, windowless office between Sweet Sally's Bakery and the Post Office. The hand-painted sign on the door caught his attention. PICKLER INVESTIGATIONS. Bubba Pickler had been recommended by Chuck. More accurately, he'd been identified as the only licensed investigator in Barton.

Joe took a chance and knocked. After a time, he heard footsteps before the door opened to reveal a large man who, from all appearances, appeared to have just awoken. His rotund physique was stuffed into a rumpled beige suit. Most of his shirt tail was out, and leather suspenders strained against his belly. A yellow paisley tie hung loosely around his neck.

He squinted into the sunlight from the dark room. "How can I help you, sir?"

"Sorry to pop in unannounced, Mr. Pickler. I'm Joe Turner. We spoke on the phone about the Ledbetter case."

"Oh yeah," he said, rubbing his face with a thick hand. "I'm afraid you caught me catching up on my shuteye after an all-night stakeout. C'mon in," he said, clicking a light. Joe followed him into the one-room office. "Have a seat," he said, gesturing to two chairs, each covered with files and newspapers. Pickler ambled behind his desk and eased himself into a large leather chair, no doubt the site of his shuteye. "So, you got the short straw representing the Ledbetter kid?"

"Which is why I need a good investigator," Joe said, sitting on the edge of a chair.

Pickler sighed, resting folded hands on his belly. "More like an act of God," he said. "I heard he confessed."

"That seems to be the scuttlebutt, but I'm not sure how anyone would know yet."

The big man shrugged. "Holler whispers, I s'pose. Where is it you're from, Mr. Turner? New York?"

"San Francisco."

"Well," he said, ignoring the correction, "Barton's not New York. More than likely, that information came from Linda McCain, the secretary in the DA's office or Officer Simpkin's wife, who runs a salon over on Maple. Could have even been Judge Boniface himself. He plays golf with the football coaches, and they tend to know things first."

"I see your point, Mr. Pickler. It's a small town. I don't think I had appreciated the importance of the football angle. The victim being the team's star quarterback…" Joe hesitated.

"Probably means your client can't get a fair trial." His matter-of-fact tone was unsettling. "Here in Barton, we only got two sports, football and preseason football."

"I've noticed. By the way, what's the significance of the 'High Bar' slogan?"

Pickler took a pouch of tobacco from his desk and put a brown wad in his cheek. "Started in the fifties after Barton had just won the first state championship. Back when the mill was running, 'high bar' used to be a steel mill industry term for perfectly forged steel. It was a rallying cry for the team. Over time, it became a phrase people just said to one another, like howdy. I reckon the Auburn Tigers have their 'war eagle,' Ole Miss their 'hotty toddy,' and we got our 'high bar.'"

Joe was nodding. "That makes sense. I was beginning to think half the town was named Bart."

"Yeah, you got your work cut out for you." Pickler leaned to his right to release a stream of brown saliva into a brass bowl on the floor. "Your client being a Ledbetter doesn't help," he added.

"The family seems very prosperous. Is there resentment?"

"I never had a problem with them." Pickler shrugged, and Joe sensed the opposite. "They tend to throw their weight around a bit. No offense, but hiring an out-of-town attorney, for example."

"No offense taken, but it sounds like you might be hard pressed to find a local attorney who would take the case." Pickler nodded, acknowledging his point. "So, Mr. Pickler, it sounds like your local knowledge would be very helpful to me. Are you interested in working for the defense team?"

The private eye reclined in his chair and rubbed his face. "Mr. Turner, you seem like you'd be great to work for, and God knows I could use the money, but I just don't think I'm up for the headache." He reached into a jacket pocket and placed a business card on his desk in front of Joe. "But if you run into any roadblocks you can't get around, give me a call."

Joe stood. "Okay. Anyone you'd recommend?"

"The only other P.I. in town is Harrick, over on Elm, but he's crooked," he said, walking Joe to the door. "Maybe try over in Millington, the next town to the east. At least he won't be a Steelers fan."

"Thanks again," Joe said, and the two shook hands.

"Hey, tell me, Mr. Turner," Pickler said as Joe was turning to leave, "have the Ledbetters asked any questions about the jury selection process?"

Joe smiled and looked the investigator in the eye. "No," he said, holding his stare. "What a strange thing to ask."

CHAPTER 5

Day One

"This sucks." The stout man crossed his thick forearms and leaned back, exhaling as his eyes moved to the ceiling.

"I think that's all of us," Jack Painter said, a bit too cheerfully as the last in line filed into the small room and took seats around a rectangular table.

"Wow. This is all so much, isn't it?" the schoolteacher asked no one in particular.

"It is quite something, indeed," the Indian woman to her right agreed. "I'm relieved we can finally talk about the case. I'm Priya Manjeer, by the way," the engineer said, nodding a greeting.

"Pleasure. Ellen Graves."

"They really cram you in here, don't they?" the big man muttered to himself, wriggling in his seat as he glanced around the room. The table and chairs took up most of the space, reaching to within a few feet of the walls on all sides. A whiteboard ran the length of one long wall.

"Are you claustrophobic?" Priya asked from across the table, getting a blank stare in return. "It's a fear of…"

"I'm allergic to wasting time," came the gruff reply.

Priya arched her eyebrows and glanced at her new friend.

"Hey," Jack called from the end of the table, still chipper, "I'm just talking here, but I thought as a first step, we might go around the room and introduce ourselves." No one answered. "Great," he continued, undaunted. "I'm…"

"I'll go," the big man cut in. "I'm Dirk Pinion. I'm a construction foreman. And by the way, he's guilty. Next," he said, gesturing to the older man to his left with perfect posture and a crew cut.

"I'm Frank Burleson, United States Navy, retired," he said formally, his raspy voice recalling John Wayne.

To Burleson's left, at the end of the table, a slender young man slouched in his seat and slowly turned to face the wall. He placed a hand to his forehead, as if shielding himself from the group's stares. "I'm Quinn," he mumbled.

After a few awkward moments of wondering if Quinn was finished, the petite woman next to him spoke up. "I'm Sara Epstein," she said, tucking a lock of blue hair behind her ear. "I'm a social worker and a homeless advocate, and I'm here to make sure the defendant gets a fair trial," she added with a steely glare at Dirk, who snorted audibly and rolled his eyes.

"My name is Elston Arbett." The distinguished black man seated across from Burleson straightened his tie. "I'm a retired tax attorney."

To his left, the engineer, Priya, introduced herself. Next was Ellen, the soft-spoken schoolteacher, who mentioned again that she felt overwhelmed.

"And how about you?" Jack asked from the end of the table, gesturing to a man in his twenties on his left.

"Wait, why don't you go?" asked Sara, from the other end of the table, sounding annoyed.

"Excuse me?" asked Jack, his fake smile losing warmth.

"We're going around the room, right?" asked the social worker. "Why wouldn't you go next?"

"Okaay." Jack scanned the room for sympathetic faces. "I'm Jack Painter. I'm a bit of a jack-of-all-trades, I suppose," he said, embarking on a well-practiced spiel. "Right now, I'm running the Echo Insurance agency here in town."

"And I'm Duncan Morris," the young man to Jack's left said with a wave. "I'm a paramedic. But I thought about teaching." He smiled across the table at Ellen.

"So, I believe the jury instruction said we should choose a foreman," Jack said to the group.

"Foreperson, actually," Sara corrected.

"Of course, of course," Jack said, still beaming. "Actually, Elston, since you're an attorney, I was going to suggest you take that role."

"Were you listening yesterday?" Elston asked, slowing shaking his head with a dour expression. "I told you I was a tax attorney. I'll pass."

"Okay, any volunteers?" Jack asked. There was silence as all nine at the table averted their eyes. "Ellen, how about you? I think the job is mainly about keeping the discussion on the rails. With your teaching experience, you'd be perfect."

"Oh, I couldn't," she said. "This is all too much for me."

More silence followed. Jack glanced at the clock on the wall above the whiteboard. "Well gang, it's 5:00 p.m. I guess we'll reconvene …"

"Dude," Sara cut in, exasperated. "It's so painfully obvious to everyone here that you're desperate to be the foreperson. So just do it already."

Jack looked around the group with palms up. "Huh?"

Sara rolled her eyes. "Oh, please. Your suggestions for foreperson were someone who had apparently already told you he wouldn't do it, and no offense—is it Ellen?—the person least likely to agree to it. But no one objects, am I right?" Sara asked, looking around the table. "Good. Congrats, Jack! Your relentlessly positive campaign of ass-kissing worked. You, Jack Painter, are the foreperson."

CHAPTER 6

Later that evening, Joe decided on a run to clear his head and acquaint himself with Barton. He found a trail that ran along the edge of the Mulberry River. Beyond the river lay the hollers, as the locals referred to them—a maze of dark and narrow canyons canopied by pine, ash, and gum trees. According to Chuck, the hollers were inhabited by generations of hillbillies who lived off the grid. Beyond the hollers, the Oconee National Forest stretched half-way across the state.

Joe passed a few other runners and cyclists on the trail, all nodding friendly greetings of, "Hey," and, "High bar." He decided against music, enjoying the quiet and the occasional sounds of wildlife. Opting for a playlist for the last mile, he was fumbling with his earbuds as he passed a slower runner at a bend in the trail. He saw the oncoming bicycle in the nick of time and dodged to his right to avoid it. Its rider, a white-haired man with a headband, came out of his pedals. His bike veered off the trail, riding into a bush at low speed.

Joe approached, preparing an apology.

"Asshole!" the man called behind him, working his way out of the bushes while straddling his bike.

So much for that, Joe thought. "Learn how to ride a bike, fuckhead!" he snapped and turned on his heels to finish the run.

Back home, after recovering, he grabbed his phone and texted Chuck.

—I need an investigator. Pickler is out. So, if you want me to represent your kin, you best hop on the next flight to your backwards-ass hometown quick as a blink and start turning over rocks.

Before he'd finished, Joe was pleased to see Eddy's name pop up on his phone. He'd been dating the archaeologist for almost two years. Whip smart with a wicked sense of humor, she made Joe feel relaxed and excited all at once. And despite Chuck's constant reminders that in the looks department, she was out of Joe's league, he'd stopped worrying about it. So far, the worst part about Barton was missing her.

"Hi, gorgeous woman! How are you?"

"Missing you terribly, Turner."

"Same here. Missin' you somepin fierce."

Eddy laughed. "Listen to you. A drawl already. Seriously, how is it?"

"The people are really friendly." Most people, Joe thought to himself, recalling the cyclist.

"So, should I dye that purple streak out of my hair?"

Joe laughed. "I'm pretty sure it's illegal, but you can wear a cap."

"And the case?"

"Going to be rough. Chuck left out that his nephew killed the town hero. Allegedly."

"Of course."

The two talked for a half hour and made plans for Eddy to visit the following week. She'd taken a research position at Cal last spring and had business at the Southeast Archaeological Center in Tallahassee, Florida.

Later, Joe sat perusing the police reports over a beer and a pizza slice. From *The Barton Herald's* extensive coverage of the murder, he already knew that Justin Holt was shot in his home at about 11:50 p.m. during a football team sleepover party to kick off the season.

The reports, though not as thorough as Joe was used to in a homicide case, were clearly written and professional. Drafted by officers with full knowledge that someday some sleazy defense attorney would be parsing their words, the reports told of a fair investigation that led to one inescapable conclusion: Stanley Carl Ledbetter shot and killed Justin Holt.

CHAPTER 7

August 26, 2025. The Night of the Murder
Police officers, dispatched to the Holt residence at 11:57 p.m., arrived to find most of the team sleeping in the main house, a grand, three-story colonial. A few teammates and Justin's distraught father led veteran officer Darrell Billups to a stand-alone structure in the backyard. Once servants' quarters, it served as Justin's bedroom.

As the officers arrived, paramedics were wheeling the victim out on a gurney to a waiting ambulance. Young Justin, shoeless and shirtless, wearing gray Barton High sweatpants, had suffered a single gunshot wound to his chest. His sister had noticed his open bedroom door and found him.

Finding Justin with a faint pulse, the paramedics worked feverishly to staunch the bleeding and intubate him. On the way to the hospital, he flatlined. The paramedics radioed Officer Billups. It was now a murder investigation.

Police officers and Daulton County deputy sheriffs set up a perimeter and processed the crime scene. All eight members of the Barton Police Department were on hand. They began canvassing the far-flung residences on the country road. As Billups began organizing the investigation, he wondered why no one heard the gunshots.

As Justin's teammates awakened, a sense of disbelief set in. School counselors were summoned, and parents arrived to collect their children. The police interviewed Justin's family and a few teammates, scheduling interviews with others for later in the day. Justin's parents gave the police a list of all the attendees. The couple had taken roll and collected car keys out of concern for drunk driving. The only person unaccounted for was the team manager, Carl Ledbetter, who had been dropped off at the party by his mother.

At the county coroner's officer in neighboring Gridley, orderlies cut off Justin's sweatpants and underwear and vacuumed them for trace evidence. They swabbed his hands for gunshot-residue and clipped his fingernails for DNA testing.

Later in the morning, Deputy Sheriff Dave Neff knocked on the door of Sinclair Lewis, who lived a quarter mile east of the Holts' on Chance Avenue, the country road that wound along the edge of the forest west of town.

Lewis had lived most of his seventy-two years there on his small pig farm. "What's all the ruckus?" he asked from inside his front door.

"Sorry to bother you at this hour, sir. There's been a shooting up at the Holts'. We're just canvassing on the off chance someone saw something."

Stooped and leaning on a cane, Lewis studied the officer, squinting up at him. "Neff," he finally said, reading the deputy's nameplate. "There was a Dell Neff. Used to manage the Ice Burgie."

"No, that's ..."

"Known Dell for years. We used to hunt hogs over in the hollers."

"Well, sir, I don't suppose you heard or saw anything? Would have been a few hours ago."

The old man stroked his chin. "Matter of fact, I did," he said. "I woke up around then to piss. Must have heard the gunshots," he said, pushing open the screen to join the officer on the porch. "I came out in the front room," Lewis said, gesturing through an open window with his cane. He was clearly enjoying the attention. "It's dead quiet out here at nighttime, and I leave the windows open this time of year. Pretty quick, I hear footsteps out on the street. I walk out on my porch, and here comes this guy, jogging right down the middle of the road."

"Could you describe him?"

"Well, he was a medium-sized feller, I'd say."

The deputy waited for more, then prompted the witness. "Height, weight, complexion, hair color, facial hair?"

Lewis shook his head. "No sir, nothing about his appearance really stuck out. But I could identify him if I saw him again. I got a memory for faces," he added, tapping his head with his index finger.

"Which way was he jogging?" Neff asked, now jotting down notes on a pad.

"I'll be damned if he wasn't running north," Lewis said, casting wide eyes toward the officer. "Could damn well have been coming from the Holts'."

CHAPTER 8

As Joe flipped through the pages of the police report, the case against his client took shape. The witness, Lewis, was shown a photograph of Carl and immediately identified him as the jogger. Given the witness's vague description, though, it wasn't the strongest evidence.

Of greater concern was Officer Billups' interaction with Carl later the following morning. Joe wondered if Carl had been home alone when the officer talked to him. Having met Carl's mother, he couldn't imagine her consenting to the interview. The report noted that when asked if he had a reason to want to harm Justin Holt, Carl had refused to answer the question several times. "Yikes," Joe whispered to himself.

After his interview, police technicians swabbed Carl's hands for traces of gunshot residue, the particles of gunpowder and primer that are expelled from the muzzle of a gun. Often landing on a shooter's hands, GSR can be compelling evidence.

Joe's eyes travelled rapidly over the report, falling on a heading on the last page labeled "GSR Findings." Joe grabbed his beer and downed it before reading on. "Carl Ledbetter's hands were each swabbed. The samples were labeled and stored separately. Both the right and left hands tested positive for gunshot residue."

Chapter 9

Joe's shirt stuck to the middle of his back as he climbed the steps of the Daulton County courthouse. He wiped his brow and cursed his decision to make the ten-minute walk to the nondescript three-story building at the north end of town.

"Hot enough for ya?" came a friendly voice from the top of the stairs. The speaker was an attractive woman in her thirties, wearing a tan suit and heels. "You must be Mr. Turner. Melissa Pettigrew," she said, extending a hand. "We spoke on the phone."

"Pleasure. Call me Joe."

"I was just arriving when I saw an unfamiliar face. Figured it was you." To Joe, her drawl seemed sharper and less refined than Aubrey Ledbetter's.

"Yeah," he said, wiping his brow, "I suppose I've got city slicker tattooed on my forehead."

She laughed. "Maybe a little. A proper Southern gentleman would carry a handkerchief, but you're new here."

Joe shrugged. "I'm not proper, Southern, or a gentleman, I'm afraid."

"C'mon and I'll introduce you to Judge Boniface."

Joe followed her into the cool, sterile rectangular building with large opaque windows and a floor of the beige vinyl squares favored in the seventies. "If you pictured a classic Southern courthouse, sorry to disappoint."

"Yeah, not exactly what Harper Lee wrote about. At least it's air-conditioned. So, we already know the judge who'll be trying our case?"

Pettigrew looked at him and smiled. "Only judge in town. There's Commissioner Tuggle up on the third floor who handles traffic cases, but he should stick to traffic, if you know what I mean."

"Not a legal giant?"

"I think he may have a relative who's a paralegal, but I'm not even sure of that."

Joe laughed, relieved that his adversary seemed pleasant.

"Yeah, this used to be the main county courthouse, but now that's over in Beaconsville. This is just a satellite court now. One department. One judge."

"And I assume one DA?"

"Yes, sir. Just me and my assistant."

After a short walk, they arrived at Department One, where a dozen or so people had gathered in the hallway, presumably participants in the morning calendar. Pettigrew unlocked the door, and Joe followed her inside a courtroom that had more character than he'd imagined.

Fold-down theatre-style seats occupied the gallery, likely retrieved from a previous courthouse. The well of the courtroom was spacious, with a traditional jury box, witness stand, and an elevated bench. Above it, a large brass Georgia state seal hung between the state and American flags.

"Hey, Barbara," the DA said, greeting a middle-aged woman at the clerk's desk. She introduced Joe, who followed her toward the judge's chambers.

When they entered, the Honorable Franklin Boniface's large leather office chair faced away from them. It slowly spun toward them to reveal a jarring sight for Joe. He wasn't wearing a headband, but it was definitely the asshole on the bicycle.

CHAPTER 10

August 24, 2025. Two Days Before the Murder
"Carl, any preference on the pizza tonight?" Carl's dad, Matt, waited in silence. "Carl, I know you can hear me. What kind of pizza, bud?"

Across the kitchen island from her husband, Aubrey sat, reading the paper and smiling. "Welcome to my world, honey. There's a Cubs game today. You know how he gets."

"It doesn't start for a half hour," Matt said, exasperated.

"Well, you're clearly not much of a fan." She walked to where Carl sat in the family room, leaned over the couch, and removed the earbuds from her son's ears.

"Oh, hi, Mom."

"Hello, dear. Big game today?"

"Statistically, they all count the same, so I've never understood the term big game. The possible exception is when you play a rival opponent. In that case, the game presents not only an opportunity for a Cubs win but also a loss for said opponent, thus effectuating a full game swing in the standings."

"Pepperoni pizza?"

"Yes, please. And by the way, I've never understood why baseball games are referred to as half games. As in 'the Cubs are two and a half games behind the Cardinals.' The nomenclature should be such that each win or loss is a game since there's no such thing as a half game."

"That's actually interesting, Carl," Matt said. "But the idea is that if one team is 3-1 and another is 2-2, that's the difference of one full game. But if one team is 3-1 and the other is 2-1, it's only a half game."

"But that's the point. It's not a half game. The team that is 2-1 needs to win one full game to be tied. Until then, they should be one game behind. The team that is 2-2 should be said to be two games back of the team that's 3-1, as a tie in the standings would only result if one team won and the other lost, making them both 3-2."

"As usual, you win, Carl."

"Thanks, Dad. Now if you'll excuse me," he said, putting in his earbuds and adjusting his Cubs cap, "I'm missing the pregame show. The radio version is far superior."

"Carl, real quick, hon, before we lose you. The big preseason football party is tomorrow night. I know the team would love you to be there."

"No, Mom. The Cubs have a day game, which might go extra innings. The schedule is on the fridge. If everyone commits it to memory, it will avoid confusion."

CHAPTER 11

"Franklin Boniface," the judge said, standing to extend a hand.

Joe's mind raced, reliving the incident. He'd had his ball cap pulled down low, and hopefully the judge had been more concerned with not crashing. "My pleasure, Judge. Joe Turner." Was it his imagination or did the judge pause slightly, eyeing him.

"Well, Mr. Turner, I hear you're from out of town? New York, is it?"

"Actually, I'm from San Francisco."

"Ah, my wife and I were in the Big Apple just last week," the judge said talking over him, "dropping our daughter off at NYU." Clearly, the town rumor mill had him a New Yorker, and Joe thought he may as well stop denying it.

"Congratulations, NYU is a fine school."

"Well, I think you'll find our little corner of the legal world a comfortable place to practice."

As the judge spoke, Joe took in his chambers. The theme was golf and, not surprisingly, the Barton football team. A helmet rested on a bookshelf behind his desk, and a team photo hung on the wall to his left, under a banner identifying the previous year's state champions.

"So, Melissa, I saw your office indicted, so no need for a preliminary hearing. When do y'all figure we can get this show on the road?"

"Oh, Judge, I don't know. I was thinking two to three weeks?" Pettigrew said, looking Joe's way to include him in the conversation.

"Really?" the judge asked, frowning. "I was thinking more like a week to ten days."

"You don't mean for trial?" Joe asked with genuine disbelief.

"Sure, for trial." Boniface smiled. "We tend not to mess around here, Mr. Turner," the judge said while looking at Pettigrew. "I know it may be a quicker pace than you're used to, but down here in Georgia, we don't waste a lot of time and money. We're not having the OJ trial here," he said, chuckling. "We're going to get some good, honest, God-fearing people on the jury and give them the evidence."

Joe breathed deeply, willing himself to stick to the most pressing issue. "So, Judge," he said, forcing a smile, "everyone here in Barton has been very welcoming. But I haven't even met my client yet. I know there must be DNA testing that's still in the works. I haven't even received the police reports from Ms. Pettigrew yet." He was choosing his words carefully. "Trying this case on that schedule is just not realistic."

"Did I ever tell you about old Judge Duffy?" Boniface asked the DA. Pettigrew smiled into a grimace, which Joe knew meant she'd heard about Judge Duffy several times. And why was the judge not looking at him?

"Old Judge Duffy was one ornery SOB. One time when I was DA, we ran out of jurors, so he went outside and had his deputy start pulling people in off the street."

The judge spun his chair to retrieve a large fountain drink and drank loudly through a straw. "Look, you two," he said, eyes still on Pettigrew, "I'm willing to be reasonable. But this community has suffered an enormous blow. People are hurting, and they need some closure. I'll give y'all three weeks but not a day more. September twenty-sixth for trial. I'll see you back here in a week for a status conference."

Outside the courtroom, Joe was fuming. So, this town needed a guilty verdict so they could get on with the football season. "Are we going to go on the record?" he asked Pettigrew, who appeared to be walking out of the courtroom.

"Oh no. Barbara will take care of the record," she said, smiling at his confusion. "I guess everything is a little more casual here than you're used to. Welcome to Barton."

CHAPTER 12

"It was a fucking nightmare, Busier. I'm not sure he recognized me, but it was definitely him. I've literally never been in the presence of a bigger asshole in my life. He wouldn't even address me. It was as if he refused to acknowledge my presence." Joe had called Eddy on his walk home to vent.

"Sorry, babe. Sounds like a d-bag. First, the bike incident and now this. His mom probably left him in a hot car when he was five."

"Oh, and he wants to get the trial over with so that quote, 'the community can have closure.' In other words, we need to get your client convicted ASAP."

"Well, they've got a football season to play, right?"

"Exactly. Speaking of my client, I'm off to meet him now. Any advice?"

"Just remember people with autism are usually pretty terrible socially. Try not to be offended."

"There's no way he will offend me more than Judge Fuckface."

"And there's the nickname I was waiting for! Also, maybe try a different route for your run?"

Joe laughed. "Bye."

Soon, he was driving his rental up the private road north of town that led to the Ledbetter estate. For a quarter mile, the paved road—much smoother than the public roads—wound through a precisely manicured lawn where soaring pines and magnolias rose from clusters of dormant azaleas. After two miles, a guard waved him through a gate, and he soon arrived at a sparkling but modest two-story home with dormer windows above a wraparound porch. It certainly wasn't the grand Southern home Joe had been expecting, and he was relieved to avoid the feel of a plantation.

"Mr. Turner?" An affable looking man in his forties came down off the porch to greet him. He wore khaki pants and a dark green polo shirt with a coat of arms on the chest.

"Hello. Mr. Ledbetter?" Joe asked as they shook hands.

"Aldridge Bain, at your service. I manage the property here at Bellcrest. Carl will arrive shortly," he said, checking his watch. "Ms. Ledbetter thought you'd have more privacy here at the guest house."

Ah, the guest house. Of course.

"May I offer you a cold drink?" Bain asked, gesturing to a pitcher on the porch.

"No thanks, I'm fine." To his left, an electric golf cart driven by a man dressed identically to Mr. Bain silently cruised to a stop. A young man in his late teens got out of the passenger seat and, without a sideways glance, strode into the house with an odd forward-leaning gait.

Bain flashed a knowing smile and gestured for Joe to follow him into the home. "I assume you know about his condition?"

"High-functioning on the autistic spectrum is what I've been told."

Bain nodded. "He'll be in the parlor. First on the left."

Carl was seated on a sofa when Joe entered the well-appointed and dimly lit room. He wore khaki pants and a starched white shirt. A blue blazer hung from his spindly frame. Black hair that needed a shampoo poked out beneath a faded Chicago Cubs cap, pulled down low on his forehead, nearly touching his black-framed glasses. He stood when Joe approached.

"Hello, Carl. I'm Joe. Thank you for standing. Such nice Southern manners," he said, taking his hand.

Carl bowed slightly. "Thank you. Social conventions are important to my mother, so I practice them scrupulously," he said in a hoarse monotone. "Except for taking off my Cubs cap," he added without the hint of a smile.

"I noticed the cap. I'm a Red Sox fan myself. Sort of the Cubs of the American League, right?"

Carl frowned. "I can see why you might say that as both franchises recently won World Series after prolonged droughts. However, while the Red Sox have won, I believe, eight championships in their 122 years, the Cubs have only three in their 147-year history."

"Wow, Carl. You know a lot about baseball," Joe said, taking a seat in a chair opposite the sofa. "But now, I thought we'd talk about the night your teammate, Justin, was killed."

Carl eyed his visitor. "I am relieved to hear you do not wish to talk about how I feel. Technically, Justin was not my teammate. Although, as team manager, I am affiliated with the Barton High School football team."

"I see," Joe said, removing a notepad from his satchel. And I know you two were close. I'm sorry for your loss."

Carl looked at him as if he'd just commented on the stock market. "Statistically, he died quite young. In Georgia, the average human life expectancy is 77 years.

That's about eighteen months less than the national average. I would guess that's because of the high incidence of tobacco use and obesity in our state."

Joe smiled to himself. Carl was as advertised. "You certainly know a lot of facts, Carl. So, where and when did you last see Justin?"

Carl dug in his pants pocket and produced a well-worn baseball. "I think around midnight on the night he was shot," he said, clutching the ball. "He was out in his bedroom. It's separate from the main residence."

"Did you notice anything unusual about Justin or his bedroom?"

Carl stared into space, recalling the evening. "No," he finally said. "Justin and the room appeared as expected."

"Did you see any other players around?"

"I did not," he said and began rocking slightly in his seat.

"Carl, do you always keep a baseball in your pocket?"

"During counseling sessions, mostly."

"You know," Joe said, sensing his client's anxiety, "If I'm not mistaken, the Cubs beat my Red Sox just a few weeks ago, right?"

"Yes. Twice, in fact," Carl answered.

Joe nodded, and the two sat in silence for a few minutes. So much for baseball talk. "Carl, can you think of any reason in the world why anyone on the team would want to harm Justin?"

"Thirty percent of murders are committed by a friend or acquaintance of the victim, so you are right to ask that question. But no, I cannot."

"Did Justin have a girlfriend?" Joe asked.

"Yes. Karen Sarkliss. She is quite a wonderful person."

Joe smiled. The comment seemed completely out of character.

"Tell me, Carl," Joe asked, trying a question Carl might hear on cross examination, "What were you doing in Justin's bedroom so late at night?"

"I went there to thank him for the party. Social conventions are important to my mother, so I practice them scrupulously. Except for taking off my Cubs cap, as I mentioned previously."

"I see."

"So, Carl, there's a witness who says he saw you running down the street away from the Holt's house just after the murder. Could this be true?"

"Yes, it's possible that's true."

"I'm sorry," Joe said, confused.

"Yes," Carl said, "whether the person saw me I could not say. I have no way of knowing whether they were in a position or location that would allow them to see me."

Joe was beginning to realize the extent of his new client's literal interpretations. "So, Carl, you were running away, but you have no way of knowing whether anyone saw you?"

"Correct."

"And why were you running away from the scene?"

"Because I needed to get home to feed my fish."

Joe blinked once slowly. "So," he said, still processing the answer, "after you saw Justin, at midnight, you decided you needed to run home to feed your fish?"

"Yes, I just said that," came the matter-of-fact reply.

Joe pinched the bridge of his nose imagining a courtroom full of people erupting in laughter after his client's testimony. "Had you just realized the fish needed feeding?"

"Yes, a fish tank in the Holt's home reminded me. I had planned to ask my dad to feed the fish that evening, but I neglected to do so. I had planned to spend the night at the Holt's with my teammates."

"How far is it from the Holt residence to your house?"

"Approximately four and a half miles."

"Did you consider the fish food thing an emergency?"

"No."

"Then why run home? Why not walk?"

Carl looked skyward, searching his memory. "I suppose I just wanted to feed the fish as soon as possible."

Joe thought of the gunshot residue. The only explanation was that, after the murder, the shooter transferred the gunshot residue to Carl's hands with a handshake. But if Carl had left the party while Justin was alive, this was impossible.

Joe ended his interview with Carl for now. He thought it made sense to talk more after he'd listened to his statement to the police. That, and he'd accumulated enough bad news for one day. "Carl, it's been a pleasure," he said, standing. "I'm sure I'll have some more questions for you another time."

Carl was out of his seat. "The pleasure has been mine," he said, as if reading the line, no doubt penned by his mother. Then, without another word, he walked briskly out of the room, pulling on the bill of his Cubs cap as he went.

CHAPTER 13

"So, Chuck, what the actual fuck is such a big deal about high school football around here? I don't get it?" Joe's investigator had arrived the night before, and the two were on their way to meet with the high school football coaches.

"Don't reckon you would," Chuck said, guiding his rental past Barton High, a single story building painted gray with blue trim, with low slung corridors branching out from a main hallway.

"Seriously, Chuck, 'reckon?' You've been here less than twenty-four hours."

Chuck laughed. "Sorry, but I did spend a good chunk of my life here. I was eighteen before I knew I could leave."

Chuck parked outside a modest building with a stenciled "Physical Education" in large letters across the wall at the edge of its flat roof. Approaching the entrance, Joe caught sight of the top of a stadium, looming high behind the building, and stopped in his tracks. "Jesus."

"High bar and damnation," Chuck whispered, gazing upwards. "I heard they put in a new stadium a few years ago. Didn't know it was the damn Super Dome."

Inside, Chuck knocked on a door labeled, "Steeler Football."

"They can't possibly fill that stadium for games, can they?" Joe asked.

"For playoff games, I'll bet they come close. Lots of hillbillies in those hollers."

The door opened to reveal a middle-aged man that could only have been a football coach. He wore a gray polo shirt with a blue block "B" on his chest, and blue polyester shorts. "Hi folks! C'mon in. I'm Coach Burgess," he said, shaking hands as Joe and Chuck made their introductions.

The coach led them into a cramped office where they took seats opposite his desk. "Argenal," the coach said, repeating Chuck's surname. "Not *the* Chuck Argenal. The Rifleman?"

"That was an awful long time ago," Chuck said, glancing at Joe sheepishly.

"Hot damn, high bar!" the coach said, suddenly beaming. "I didn't know I was in the presence of greatness."

"Oh, you know how stories get told. I…"

"Arn!" Burgess called from his desk. A stocky coach in his forties came to the doorway. "This here's Mr. Turner and Chuck Argenal."

Stuckey's eyes widened as he took Chuck's hand. "Well hey! Wow, um, welcome," he said, stammering. "It's truly an honor. You started it all back in '75. High bar," he added, still pumping Chuck's hand.

"Well, the presence of greatness," Joe put in, reveling in his investigator's uneasiness. "I had no idea."

"You're kiddin'," Coach Burgess said, as if Joe had failed to recognize a former president. "This man is a Steeler legend. Quarterbacked us to our first two state titles. So, you played for old Coach Thurber. I hear he was a ball buster."

"So, guys," Chuck said, desperate to change the subject, "Joe and I just have a few questions about the Holt case."

"Oh, that's okay, Rifleman." Joe grinned at his friend. "What was it like back in seventy-five? Did you wear leather helmets?"

"So," Chuck said, ignoring him, "as you know, Mr. Turner represents the Ledbetter kid, so we were curious as to your thoughts on the matter."

"Well, first of all, we are absolutely at your service. Full cooperation. Whatever you need."

"Yessir," added Coach Stuckey, still standing in the doorway.

"Obviously," Burgess continued, "it was a terrible tragedy. Hit our team so hard. Now Carl, there's no doubt he's wound pretty tight. But he's a good kid. Just can't see him doing this."

"Did you ever notice any friction between Carl and Justin, or Justin and another member of the team?" Joe asked.

Coach Burgess took off his ball cap and rubbed his bald head. "Minor scraps but nothing worth mentioning."

"We're a pretty tight-knit group," said Stuckey. "It's just hard for me to imagine any player killing a teammate."

"Had you noticed anything unusual about Justin Holt? Did he seem distracted or troubled?"

"No." Burgess shrugged. "Not much bothered Justin. Had his pick of colleges for next year. Dating the head cheerleader. He had the world by the tail, really." The coach stared into space, lost in a memory.

"If I were you, I'd take a hard look at that Tettleton kid," Burgess finally said.

"The Tettletons are still around?" Chuck asked.

"Yeah, and one of them has made it a mission to mess with the football team. We're pretty sure he shot out the window of the team room last year, but we couldn't prove it."

"Sounds like a Tettleton," Chuck said, standing. "Well, we sure do thank you. For us, information is vital. I know it's a lot to ask, but do you think it would be possible to set up some interviews with the players who were at the party."

"Absolutely," Burgess said as he stood. "Anything you need." Joe and Chuck gave the coaches their business cards and showed themselves out.

"So, that was easier than I expected," Chuck said as they drove away from the high school.

"Thanks to you, Rifleman," Joe said, chuckling. "High bar!" he added, trying a Southern drawl. "I truly had no idea you were a Steeler legend."

"Very funny. Big fish, small pond."

"Who are the Tettletons?" Joe asked.

"Clan of mangy hillbillies that live in a holler west of town. They mainly keep to themselves, but once in a while, they take the opportunity to terrorize the locals."

"They sound charming. So, about your football exploits. Did you play in college?"

"Two years at Savannah State before I blew out my knee. Now, speaking of quarterbacks, it turns out the current QB1 at Barton High is Coach Stuckey's son, Luke."

"Interesting. I thought I recognized that name from a story in the *Herald*."

"Locals seem to think he's no Justin Holt but still damn good. In line for a scholarship."

"So, what does this mean for us? You're not suggesting Luke wanted Justin dead just so he could play quarterback."

"I'm just spit balling. Luke's a senior. If Justin were alive and Luke didn't get a chance to play this year, that would leave him without a chance to impress colleges." Chuck shrugged. "Like I said, I'm just flappin' my gums."

The two rode in silence for a while. Passing through the town square, Joe gazed up at the water tower where "High Bar" was painted in blue block letters. "You know, Chuck, a week ago I would have said you were crazy. But…" His voice trailed off.

"Yeah," he said, "these folks love their football."

CHAPTER 14

Day Two

"I say we take a vote," Dirk said, cracking his knuckles as the group settled around the table.

"Now?" Jack, the self-appointed foreperson asked. "Isn't that a little premature?"

"It's a lot premature," declared Sara firmly. "We haven't even discussed the evidence," added the social worker.

"It does seem like, given the stakes, we should at least talk about the case first," said Ellen, rubbing her temples.

Dirk sighed loudly. "Look, y'all, if we take a vote and we all agree he's guilty, what's there to discuss?"

"Well," Ellen answered quietly, "maybe we could go around the room…"

"Oh, Jesus!" Dirk cut in loudly. "We already did that!" he growled, slamming both hands on the table. The big man rose from his chair and walked toward the door. There, he stood facing away from the others, his face in his hands.

The outburst brought silence from the others, and they eyed him wearily.

"So," Jack began, "I'm not suggesting that we waste anyone's time. But if we vote now and march out there with a verdict after less than two hours of deliberation, how's that gonna look?"

Dirk walked back to his chair, sat down heavily, and crossed his arms.

"This is just such a big deal," Ellen said, wringing her hands. "I just think since the decision is so important—for the defendant and the victim's family we need to talk about it a bit."

Across the table, Duncan, the young paramedic, smiled her way. "I totally agree with that. It's just such a big deal, right?"

Dirk rolled his eyes. "Shocker," he said under his breath. "Whatever, fine," he said, shaking his head.

"Okay, I'll start," Jack began from the head of the table. "I've just been so impressed with this whole process—the police, the investigation, the judge, the attorneys. I'm just proud to be a part of this."

"Okay," Sara said from the other end of the table, drawing out the word. "Whatever the hell that means."

"I'm sorry, I'm just being honest," Jack responded defensively.

"Well, what was your impression of the evidence? That's sort of why we're here."

"I was just very impressed by everyone's presentation," Jack said meekly, drawing several smirks from around the table.

"So, I'll go," Dirk said with a heavy sigh. "Obviously, the kid is guilty. The evidence is cut and dried. There's witnesses, scientific evidence. Honestly, I don't know why we're still here."

To his left, Mr. Burleson, the retired navy officer, nodded. "I agree. I don't know that it's obvious, but it seems like you'd have to believe a lot of coincidences to find him innocent."

"Not guilty," corrected Sara. "To acquit, we don't have to find that he didn't do it, just that the prosecution hasn't proven it beyond a reasonable doubt."

"So, let me guess." Dirk's tone dripped with disgust. "You'd vote not guilty."

"I'm not sure," the social worker answered. "I don't think I'm at guilty yet, but I could be convinced. What about you, Quinn?" she asked the young man to her right. He slowly backed his chair into the corner and clutched his backpack to his chest, as if shielding himself from the others.

"Yeah, that's a no go," Dirk muttered.

"Excuse me," Sara said tersely. "I value everyone's opinion, and so should you."

To Sara's left, Elston, the retired attorney, spoke up. "I know the evidence is compelling, but my gut is telling me that kid isn't capable of this."

Priya nodded. "Not guilty for me. I feel like there are some things that don't make sense."

"I don't know. Elston has a point," said Ellen, "but on the other hand, I tend to think where there's smoke, there's fire. I just feel so bad for the victim's family."

"Which we were specifically told we couldn't consider," countered Elston. "How about you, young man? Sorry, I forgot your name."

"No worries. It's Duncan. No matter what you think about the scientific evidence, for me the most important evidence is the fact that he was running away from the crime scene right after the murder. My first impression is guilty," he said, stealing a glance at Ellen.

"Okay, excellent," Jack said, "I think that was productive. "Now I thought…"

Dirk snorted. "Jack, you realize you and the mute in the corner…"

"Quinn. His name is Quinn," Sara said crossly.

"Fine. You and Quinn are the only people who refused to say what they think."

"I haven't made up my mind yet, Dirk," Jack said, managing a smile. "If you insist, I'd say guilty, but I was hoping we could go over the evidence. I know I took some pretty good notes, but my memory isn't perfect."

"All of it?" Dirk moaned, shaking his head. "It was a fourteen-day trial."

"Yes, all of it," Sara said. "That's what juries do."

"Okay," Jack said, cheerfully. "The first witness was Officer Billups…"

CHAPTER 15

Back in his temporary home, Joe made himself a gin and tonic and moped to the couch. He missed Eddy. When they met, her work as an archaeologist meant lots of travel. But since taking the professorship, they hadn't been apart for more than a few days. Joe also hated the fact that he liked Carl so much. That always added stress to trials.

He smiled, recalling Carl's strictly literal interpretations. His client was challenging, to be sure. Joe considered his mother's comment that he was incapable of expressing emotion. He thought of Karen, the "quite wonderful person," and wondered whether this made for a sad and empty life for him.

Joe also thought there was a little more to Carl than met the eye. He seemed to have a certain self-awareness about him that was endearing. Part of Joe wondered whether Carl's mechanical explanation for his manners was meant to be ironic—his own comment on what he thought of conventions.

As Joe sipped his drink, his thoughts moved to the trial. Judge Boniface's ridiculous schedule was weighing on his mind. He imagined learning about new evidence hours before his opening statement then pictured the judge's jowly face calling him an asshole from his bicycle. He opened his laptop and emailed Melissa Pettigrew, reminding her of the urgency of obtaining the DNA results. So far, he liked the DA, and it made him uncomfortable. His first instinct with most prosecutors was distrust, which kept him sharp. So he thought, anyway.

The worst news of the day came in an email attachment from Pettigrew. It was a recording of Carl's interrogation. He was sure that his parents wouldn't have allowed that to happen had they been home. But the night of the party, Aubrey and Matt had hopped on their jet for a romantic night at the Four Seasons in Atlanta. Ever since speaking to Carl, Joe had been dreading finding out what he had told the police.

He opened his laptop on the coffee table and put in his earbuds. After advising him of his right to remain silent, the officer asked Carl if he knew why they were at his house at seven o'clock on a Saturday morning.

"Yes," he said. "I assume it's about what happened to Justin."

"Oh fuck, Carl," Joe said aloud and covered his face with his hand. At that moment, for the first time, he considered the very real possibility that Carl Ledbetter had murdered Justin Holt.

As with most of his cases, he hadn't asked his client directly. Practically, it made little sense to ask. If Carl confessed to the murder to Joe then later testified that he was innocent, Joe would have to withdraw from the case to avoid suborning perjury.

Until now, it had never occurred to him that Carl was guilty. Maybe Carl just seemed too emotionally unsophisticated to conjure evil. Whatever the reason, when Carl had told him that Karen was "quite a wonderful person," Joe was certain he wasn't listening to the words of a murderer. Now, though, he wondered.

Remarkably, the officers hadn't followed up by asking how Carl knew their purpose. Maybe they assumed the news had reached him, unaware that Carl didn't own a cell phone.

Next, the police confronted him with the witness, Sinclair Lewis. "Old Mr. Lewis saw you running down the street away from the murder scene," the officer had said. Cringing, Joe braced himself for the fish feeding explanation. Instead, there was silence. After thirty seconds, Joe smiled to himself, knowing the reason. Another half minute passed before the officer spoke again. "Did you not hear my question, Carl?"

"Of course I heard you," Carl said, clearly confused. "I was sitting right here. It was not a question. It was a statement."

"Okay, Carl, your silence speaks volumes."

"That doesn't make any sense."

"Carl," the officer said, exasperated, "Can you think of any reason why you would want to hurt Justin Holt?" More silence. As described in the police report, the officer asked his question four times. Each time it was met with silence.

Joe sighed, recalling his mother's words—sometimes, Carl's mind gets stuck in a loop. As he sat, listening to the silence on the tape, Joe had no doubt Carl was searching every crevice of his mind for any reason he would want to hurt Justin, even knowing there was none.

Finally, the officer asked Carl about his knowledge of guns and silencers. "Although I don't own a gun, I've had ample experience shooting at the range. My father takes me there sometimes. I'm familiar with many guns but prefer a Glock 19 for target practice. Of course, I'm familiar with silencers as well. They are important for ear protection at the range, and my ears are particularly sensitive to loud noises. I prefer the Rugged Obsidian 9, utilized at its full configuration. It makes the firearm heavier, of course, but I've found that using the short-length option is suboptimal." Although Carl was just getting started, the officer cut him off and ended the interview.

Joe downed the last of his drink and considered whether Carl should testify. The town rumor that he'd confessed was technically inaccurate. Still, Carl's silence in the face of the accusations could only be explained by his testimony. That way, the jury could observe the way his mind worked firsthand.

But there seemed even better reasons to keep Carl off the witness stand. He'd managed not to admit running away from the scene immediately after the murder. Depending on the strength of Sinclair Lewis's identification, this was the most damning piece of evidence to date. Perhaps the identification could be called into question. But if Carl testified, the jury would learn that he had run home, not to flee a murder scene but to feed his fish.

Joe texted Chuck, asking him to interview Lewis and the hillbilly, Tettleton, tomorrow. Then he smiled at his favorite moment from the day: Karen Sarkliss is quite a wonderful person.

CHAPTER 16

As Chuck guided his rented pickup through downtown Barton, passing the Methodist Church, the Barton Burgee, and the Bronze Cue, he marveled at the lack of change the place had undergone since he left. A few fast-food places had sprung up on the south end of town, but mostly, the town had resisted the megastores, staying loyal to the local businesses that had been around since Chuck was a boy. Nearly a half century later, Barton appeared to be the same sleepy, charming, gossipy, football-crazy town. "Even the Tettletons," Chuck whispered to himself, referencing the purpose of his current errand.

The Tettletons lived deep in a holler west of town, tenaciously protecting their privacy. Their children usually attended school in Barton through middle school, sometimes longer, never participating in sports or clubs. Stealing was a way of life for the family—mostly food, gasoline, or lumber. But they never stole more than they needed, and the locals tolerated it. Persistent rumors swirled that they grew poppies and sold them to the Georgia Mob, but if that was the case, local law enforcement looked the other way. A trip to their holler was more trouble than it was worth.

Chuck had grown up in the next holler from the Tettletons, so he knew the family better than most. The football coach's suspicion that a Tettleton had committed the Justin Holt murder didn't square with what he knew of them. It wasn't that they were averse to violence. Chuck knew they learned to fight when they were young and never backed down from a "slicker"—their name for the townsfolk of Barton. Growing up in Barton, Chuck had never considered the irony of Bartonites being called city slickers.

But while the Tettletons didn't shy from a fight, they usually reserved violence for those who offended them—trespassed on their property, stole from their garden, or harmed a family member. Once, one of Chuck's high school classmates had gotten frisky with a freshman, Maylene Tettleton. In the middle of the school day, a truckload of Tettletons stood guard while Maylene's twin, Rodney, took revenge with his fists. Whatever the motive for the Holt murder, it seemed well outside the Tettleton issue box.

Chuck also knew nothing happened in Barton without the Tettletons knowing about it. While they steered clear of town business, their family network kept them well informed. More than once, the local police had relied on the family for leads in solving crimes. The Tettletons cooperated when it benefited them.

West of town, Chuck turned right off County Route 6 onto a gravel road that climbed Jenner Hill then dead-ended at the shooting range. Beyond the range, he eased his truck down a narrow dirt road, its beginning barely visible amongst a grove of loblolly pines. Hairpin switchbacks led him downhill, descending into the shade of privet, hickory, and black oaks.

Arriving at a fork in the road, Chuck parked and paused outside, inhaling the familiar scent of the forest. He set off on foot and soon veered from the footpath, padding across the damp detritus of the forest floor. After a quarter mile, he crossed Pugh Creek and descended into Otis Holler, where the dark canopy tunneled over the trail. Now on Tettleton property, he took a white handkerchief from his pocket, letting it flutter in the soft breeze as he walked.

Just as he was thinking it was likely the Tettleton's already had eyes on him, a metallic clack ripped through nature's soft murmurs. Chuck froze as the teenage boy stepped out from behind a pine tree pointing a shotgun at his chest. "Who the fuck are you?" Lean and sinewy, he wore cargo shorts, a white sleeveless shirt, and, as was the Tettleton custom, no shoes. His stringy brown hair was pulled back in a ponytail.

"Chuck Argenal. I come peaceful," he said, showing the handkerchief. "I know your granddad, Eustis."

"Well, you're in our holler," the boy said, holding the gun steady. "I oughta shoot you for that. What you want?"

"Just to visit with your people."

The boy looked Chuck up and down. "Bullshit, old man. You best tell me what you want."

The Tettleton's were not known for idle threats, and Chuck's instinct was to tell the truth. "I came out to speak to your family about the murder that happened in town."

The boy raised the gun level with Chuck's head. "Pow!" he yelled, and Chuck jumped out of his skin then collapsed to his knees, breathing heavily, as the boy smirked. "Put this on," the boy said, throwing a black rag Chuck's way.

Once blindfolded, a gentle push from behind and Chuck was walking, feeling for the ground under his feet.

After stumbling twice—the second time into a patch of burweed, he adjusted the blindfold up on his face so he could make out the trail beneath him.

After a fifteen-minute walk up and down sloping hills, he was jerked to a stop, his blindfold removed. Rubbing his stinging face and arms, Chuck took in his surroundings. He was in the middle of a small clearing in the thick forest. Before him was a picnic table and benches. Chuck smiled to himself as he read "U.S. Park Service" stenciled on the table.

"Chuck Argenal," a gravelly voice said behind him. Chuck turned to find a middle-aged man approaching, limping with the aid of a cane.

"Eustis?" Chuck asked.

"Hell, I haven't changed that much, have I, you old rattlesnake?" he said, taking Chuck's hand.

"Grandpa, you know this slicker?" Chuck's kidnapper asked.

"Yeah, we ain't friends, necessarily, but he's only half slicker. Grew up in Bunkers Holler. Didn't my daddy shoot at you once for trespassing?" Eustis asked with a smile.

"At me?" Chuck exclaimed. "Filled my fourteen-year-old ass with buckshot!"

Eustis laughed and took a seat on the bench. "And yet here you are again. What's ya huntin'?"

"Investigating the murder in Barton."

"Yeah, our people seen you snoopin' around town."

"Well, what can you tell me about the murder? I hear one of your boys has a beef with the football team."

Tettleton nodded. "That'd be Clem, Del here's half-brother. You're lucky it wasn't him who came across you today. One of them angry young ones. Might not be rowing with both oars in the water."

"Is he good for the murder?"

"I honestly don't know."

"What's your gut say, Eustis?"

Tettleton rubbed his face, grimacing as he thought for a time. "Could be that Clem got mad and killed him," he finally said with a shrug. "Wouldn't surprise me. On the other hand, us Tettletons are raised with rules. Rules about shit that matters, not slicker rules about what drugs you can put in your body or how many fish you can catch. Our rules are about being loyal to your family, respecting your elders. We got rules about taking a life too. Not liking someone don't cut it. Then, again, Clem smokes too much of the hippy lettuce. Messes with your faculties. Who knows?"

Tettleton stood. "Seems to me if you find out why this kid was murdered, that's a start," he said, leaning on his cane. "Did the kid break a slicker rule or a hillbilly rule?" The men shook hands. "I'll get Del to walk you back," he said walking away.

"That's okay, Eustis, I'll manage," Chuck said, standing. "I peeked under the blindfold."

Tettleton chuckled. "I never did trust you," he called over his shoulder.

CHAPTER 17

Monday morning found Joe waiting outside Department One. Two men and a woman sat on a bench in the hallway. Neither appeared to be attorneys, so Joe assumed they were criminal defendants and wondered how they'd run afoul of the law.

"Morning, Joe," called Melissa Pettigrew cheerfully from down the hall. She wore a blue suit and carried some files and a pink bakery box.

"Good morning, Melissa."

Pettigrew unlocked the courtroom and turned to address the people on the bench. "Y'all were cited over the weekend to appear today?" All three nodded. "I'll come back and open the department to the public in about fifteen minutes."

"Busy day," Pettigrew said to Joe, once inside the courtroom, and he couldn't tell if she was joking.

"I have a supplemental police report for you," she said, handing him an envelope.

"Oooh, you brought Sweet Sally's?" called Barbara from the clerk's desk. As usual, she was the sole occupant of the courtroom.

"I surely did," the DA said, opening the box for the clerk.

"The judge said to go on back," she said, lifting a gooey pecan sweet roll onto a paper plate.

In his chambers, Judge Boniface swiveled his chair to greet them. "Morning, you two," he said, his eyes glued to the pink box. "Melissa, you're going to be the death of me," he said, producing three small paper plates from his desk." That will take a few miles on the bike to burn off, Joe thought to himself.

"Joe, dig in," said Pettigrew.

"Oh, no thanks." Both judge and attorney froze and looked at him like he had three heads.

"You don't understand," Pettigrew said, serving him. "'No thank you,' is not an option when it comes to Sweet Sally's world-famous pecan sweet rolls. Unless you're celiac or there's some sort of religious objection, I'm afraid I'm going to have to insist," the prosecutor said.

Joe smiled. In their own way, these two were charmers. "Well, then, I suppose I haven't a choice. But, Judge, I would like to take up the timing of the trial again," he said, taking his first bite. "I just…" He paused and closed his eyes, overwhelmed by the warm, fresh-baked buttery sweetness. "Wow," he said, as his hosts smiled and nodded.

"One discovery question," said Joe, after collecting himself. "I didn't see any witness statements from the football coaches. I believe both Coach Burgess and Coach Stuckey were at the party, right?"

"Yeah, but I'm pretty sure they left earlier," Pettigrew said. "Probably weren't around when the police arrived."

"Yeah, they did," said Boniface. "Er, I assumed they did," he added quickly.

"Still, it'd be nice to know whether they noticed anything. Anyway, Judge, I also have to ask that the trial be pushed to a later date. I simply cannot be ready, and I don't see how the prosecution can either. We're two weeks away from jury selection and don't even have the DNA results yet."

Boniface turned to the DA. "When will you have the DNA back?"

"Likely early next week."

The judge shrugged. "So that'll give you a week. Plenty of time," he said, addressing Pettigrew before taking another bite of sweet roll.

This guy literally refuses to acknowledge my presence, thought Joe. "To hire and prepare an expert witness to deal with DNA, Judge? Respectfully, I disagree."

The big man leaned back in his chair, resting folded hands on his belly. "Seems to me this is a case that should settle," he said. "Melissa, could you live with a manslaughter and, say, twenty years?"

"I could be talked into that, Judge."

"Mr. Turner," Boniface said, staring at the ceiling, "I wouldn't presume to tell you how to do your job, but your client is running away from the scene, he's got gunshot residue on his hands, and I'm hearing he damn-near confessed. Your client would avoid a life sentence, likely paroled in fifteen."

Joe seethed. Glad to hear you're unbiased, you buffoon! But he willed himself not to lash out. "Judge, it's difficult to evaluate the case when I don't have all the evidence. Just this morning, I was given more police reports. It seems like the investigation is ongoing."

"Sorry, Mr. Turner," the judge said, finally glancing his way, "we've already sent out extra juror summonses. The town expects this to happen and needs it to happen. The trial date will remain."

"Then I'd like to make a record, Your Honor?"

"You'd what?"

"I'd like to go on the record with a motion to continue. I don't believe I can meet the constitutional requirement of effective assistance of counsel on this schedule, and I'd like to make a record of that." You know, like they do in a real courtroom, he wanted to add.

The judge smiled condescendingly. "Well, we aren't set up for that today. Our court reporter, Inez, comes Tuesdays and Thursdays. She has the morning shift at Nadine's on Mondays."

"Of course she does," Joe whispered under his breath. "Then can I come back tomorrow?" he asked, standing to leave.

"Tomorrow I've got a judge's conference over in Athens. I can give you next Thursday."

"Fine," Joe said curtly and walked out, trailed by Pettigrew.

The DA caught up to him in the hallway outside court. "I guess this place isn't exactly what you're used to. We just don't have…"

Joe spun to face her. "The problem is, no matter how down-home and friendly everyone is, no matter how much this podunk little place tries its best to be a real courthouse and give my client a real trial, if my client is convicted," he said, hearing his voice rise, "he's going to a real fucking prison for a very long time, and that's not going to happen on my watch!" Joe turned to leave.

"Okay, then," Pettigrew called after him. "Looks like we got a shootin' match."

Joe rolled his eyes. "Jesus, do they ever stop?" he said to himself, walking away.

CHAPTER 18

On the walk back to the house, Joe vowed to kick Melissa Pettigrew's ass in court. Something about the tone of her last comment had made her down-home routine seem phony. And Joe hated almost nothing more than phony. He half suspected it was just him, getting himself fired up for trial, but didn't care.

After a lunch of cold pizza, he changed into jeans and his favorite Nirvana concert T-shirt and cracked a beer. He walked barefoot to the front porch of the Victorian and settled into an Adirondack chair with the new police report.

Supplemental police reports, drafted after a suspect had been identified, rarely brought good news, so Joe braced himself with a long drink. The report documented the second statement of a football player named Butch Ford. After telling the police he hadn't noticed anything unusual on the night of the murder, his parents took him to the station a week later.

Now he said that around midnight—he couldn't be sure of the time—he needed to use the bathroom. Finding the facilities in the main house occupied, he walked into the backyard to relieve himself in some bushes. Standing next to an open window of Justin's bedroom, Ford heard someone say, "Hi, Carl." He hadn't mentioned this to the police because he hadn't considered it important. "I didn't hear any gunshots," his statement read, "but when I heard about the time of death and rumors about a silencer, I figured I should speak up."

"Fuck," Joe exhaled. The testimony would be devastating—another pebble in a growing pile of evidence against Carl. The judge's proposed plea agreement was beginning to sound better. He dreaded the idea of suggesting to Aubrey Ledbetter that her son, already faced with so many obstacles in life, sign up for twenty years in prison.

Carl, Joe knew, would take it in stride. He might not accept the plea bargain, but his reaction would be unemotional. This brought Joe a certain amount of comfort but also sadness.

"Hi there!"

Shaken from his thoughts by the familiar, sweet voice, Joe looked down from his porch to see Eddy walking up the stone path to the house. "Oh my gosh," he said and raced to her for a long embrace. "You have no idea how happy I am to see you. And look at you," he said, taking in his girlfriend's belt buckle and boots. "You'll fit right in here."

"These rags? Why thanks, darlin," Eddy said in a drawl. "I just threw on what came natural."

"Well, come on in," Joe said, leading her inside by the hand. "I'll have to try to get you out of them."

The last thoughts of the Carl Ledbetter case had just left Joe's mind when Chuck's voice snuck through the front door just before it closed. "Hi, you two," he called from his parking spot on the street.

Joe closed his eyes and sighed. "To be continued."

"Hi, Chuck," Eddy said as he climbed the porch steps. "How's my favorite P.I. from Barton, Georgia, who loves movie lines?"

He laughed. "Eddy, there's no place like home, you dig?"

"Ah, archaeology humor. And thanks, Dorothy. Even I know that one. So, how does it look for, what's his name, Carl?"

Joe had ducked into the house and now appeared with three beers. "Bleak," he said.

"Okay, run it down for me," Eddy said. "I'm the jury."

Joe beamed. He loved his partner's enthusiasm for his work. "Chuck, maybe it will sound less bleak coming from you."

"Well," the P.I. began, "Justin Holt was shot at close range in the middle of the night at a football slumber party in his bedroom, which is separate from the main residence. Like a guest house. To avoid drinking and driving by the boys, Justin's parents made sure they kept track of them, confiscating car keys, that sort of thing. Carl was the only one missing. A neighbor saw him running away from the scene. Later that morning, the cops found gunshot residue on his hands, and his statement was incriminating."

Eddy sipped her beer while Joe filled them in on the latest witness statement.

"Yikes," said Eddy. "For the defense, Mr. Turner?"

"Carl loves the team and would never hurt a fly. His mother says so," he said, managing a straight face. "He's autistic, which accounts for his incriminating statement."

"If he's on the spectrum, can he accurately articulate what happened?" asked Eddy.

Joe thought about Carl's statement about going home to feed his fish. "Not exactly," he said.

"And the gunshot residue?" Eddy asked, cringing.

"Working on that," said Joe. "Oh, and there might be Carl's DNA under the victim's fingernails, but I likely won't know until the eve of trial. Any other questions, babe?"

"Yeah," Eddy deadpanned. "How does Carl look in blue?"

Joe laughed, shaking his head. "Chuck, how are we coming on blaming someone else?"

The investigator sipped his beer. "So, I met with the crazy hillbilly's people today. Clem Tettleton is crazy enough to kill and hates the football team. Apparently, he's going to contact me, which is disconcerting."

"How are the player interviews coming along?" Joe asked.

"I'm writing them up. All done except for the Stuckey kid. Wasn't available," he said, shooting Joe a look.

"That's interesting."

"What's interesting?" asked Eddy.

"Chuck's got this crazy-ass theory that the second-string quarterback killed the star."

"Oooh, I like it," said Eddy. "A Nancy Kerrigan tale."

Joe rolled his eyes. "Yeah, unfortunately, I'm the one that would have to sell this to a jury. Chuck, can you also interview the football coaches, also known as Judge Boniface's golfing buddies?"

"Sure. I'll let you guys catch up," he said, heading off the porch.

When he'd gone, Joe and Eddy embraced again. "Where were we?" Joe asked.

"Oh, how cliché."

Joe laughed. "True, it must be a movie line."

"Oh, why don't I go ask Chuck," Eddy said, pretending to pull away.

"Very funny. As they say here in Barton," he said, leading his girlfriend inside "let's have a mess a fun."

CHAPTER 19

Daulton County Deputy Sheriff Clint Shrag eased his cruiser to a stop on the gravel in front of the dilapidated house and sighed, having drawn the day's short straw. His department was well familiar with Sinclair Lewis, who lived by himself on Chance Avenue, and it wasn't the deputy's first visit.

Lewis had the sheriff's department on speed dial and was forever reporting the minor transgressions of his neighbors or potential safety hazards, from downed power lines to deep potholes. It wasn't as if the retired crop duster was unpleasant. The lonely widower of nine years was as nice as pie and usually had a pitcher of sweet tea on his porch. The difficulty was limiting the visits to less than an hour.

And today's wasn't just a report of the Judson's mule kicking a hole in his fence. Although the Barton Police Department was handling the Justin Holt homicide, the request to re-interview Lewis, living as he did in unincorporated Barton, had fallen to the sheriff's department.

"Right on time, Deputy Shrag. Good to see you again," Lewis called from the swing on his front porch.

"Mr. Lewis, good morning." The deputy hoped to dive right in. "I understand you may have some more information about your observations on the night of the Holt homicide."

Lewis was having none of it. "Come and have a glass of tea, Deputy. Nothing like an early fall morning," he said, pouring a glass as the deputy took a seat on a high-backed chair on the porch. "My brother says the leaves are starting to turn up in Tallulah."

"So, Mr. Lewis…"

"They say that leaves turn first at the higher elevations because of the colder weather. Call me Sin," Lewis said breaking into a smile. "When my mama named me Sinclair, she surely didn't intend that people would call me Sin, but they always have."

"I remember you telling me that. Okay, Sin, that's what I'll call you," the deputy said, taking a sip and settling back in his chair. It was clear the conversation would proceed at his host's pace.

"You know, I knew an Earnest Shrag growing up in Valdosta."

"Yessir, we talked about that last time I was here. I don't know an Earnest, but I do have family down in Thomasville. This is some good tea, by the way."

"That's right, I'd forgotten that," Lewis said. "Well, Deputy, speaking of my memory, I'd imagine you'd like to get to the matter at hand."

"Yeah, the sergeant said you had some more information about what you saw the night of the Holt homicide."

"Funny how the memory works, isn't it, Deputy? I suppose when that officer interviewed me early that morning, I wasn't at my best. Had been up all night, thinking about what I'd seen, hadn't had my coffee yet. Anyhow, as I look back on what I saw now, I realize I forgot to include a detail that I'm sure is important. Fact is, I feel damn stupid about it now." Lewis paused for a sip of tea, and the officer noticed his palsied hand rattling the ice in his glass.

"Aw, Mr...., Sin," the deputy said, correcting himself, "you oughtn't worry about that. Memory is a funny thing. Just the other day, I saw Deputy Leonard's wife across the street. I've known Becky for years, but for the life of me, I couldn't think of her name."

"Well, that's nice of you to say, Deputy. My wife used to say nice things like that to me." Lewis sat quietly for a full minute, lost in thought.

"So," Deputy Shrag said gingerly, "what was it that you recall now about that night?"

The deputy's voice startled Lewis from his thoughts. "Oh, well, yes," he said, focusing again. "Before I forget, I wondered when I'd be hearing from the prosecutor. I read in the *Herald* that the trial is coming up soon, and I imagine she'd want to come out and interview me," he said hopefully. "I was a bit surprised I hadn't heard from her yet."

"Yessir, I'm sure they'll be in touch. I really don't have much contact with the DA's Office. So, Mr. Lewis" the deputy said, losing patience "what was it you saw?"

Resigned to the visit's end, a wan smile spread across the old man's face. "As I look back now—and I can see it plain as day—this kid is running smack dab in the middle of the street and has something in his..." Lewis paused and stared at the ceiling. "Would have been his right hand. He was holding it out in front of him, sort of away from his body like it was something foul, like a dirty diaper. I saw it reflecting off the moonlight, clear as day."

Lewis paused to sip his tea, as if knowing the officer was on the edge of his seat. "I'll be damned if he wasn't toting a gun."

CHAPTER 20

Eddy rolled to her side, peering up from under a comforter. "Damn, Turner. Love 'em and leave 'em," she said through a yawn, spying her boyfriend getting dressed.

"Haven't got a coffee maker yet," Joe said, pulling on his sneakers. He knelt and kissed Eddy's head. "Back in a few."

"Don't suppose there's any chance of a bagel and lox?"

"None you'd want. How about biscuits and gravy?"

"Hard pass."

As had been his routine, Joe walked the three blocks to Sweet Sally's, where the line spilled onto the sidewalk outside. He took his place behind a buxom woman with lots of peroxided curls who was on her phone complaining loudly about some recent ordeal.

Soon, Eddy appeared by his side, wearing sweatpants and a T-shirt. "Look who got up," he said.

"Yeah, I figured I'd come sample the culture."

"Enjoy," he said, raising his eyebrows toward the big hair ahead of them.

"Probably a suboptimal pedicure," Eddy whispered.

So far, Joe had resisted another pecan sweet roll, but as they made their way to the bakery door, the sweet wafts of butter and brown sugar made their mouths water.

"Hey, Monica." Ahead of them, a man carrying a pink box touched his John Deere cap and bowed slightly to the blonde curls.

"High bar, Jason. The office is gonna love you this morning." She'd dropped her phone in her designer bag and switched her tone to syrupy sweet.

"Gotta keep 'em happy. How's our QB1? Ready for Friday?"

"Luke is just fine. You're so sweet to ask" she said, touching the man's forearm. "This whole thing has been a lot, but you know, when it comes to football, that boy has one speed. He can't wait to get on the field."

"Good to hear. Take care, now."

"You too!"

Luke Stuckey's mom, Joe thought to himself, as the woman greeted more adoring fans on their way out of the bakery. Football royalty.

"Is it gonna be UGA for Luke next year?" asked another. "That's some tall cotton."

"I surely hope so, Brady, but he probably won't decide until after the season. These recruiters are just relentless," she said dramatically. "It's honestly becoming a bit much."

After Joe and Eddy ordered two large coffees and sweet rolls, they walked to the far wall where Monica Stuckey was busy pouring cream and a heavy stream of sugar in her coffee. She made eye contact with Joe, bright red lips forming a smile that didn't reach her eyes.

"Joe? Eddy?" a young man called from behind the counter. After he had collected their coffees and sweet rolls, Joe felt a hand on his shoulder.

"Joe, you must be that big city attorney of Carl Ledbetter's," Monica Stuckey said, forcing a bigger smile. Up close, her cheeks appeared dusted with some sort of glitter.

"Yes, Joe Turner." He felt vaguely insulted.

"I'm Monica Stuckey. I believe you met my husband, Coach Stuckey."

"Yes, all the coaches were very helpful. And this is my friend, Eddy Busier."

"Eddy, what an unusual name," she said as if tasting aspirin.

Eddy blinked slowly, summoning restraint. "It's short for Ed…"

"Well, we just love Carl," Monica said, talking over her. "We're close with the Ledbetters, and we're just ever so thankful for you. If there's anything I can do, please don't hesitate," she said, her eyes shifting to Eddy's ponytail then down to her canvas sneakers and back up again.

"Thanks," Joe said pleasantly, "and since you mentioned it, I'd like to interview Luke."

"Excuse me?" The fake smile changed its shape ever so slightly.

"We're interviewing all the football players, and I believe Luke is the last one."

"Oh, absolutely, of course," she said, leaning in to whisper. "As QB1 in this football-crazy town, Luke's got a full plate, but of course, I will surely make sure he's available for that. Now you take care," she added, leaving Joe with the distinct impression she'd do no such thing.

On the walk back to their house, Chuck called. "Sweet Sally's," he said. "Nothing better. I'm on my way to interview the crazy hillbilly. Anything else pressing?"

"Can you interview Luke Stuckey soon?" Joe asked, still thinking about his unpleasant encounter with his mom.

"Trying. He's got football practice, weights, throwing sessions with some private coach. The kid's busier than a one-legged man in an ass-kicking contest. Why? You coming around to my theory?"

"Not exactly, but we need to pin this murder on someone other than our client."

Chuck laughed. "That's the spirit. I'll round up the usual suspects."

"Movie line, I assume?"

"Casablanca."

"See ya, Chuck."

Back at their temporary home, Joe and Eddy sat on the porch swing, sipping their coffee. Joe handed over the sweet roll bag. "I've heard these aren't bad," he mentioned casually, suppressing a smile.

"Thanks. You know, I was thinking about that judge," Eddy began, pausing for her first bite. "It seems to me …" She closed her eyes as she chewed. "Oh my God."

CHAPTER 21

After a run, Joe was at his computer when an email from Pettigrew arrived with two attachments. The first contained photos of the crime scene. They showed what appeared to be a typical teenager's bedroom—clothes on the floor, sports posters on the wall, and trophies on a dresser. A bed appeared made, more or less—at least not yet slept in that night. In the middle of the room, a puddle of blood stained the hardwood floor, its edges brown from oxidation. Blood-soaked towels lay wadded nearby. A few feet away, a yellow evidence marker lay next to a spent shell casing.

Other photos showed the victim before the autopsy, dressed as he was when found. Barefoot, he wore gray sweatpants with the blue Steeler block "B" logo on the thigh. He was shirtless, his athletic frame splayed on a cold metal table. Joe clicked through the close-up shots of the body, hoping each photo was the last. He paused on one, struck by the heartbreaking expression on the boy's handsome face, centered in the frame. His blue eyes were open, staring into space, his mouth relaxed into a look of pleading sorrow.

He opened the other attachment, hoping to see the DNA results—really anything to distract him from the sadness, but no luck. It was the coroner's report. He sighed heavily. The cold, precise description of a dead human corpse always made for depressing reading. Then came the autopsy photos.

He'd tried various methods to get through them. Sometimes he'd trick himself into pretending he was reading about the guinea pig he'd dissected in high school biology. It never worked for long.

Justin Cassady Holt drew his last breath at age seventeen when a bullet caused a catastrophic injury to his heart. "A single bullet wound, entered on the left side of the chest upwards at a twenty percent angle, travelling through the aortic ventricle before lodging near the thoracic vertebrae."

The report noted that stippling—a pattern of gunshot residue burned into the skin—was apparent at the point of entry. The victim suffered a contusion to the back of his head, likely suffered when he fell from a standing position in the middle of the room.

Finally, the report noted a superficial scratch on Justin Holts' body. Never breaking the skin, the claw mark appeared to have been made by a single fingernail, beginning on his chest and traveling down to his waistline. The area had been scraped, and samples were obtained for DNA testing.

Joe thought about the victim. A young, vibrant soul reduced to a cold sack of bones and flesh on a metal table. He walked to the refrigerator for a beer.

"Start a movie soon?" Eddy called from the couch.

"Five minutes, babe."

"Is that lawyer time or real time?"

"Real," Joe called back. "I need to get this over with," he whispered to himself. He downed half the beer then took stock of the report. Justin Holt almost assuredly knew his killer, who had shot him from point blank range. The upward angle of the bullet probably meant the killer was shorter than the 6'2" quarterback, which didn't exactly narrow the suspect pool.

Joe sat back in his chair and sighed. Not only had the report been as depressing as he'd feared, it wasn't at all helpful to the cause. Carl knew Justin and was shorter. Not to mention the gunshot residue on his hands, the "Hi, Carl" witness, and the neighbor who saw him running from the murder scene.

"Time's up, babe," Eddy called from the couch.

Joe closed his laptop. "Good. How about a romcom?"

CHAPTER 22

One Month Before the Murder
Sometimes, Justin Holt felt like he was living in a beer commercial. Not that he drank much beer, of course. But the cheerleaders, pep band, rallies, and local television interviews were incessant. The attention had been fun in the beginning, after his breakout season when the team won their first of three consecutive Georgia State Small School championships. But now, between football practices, football games and everything that came with it, it was, as his mother said recently, a bit much.

Justin was particularly dreading the upcoming made-for-media event where he would reveal his college choice, or more accurately, his college football choice. As he understood it, he would be seated at a table with three baseball caps on the table in front of him, one each from his final three—Georgia, Alabama, and Vanderbilt. Then he would reveal his destination by putting on the Georgia Bulldogs cap to thunderous applause.

Truth be told, he would prefer to attend his mom's alma mater, Vanderbilt, and study English. But it had been made clear that Vanderbilt, given the state of the Commodore football program, would be the equivalent of professional suicide. To which Justin responded in his private moments, "Professional suicide? Really? I'm seventeen!"

More than once lately, Justin had wished that God hadn't given him the unique ability to throw an oblong inflatable vessel farther and more accurately than just about everyone. Everyone he'd met, anyway. Sometimes he wished he'd had just ordinary talent, like his backup, Luke Stuckey. Luke loved football, and he'd made himself great. He'd had a private coach for as long as Justin could remember and was a slave to his maniacal father's practice regimen. Anyway, sometimes Justin regretted his gift.

CHAPTER 23

Joe rolled down the passenger window as Chuck's truck made its way south on Maple Street on their way to the Holt estate. They wouldn't knock on their door, but Joe wanted to understand the possible escape routes of the killer.

The sun warmed Joe's face, and crisp, fragrant air made for a true fall day he rarely saw in California. The modest houses in Barton soon gave way to a countryside of forested rolling hills, dotted with small farms and homesteads.

"How was Tettleton?" he asked, remembering Chuck's scheduled meeting.

"He no-showed, of course, but I spoke to his sister. Turns out he's sort of a half-Tettleton but every bit as yellow-bellied. Usually stays with his mom down in Hell's Holler."

"Sounds lovely."

"The good news is, according to his sister, he hates, and I mean hates, everything about the football team. Apparently played his freshman year then got kicked off the team for shoplifting a case of beer while wearing his team jersey."

"And I assume there's bad news?" Joe asked.

"Not sure yet but he might have an alibi. He's on probation with a curfew. He left me a colorful voicemail claiming his GPS ankle monitor will show he was home by midnight. I'll confirm with the probation department."

"Estimated time of death was 11:50 p.m. So, I take it he couldn't have committed the murder and made it home in time to check in at midnight?"

"It's a thirty-minute drive, but he might have made it," the investigator said cryptically. He turned down a gravel road where a rusty road sign nailed to a maple tree read Chance Avenue. The road rose gently up a foothill, bordered on both sides by a brilliant forest of hickory and maple trees turned shades of gold, plum, and rusty orange.

On the left at the top of a rise, the forest stopped abruptly at an apple orchard, its perfect rows bisected by a long driveway that disappeared over a rise. Chuck slowed to a stop. "This is the Holts' property. The house is just over that hill." They sat quietly, taking in the surroundings. Joe pictured Carl running toward them in the dead of night, hell bent on feeding his fish.

Chuck made a U-turn and headed back down Chance Avenue. "Down here on the right is Sinclair Lewis's house." Joe hadn't noticed the place passing it the first time. Chuck pulled to a stop in front of the house and killed the engine. "He's not home. I'll come back and talk to him another time, but feel free if you want to stretch your legs."

"How do you know he's not home?" Joe asked, getting out of the truck.

"His beat-up truck's not here. I'm sure he saves the car for church." Chuck gestured to a sedan parked under a lean-to on the side of the ramshackle house.

Joe walked to the shoulder of the gravel road and stood, listening to himself breathe, mesmerized by the absolute quiet. After a minute, he blinked himself from his trance. For one thing, he was no longer skeptical about Lewis hearing the footfalls of a jogger from inside his home. In this silence, he likely would have heard Carl's heartbeat.

Joe walked to the edge of the Lewis property, crunching red maple leaves underfoot. The low-slung home looked like it would blow over in a strong wind. Its cedar planks had long since faded gray, and a dark green tarp covered part of the sagging roof. The house was set back some forty feet from the road, and there was an unobstructed view from its porch. He didn't see any exterior lights.

One more invigorating deep breath of the brisk air and Joe returned to the truck. "Must be pretty dark here at night."

"You'd be surprised by how bright the moon can be out here," Chuck said, pulling back onto the road. He drove a few hundred feet before pulling over again. "Last stop," he said, getting out of the truck. "C'mon."

Chuck gestured toward a sign nailed to a telephone pole that read "Cabarton Ranch." Atop the sign was a floodlight and a surveillance camera pointed toward the street. "Be sure you get that footage from the DA."

"I will. Isn't that an odd place for a surveillance camera?" Joe asked.

"All the property east of the road is privately owned. The camera is to catch poachers or at least discourage them."

Joe nodded, wondering what animals were hunted.

They crossed the shoulder of the road and walked up a short ridge where an enormous oak tree, charred by a lightning strike, towered above them. A few paces past it, the hillside fell away sharply then sloped down to a deep valley in the distance.

Joe stood still at the edge of the ravine, marveling at the peacefulness of the place, inhaling the musky-sweetness of the leaves. "Down there's the hollers," Chuck said, following his gaze.

At the base of the big tree, Chuck dragged a thick limb from a leaf pile. Joe walked to him, smiling. "So, I take it you've officially lost your mind?"

Chuck continued his task, breathing heavily as he cleared away more limbs from the pile. "There it is," he said finally, brushing away leaves to reveal metal train tracks that headed toward the ridge before disappearing again into the ground.

"So," he said, catching his breath. "Way back when, there was a gold mine in this valley. When we were young and stupid, we'd hop in a miner's car and go careening down the hillside. No helmet, of course."

"Well, if you want to recapture your youth, count me out," Joe said, smirking. "What's this about?"

"So, like I said, it's about a thirty-minute drive down to Hell's Holler," he said, gesturing to the valley below. "County Route 6 is the only way. So, If Clem Tettleton was home by his midnight curfew, he's got an alibi…"

"But if he took Mr. Toad's wild ride, he could have committed the murder and still made it home."

Chuck sighed and kicked leaves from the corroded track that had clearly not been used in years. "Yeah, well, so much for that idea," he said, turning back toward the road.

"It's okay, Chuck. Love where your head's at."

"You seem awfully cheery. What, did you cause the judge to crash his bike again this morning?"

"No, I think the countryside agrees with me. It seems like…" Joe paused, distracted by the loud engine of a pale yellow, beat-up pickup careening in their direction on the gravel road. As it sped by, he saw two men standing in the bed of the pickup, shirtless and howling. Then something pinged loudly off a road sign, not ten feet away.

"Meet the Tettletons," Chuck said, approaching the road sign as the truck disappeared around a bend. He looked up at the road sign. "Looks like it could be a 9-millimeter."

"Jesus! They fired a gun?" Joe asked, wide-eyed.

"Yeah. And I didn't hear a gunshot, did you?"

CHAPTER 24

August 24, 2025, Two Days Before the Murder
"You know you're impossible to watch a game with, Carl," Matt Ledbetter joked from his easy chair.

The third inning was complete, and his son had taken out his earbuds. "Why do you say that?"

"Well, for one thing, with your earbuds, we can't communicate with each other."

"The radio announcers are more knowledgeable."

"Yes, but as I've pointed out, the radio feed is several seconds ahead of the television, so you're constantly celebrating something before it happens. It takes all the drama out of it for me."

Carl frowned. "Yes, you have said all that before many times. Why is it important to watch the game with me? There are lots of televisions in the house."

Matt smiled. Even after eighteen years, sometimes Carl's lack of social instincts still surprised him. "I just like to talk to you during the game."

Carl put his earbuds back in as the top of the fourth commenced. "Okay, Dad," he said loudly, "I have the volume down low on the radio so I can hear you. The inning is starting. What would you like to say to me?"

"Um, uh…"

"Dad, you just said you like to talk to me during the game. It's now during the game. What…" Carl paused for a fist pump after hearing of the first out. "What do you want to say?" he asked, failing to suppress a grin.

Matt laughed, realizing his son was joking. He'd been developing a sense of humor lately. Sarcasm was still mostly lost on him, but his cognitive therapy was helping.

"Okay, here's something, Carl. It seems like no one ever steals a base anymore."

"It seems like that because it's true. In 1977, the Oakland Athletics stole 341 bases. This year, even with the new rules that assist base stealers, the Texas Rangers are on pace to steal something like 130." Carl sighed. "That pitch was a strike."

"So why is that, Carl? I suppose some egghead has figured out that steals are no longer efficient?"

"It's simple math, actually." Carl sounded irritated. "A successful steal increases your chance to score by just over nineteen percent. If you're caught stealing, it decreases your chance of scoring by twenty-six percent. To make it worth the risk, you'd have to steal at a seventy-five percent success rate. So, it actually makes sense for elite base stealers." Carl stood and pumped his fist, celebrating a nice catch.

"Due to the recent limitations on pick-off attempts and the increase in base size, teams are becoming more proficient at stealing bases. So, the frequency of the steal is increasing."

"Carl," his mom called, moving in his field of vision to get his attention. "You have a visitor."

He frowned. "I'm watching the Cubs game, Mother."

"Yes, Carl, I know about your rules, but I thought you might make an exception for this visitor," she said, winking at her husband.

CHAPTER 25

"This is a little different from my high school rallies," Joe yelled over the blaring marching band that was filing into the stadium. He and Chuck stood to the side as fans with face paint and pom-poms streamed in.

"Yeah," said Chuck, bending closer to Joe's ear. "I heard they started inviting the public a while back. Now the town damn near shuts down on Wednesday afternoons."

"Well, look who's already a fan," came a voice behind them. "Hi, Joe," said Melissa Pettigrew. She wore a pinstriped gray suit and a blue Steelers cap.

"Hi, Melissa. This is my investigator, Chuck Argenal."

"High bar, Chuck. I hear you were quite a Steeler in your day."

"Back before the forward pass," Chuck said, shaking his head.

"So, I see what the judge means about the town grieving," Joe said, smirking at the raucous atmosphere.

Pettigrew chuckled. "See you in court tomorrow, counselor."

Chuck nudged Joe and cocked his head toward Arn Stuckey, who was approaching. "High bar, you two," he said. "Thanks for coming out."

"Coach." Joe nodded.

"Chuck, the DA told me you wanted to speak to me. I got time now, if you'd like," he said and led them into an office beneath the grandstand. "Truth be told, I'd rather avoid all this." He gestured above where the crowd thundered and the pep band blared.

"We just wondered if you noticed anything at all unusual that night at the party." Chuck asked.

"No, sir. Can't say that I did. Course, I was gone by about 7:00 p.m. We coaches tend to make an appearance then let the boys have their fun. Besides, it was poker night. We try to play most Fridays when it's not football season."

"Obviously, you didn't happen to see that Tettleton kid around there that night?"

"Oh, hell no. I surely would have mentioned that. My money's still on him for the killer."

"I heard he got kicked off the team last year."

"Yes, sir. It's a shame too, as athletic as he was. But couldn't keep his ass out of trouble. I remember Coach Burgess addressing the team. Tettleton's mom had bailed him out, and so he showed up at practice as if nothing had happened. Coach Burgess, he's always had a way with words. He says, 'Gentlemen, it only takes a little bit of dog shit to ruin a whole bucket of ice cream,'" Stuckey said, smiling at the memory. "'Tettleton,' he says, 'you are the dog shit in our bucket of ice cream.'

"I remember looking at that kid. He looked like he wanted to kill coach right then and there. Ever since, he's been picking fights with football players, stalking the cheerleaders, vandalizing our equipment. The kid is bad news."

"We're getting that impression," Joe chimed in. "Coach, we'd like to speak with your son about that night as well. I think he's the only team member we haven't talked to."

"Okay, sure. Luke's a bit over-scheduled, but I'll make sure I let you know a good time. In fact," the coach said, taking paper and pen from a desk drawer. "Here's the best way to reach him," he said, scribbling on the paper. "He's never far from that damn cell phone."

"Okay, thanks again, Coach. We'll let you get back to your duties."

"Okay. See y'all."

Chuck bought a bag of popcorn at the concession stand and was eating handfuls on the ride away from the stadium. "What do you think of Tettleton's little stunt with the silencer?" Joe asked.

"Hard to say. My instinct is they're just fucking with us. If crazy Clem was the killer, I don't think he would have gone that route. Then again," Chuck said, pausing to toss some popcorn in his mouth, "they are the Tettleton's, so all bets are off."

"Check his alibi when you can. And maybe good ole Coach Stuckey's too. Having met his wife, I'm not sure she would allow him to spend Fridays playing poker. Just a hunch."

"Will do."

They rode in silence for a while before Joe spoke. "You know, Chuck, I've noticed a few things about your hometown."

"Yeah, what's that?"

"Well, for one, everyone knows everyone's business."

Chuck nodded. "Holler whispers."

"I've heard that before. What's it mean?"

"Down in the deep hollers, the acoustics are like a cathedral. You can whisper down there and be heard a quarter mile away. 'Holler whispers' means everyone hears everything."

"Holler whispers," Joe said, nodding.

"What else have you noticed about Barton?" Chuck asked.

"Well, even though everyone knows everything, it seems like something is behind this murder that's under everyone's radar. Also, everyone seems ever so friendly and helpful…"

"And yet, someone is lying their ass off," Chuck said, nodding.

"Sure seems that way."

CHAPTER 26

"Sinclair Lewis?" Chuck called as he walked up the dirt driveway to the rickety house.

The old man stood at the edge of his porch, leaning forward with both hands on his cane, squinting down at the approaching stranger as his chair rocked behind him. "Can I help you?" he asked warily.

"I'm Chuck Argenal, Mr. Lewis. I was wondering if you could spare some time to talk about the Holt murder?"

"You from the *Herald*?"

"No, sir, I'm an investigator hired by the Ledbetters."

Chuck noticed a hint of disappointment on Lewis' face. "Not that I'm eager for the publicity, but you'd think the *Herald* might be interested in what I had to say." He shrugged and waved Chuck up to the porch.

"Argenal, Argenal…you Pappi's kid?" he asked, gesturing to the chair next to him. "Knew him well."

"No, sir, Pappi's my uncle." As he spoke, Chuck checked out the view of the street from the porch, much of it currently blocked by a step side pickup from the eighties.

"One of your people was hell on the football field," Lewis said, ignoring the answer. "I think it was Pappi's nephew."

"This year's team going to go all the way?" Chuck asked, happy not to relive his glory days.

Lewis snorted in disgust. "For me, the passing game has ruined football. Nobody runs the ball anymore. I hear that Stuckey kid can sling it around, so we'll probably be fine." Lewis rocked back in his chair. "But you're not here to talk football."

"No, sir. Just here to clarify some things about your statement, if that's okay?"

"Fire away," Lewis said. "Remember it like it was yesterday. I was up later than usual, sitting right here. I like to whittle at night. Or was I up to pee?" he asked himself. "Anyway, I heard the footsteps on the gravel first, then here comes this fellow," he said, raising his cane and pointing toward the road where the truck blocked his view.

"That truck was parked around back. It's out there today because that's where it died on me yesterday. Grady Richins should be here soon to tow it for me." Lewis checked his watch. "Where was I?" he asked, regaining focus. "So, here he comes, smack dab in the middle of the street, running like he stole something."

Chuck looked around the place for exterior lights, and Lewis followed his gaze. "Lots of moonlight that night," he said defensively. "I don't have to tell you about our big Georgia moons."

Chuck nodded. "You get a good look at him?"

"Yes, sir, it was the kid in the picture the officer showed me. Deputy Neff, I believe it was. Recognized him right away. Yes sir, my body's a' crumblin' but I still got the hawk eyes."

"I don't doubt that, sir. I noticed you don't wear glasses."

"Never have," Lewis said proudly. "I use a pair for reading and whittling but not for distance. I'm afraid I saw what I saw, Mr. Argenal."

At the road, a postal truck pulled up at the mailbox at the edge of the driveway. Lewis leaned forward in his seat and squinted out toward it. "Looks like that's Grady to fix my truck," he said, standing.

"I appreciate your time," Chuck said as the men shook hands. He was off the porch quickly as the postal truck rolled away, happy to avoid witnessing Lewis's embarrassment.

CHAPTER 27

Day Three

"Well, now you're just making shit up," Dirk said, shaking his head.

Across the table, Elston Arbett spread his palms. "I'm just saying, there were forty teenagers there. Anything could have happened."

"But, Elston, we should stick to the evidence," Frank countered. The former Navy man's tone was respectful. "The jury instructions clearly tell us not to speculate."

"Frank, nobody knows for sure what happened that night," the retired tax attorney countered. "To a certain extent, this is all speculation."

"I'm really having a difficult time with Carl's lack of motive," added Priya. "You just don't kill someone for no reason."

"You do if you have a screw loose," Dirk quipped. "And what's with the rocking? It looked like he was laying an egg on the witness stand."

"He's autistic!" Sara snapped, glaring at Dirk. "He's probably very intelligent."

Dirk rolled his eyes. "My bad. No offense, dude," he said, looking down the table to Quinn, drawing several groans from the jury.

Sara stood and stalked to the water cooler. "Insulting fuck," she said, loud enough for all to hear.

"Okay," Jack said from the head of the table. "Let's keep it civil. What do we all think of Mr. Lewis' testimony?" he asked, changing the subject. "He seemed to be enjoying his fifteen minutes of fame."

Frank nodded. "Sinclair hasn't been the same since Ruby died."

"I agree," put in Duncan. "He was trying a little too hard. Still, we know at least part of his testimony was true."

"That's right," Ellen said, as Duncan beamed. "He may have been enjoying himself on the stand, but he didn't seem like the type to just make stuff up. I mean, why would he make up seeing Carl carrying a gun?"

"Many times, we see what our mind wants us to see," countered Priya. "Memory is a funny thing."

Dirk sighed, disgusted. "Well shit then, why bother listening to the witnesses when we can just have our neighborhood shrink tell us what they really meant?"

"I'm an engineer, Dirk," Priya said calmly, "and I don't think that's productive. All I'm saying is that paying attention to the witnesses' motivation is important."

"Quinn, I value your opinion," Sara said gently, as the young man to her right turned away slightly and hunched his shoulders. "I know you have some ideas about all this."

He peeked up at Sara then looked around the table. He mumbled something no one could hear. "What was that? We didn't hear you," Ellen whispered.

Quinn cleared his throat and kept staring at the floor. "I'm listening," he said at a volume that was still barely audible. "If I have something to contribute, I will do so," he said in a quiet monotone.

"Okay, he speaks!" Dirk said, scanning the room for approval. "Hey, Quinn," he said, mimicking the young man's voice and cadence, "can you say guilty?" He belly laughed as the other jurors shook their heads in disgust.

"You're such a jackass!" Sara said, touching Quinn's shoulder.

"Okay," Jack said, relishing his position as referee. "Let's focus on what we know. I have to admit, the scientific evidence is compelling."

Frank, the former military man nodded. "The gunshot residue was on his hands."

"Yes, and we saw how it could have been transferred to Carl's hands," countered Sara.

"Oh God," Dirk said shaking his head, "you're buying that homo lawyer's BS hook, line and sinker. Figures." He rolled his eyes and smirked.

Sara slammed down her notebook on the table as the group fell silent. She glared at Dirk for several seconds. "You are a disgusting human being!" she said, her voice quaking. "We need a break, Jack," she said, and stormed out.

Dirk sat with a smug smile, seemingly unfazed by the events. "Well, answer me this, folks," he asked loudly as the group filed out. "How the fuck do you explain good old Carl's DNA under Justin Holt's fingernail?"

CHAPTER 28

Joe walked into the courtroom to find it empty. He took a seat in a chair behind the counsel table, wondering if Judge Boniface had decided to play nine holes. And where was Pettigrew?

After fifteen minutes, Barbara, the clerk, walked in from the hallway that led to the judge's chambers. "Oh, hello, Mr. Turner, you may as well head on back," she said, gesturing behind her. "Those two will be talking football all day if you let them."

Joe was confused for a moment. It was improper for an attorney to meet with a judge outside the presence of opposing counsel. Then again, Joe reminded himself as he walked into chambers, this was Barton.

"Afternoon, Mr. Turner. Please have a seat," the judge said from behind his desk. He wore jeans and a dress shirt. "Ms. Pettigrew here was just telling me some interesting news."

"I hope not about our case. That would be an ex parte communication."

"Well, Melissa," the judge said with a condescending smile, "you best put your big-girl pants on today. He's breaking out the Latin on us. And no, we were just talking about the Steelers. Big game coming up on Friday," the judge said as Joe seethed. Pettigrew smiled uncomfortably, clutching a manila envelope. "Melissa, what'd you bring with you there?" Boniface asked, clearly pretending not to know.

Pettigrew handed Joe the envelope. "The DNA results came in. Good news for you is your client didn't scratch the victim's chest. That DNA came back positive for a mixture of the victim and an unknown person. Bad news is we found Carl Ledbetter's DNA under Justin Holt's right middle fingernail." The DA's words floated to Joe in slow motion before slamming into his forehead.

"What DNA testing was used?" he asked, managing to keep a poker face.

"Y only," Pettigrew answered, referring to the DNA test that compared only Y chromosomes.

"This seems like a pretty thin report," Joe said, eyeing the envelope. "I'll want all the raw data and testing protocols. Also, I'll want to retest in an independent lab." Still reeling, Joe had switched to defense attorney autopilot.

"You want to what?" the judge asked, incredulous.

"I'm entitled to full discovery, Your Honor, and an independent testing of the evidence." Forgive me if I don't trust some lab in the woods that makes moonshine on weekends, he wanted to add.

"Mr. Turner, believe it or not, we have competent scientists in this state," Boniface said, as if reading his mind. "They went to college and wear white coats and everything. But, if you want to run up your client's bill, far be it from me to get in the way. Now," the judge said as he stood, "I can see you got all gussied up, and we got our court reporter here on a Thursday, just for you. So, I'll get my costume on so you can go out and play lawyer."

Joe marched into the courtroom livid. He and Pettigrew stood at the counsel table while the court reporter and part-time waitress, Inez, readied her stenograph.

"All rise. Come to order." The courtroom deputy's words echoed throughout the empty courtroom. Joe caught sight of Pettigrew suppressing a laugh. The bailiff continued, as if addressing a packed courtroom. "The Superior Court of the State of Georgia, County of Daulton, Judge Franklin Boniface presiding, is now in session. You may be seated."

The judge shook his head, looking frustrated. "Only do that for trials, Alvin. Now, Mr. Turner, I understand you have a motion."

Joe formally requested a continuance of the trial, citing an inability to provide effective representation for his client given the time constraints. He also moved to recuse the judge based on his relationship with the victim's family. Knowing Boniface would deny the motions, he made the requests solely to preserve an appeal in the event of a conviction. As he spoke in a resigned tone, his mind was far from the case law that he recited from memory.

He thought about the upcoming conversations looming with Carl and his parents. The one where he would encourage Carl to take a plea. He thought of his likable client in a cold prison cell, deprived of his Cubs games and taken from his family.

"That about it, Mr. Turner?" the judge asked, looking down at him with a bored expression. Joe didn't bother to answer. "Good. Motions denied," he said, rapping his gavel on the bench. "I'll see you two next week for trial."

On the walk back home, Joe called Chuck to inquire about the availability of his favorite DNA expert, Curtis

Berrian. Known in legal circles in the San Francisco Bay Area as Dr. Death, the former Chief Pathologist of Alameda County was a leading expert in the field.

Next, he thought of the overwhelming evidence, and an unsettling image of his client snuck into Joe's consciousness. This time, Carl's face twisted in anger as he held a gun to his victim's chest.

CHAPTER 29

Walking back to the house after court and needing to vent, Joe dialed Eddy, who was driving to the Archaeological Center in Tallahassee.

"And he actually told the DA to put her big-girl pants on?" she asked. "What a d-bag."

"Total d-bag trapped in the nineteen fifties. Everyone else here seems fairly progressive. There's one giant exception, and he's the…" Joe waited as he passed a mother and daughter on the sidewalk. "And he's the fucking judge!"

"Joe Turner, I think I know you pretty well. I don't see you making it through the trial with this buffoon without losing it. I feel like I should start raising bail money now."

"Relax, Busier, I haven't been held in contempt in two years."

Eddy laughed. "Yeah, not impressive. Just do me a favor. If you feel like you're about to say something you'll regret, instead just say, 'Judge, have a wonderful day.' Only you'll know that in your mind, you'll actually be saying, 'Go fuck yourself.'"

Joe frowned. "'Have a wonderful day.' That doesn't sound very satisfying."

"Humor me."

"Don't worry. I'll hold it together for Carl."

"For Carl? Uh oh, Turner."

"Anyway," Joe continued, ignoring the comment, "the Ledbetters will cover the bail. In other matters, would you be willing to sit in when we interview Luke Stuckey?"

"Ah, finally recognizing my incredible ability to read people. About time."

"Whatever, Busier. You minored in psych, so, what, that makes you a mind reader?"

"It was nearly a double major, and yes, I'll allow you to tap into my innate brilliance."

"Also, would you mind doing some research on this town?"

"Sure. I'll be back there the day after tomorrow. What do you need to know?"

"I'll explain later. Going to meet Chuck for coffee. Drive safely."

Joe walked into Nadine's and found Chuck waiting in a corner booth. "Of all the gin joints in all the towns in the world."

"Sorry, I should know that."

Chuck shook his head in disgust. "Casablanca again."

"Tell me something good, Chuck."

"I got two things. First, someone left an anonymous note on my car." Chuck dug the crumpled note from his shirt pocket. "Says 'Tettleton's the murderer.'"

"Okay," Joe said with reservation in his voice. "Not admissible in court, but I guess we might be on the right track."

"Yeah, there's a very faint water mark on the paper," Chuck said, holding it up to the light.

"Look at you, sleuthing away."

The private eye took another folded paper from his jacket and laid it on the table. "Same paper."

Joe looked down at the paper with the football team's letterhead stamped at the top and Luke Stuckey's phone number printed below it. "Interesting," he said. "The coaches are really selling Tettleton as the murderer. The QB2 theory just won't die."

"On the other hand," his investigator said, "the coaches might be on to something. I checked out Tettleton's social media. Turns out, the night before the murder, he posted, and I quote, 'Big party at QB1's house tomorrow. I expect a big loss before the season starts.'"

"Wow, Chuck, you buried the lead! That's incredibly ominous," he whispered, looking furtively around the restaurant behind him.

"The spelling was atrocious, but yeah," Chuck deadpanned. "Also, Dr. Death is available and interested. Says he's free for a call tomorrow around 3:00 p.m. our time."

"Great."

The two compared notes on their two alternative suspects and exchanged subpoenas and investigation ideas before parting.

As Joe walked back to the house, he took stock of the defense. The Ledbetter case was becoming a nightmare for a few reasons. First, Eddy's "Uh oh" comment had referenced Joe's use of his client's first name. He'd learned long ago to avoid emotional attachments to his clients. It could cloud judgment and lead to devastating losses.

Also, the evidence against Carl seemed insurmountable. Joe was no stranger to cases with no defense—"dead cases" in defense attorney parlance. But almost without exception, these cases involved defendants who were clearly factually guilty. Although losing was never pleasant, Joe felt far less pressure when his client's guilt was obvious. But when he and his legal pad were the only thing standing between an innocent client and a life behind bars, the stress could be unbearable.

As Joe turned down Cedar Street, the Victorian coming into view, he felt a tightness in his shoulders and a pit in his stomach that was all too familiar.

CHAPTER 30

Carl

I knew it would be bad as soon as Joe Turner said, "Carl, I'd like to talk to you about…" It was every adult's tell. If you hear that phrase, very bad news will follow. It must be in some how-to-impart-bad-news handbook somewhere.

No adult ever just blurts out bad news without the preface. It's never, "Carl, your brother died," or "Carl, we had to put Mittens to sleep," or "Carl, we need to increase the medication that makes you nauseous."

Also, the "I'd like to talk to you" introduction is reserved for only truly horrible news. They don't bother with it for mere inconveniences or mild setbacks. Plenty of times I've heard, "Carl, the Cubs game got rained out," or "Karen cancelled your tutoring today." But if the news is truly awful, it's always, "Carl, I'd like to talk to you about…." Then falls the bomb of devastation.

I don't understand why they say it. If they felt the need to say something before delivering the bad news, why don't they just say, "Carl, I'm about to impart some terrible information."

The real problem I have with the phrase is its plain and obvious meaning. "I'd like to talk to you…" could only mean that the speaker enjoys giving me the bad news that follows. Why they take pleasure in my misery, I'll never understand. There's a German word for taking delight in another's misery: schadenfreude. So, I know the feeling exists, but I confess to being at a loss to understand it.

This attorney, Joe Turner, seems nicer than most. At least he didn't speak to me like a child. Apparently, though, even he enjoyed imparting bad news.

I almost interrupted him when he'd started the sentence, "Carl, I'd like to talk to you…," and now I wish I had done so.

"Joe Turner," I wish I'd said, "you are undoubtedly about to give me some truly awful news. I know this because you just said, 'Carl, I'd like to talk to you.' My question, Joe," I fervently wished I'd asked, "is if you are going to give me bad news, why are you going to like it? If I had to tell you that your dog died, I wouldn't take any pleasure in it. In fact, quite the opposite. 'I hate to tell you this,' I'd likely say, 'but your dog died.'"

Anyway, I didn't say any of that to Joe Turner. As an aside, it is quite common for me to say only a fraction of what I am thinking. On one hand, therapists have told me this is unhealthy. However, I've found that often, when I articulate my thoughts, I unwittingly offend people.

Joe Turner's pause just after the pronouncement of his perverse glee was also very disconcerting. There is usually a pause before adults deliver the bad news. I've noticed that the bigger the pause, the more devastating the news.

It was as if they were saying, "Look, Carl, you know bad news is on the way. Otherwise, I wouldn't have told you that I would like to talk to you. Now, since this news is truly some of the worst you'll ever hear, and because I very much enjoy giving you the bad news, I'm going to savor it for as long as possible."

Joe Turner's pause had been deceiving because, given the devastating news he'd shared, it had been nowhere near long enough to give me fair warning. I agree that the elaborate coded preface and the pause that followed were stupid. However, if I am to continue to rely on it, it should be applied consistently.

Joe Turner paused for only a half second. This length of pause implied bad news akin to a cancelled vacation or the death of an obscure relative. The pause was certainly not commensurate with the news itself, which had been calamitous.

Joe Turner told me that in order to avoid being incarcerated for the rest of my life, I should take advantage of an opportunity to be incarcerated for the next twenty years. Also, in order to take advantage of this opportunity, I would have to lie and say that I killed my good friend Justin Holt.

I told him I would do no such thing. Obviously.

CHAPTER 31

"I can't imagine how it's come to this. Surely there must be something that can be done. Would more money help? Would another attorney on the case help?" Aubrey asked, desperation in her voice. The Ledbetters, Aubrey and Matt, had knocked on Joe's door shortly after he arrived home. Joe had invited them over to discuss the plea bargain. He hoped they could convince their son of its wisdom.

"No, Aubrey, and I know this is devastating to hear, but the evidence is daunting." Joe outlined the prosecution's case, highlighting Carl's DNA under the victim's fingernail, the gunshot residue on Carl's hands, and the eyewitness who saw him running away from the scene.

"I'd like to show you something," Aubrey said, handing the phone to Joe. "It's a video of last year's football banquet. Justin had just received the Most Valuable Player Award."

Joe pushed play. A handsome young man was speaking at a podium before rows of tables in a modest high school auditorium. Joe recognized Justin from the autopsy photos and cringed. In the video, his cool blue eyes sparkled below a rakish mop of sandy blond hair. A playful smile revealed perfect teeth. Speaking with poise beyond his years, he thanked his teammates and coaches, his Southern drawl deepening the sincerity of his words. Standing to his left and behind him, Joe could make out a familiar figure in a Cubs cap.

"I'd also like to thank someone else who meant the world to me this year. As y'all know, I spent the first half of the year with my arm in a sling, feeling about as worthless as a bump on a log. Anyway, one person on the team wouldn't let me feel sorry for myself. He quizzed me play calls and our hand signals every day." Justin paused to smile. "And if you know him, you know he doesn't mind repeating the plays as many times as it takes. Over and over and over.

"He also kept telling me we were going to win state. Anyway, he does so much for our team, and I wanted to make sure he was recognized. So, high bar, Carl. Please give it up for our manager, Carl Ledbetter." The room erupted in applause, and the video ended with Justin and Carl embracing in a lengthy bearhug.

Taking back her phone, Aubrey Ledbetter looked Joe in the eye. "You've been around my son, Joe," she said quietly. "He's not an emotional child. If he exhibits emotions, they're usually wrong for the occasion. Laughing loudly at funerals, that sort of thing. When he returned to our table that night, there were tears in his eyes. He looked over at me and nodded," she said, dabbing her eyes as she smiled at the memory. "He knew he was finally feeling the right emotion, and he was proud of himself for it."

Sitting next to his wife, Matt reached for Aubrey's hand and held it. "That's how I know my son is innocent," he said.

Joe was at a loss for words. The video was powerful, and yet the evidence remained.

Aubrey breathed deeply and straightened herself in her chair. "Of course, pragmatically, the plea bargain seems like the smart thing to do. But it doesn't really matter what we think."

"Well, I was hoping if Carl heard it from you two rather than a stranger, he might see the wisdom of a plea."

The Ledbetters both smiled in silence. "What am I missing?" asked Joe.

Finally, Matt spoke up. "Joe, once Carl makes up his mind, he doesn't change it."

"And by that, my husband means, not once in Carl's life has he changed his mind about anything. Ever."

Joe sighed. "I see."

"You know," Aubrey said, staring into space with watery eyes, "I very nearly kept him home that night. He'd just had the seizure the day before. I remember at the hospital after he'd slept, his first words were, 'May I still attend the party, Mama?' He was so excited to go," she said quietly. "So happy to see Karen and the team. Finally, I said he could if he agreed to take my phone."

"I'm sure he was excited," Joe said, compassion in his voice. "And of course you'd let him go. I know the team was important to him."

Aubrey nodded a thank you. "Well," she said standing, "I'll speak to Carl about this. Then you can have another run at him. I'll bring him by later in the week, if that works?"

"Sure. And I did have one question. I understand Carl was home alone when the police questioned him. When you arrived home, did you notice anything out of the ordinary?"

Aubrey hesitated ever so slightly. "No," she said, unconvincingly, "nothing comes to mind. And, Joe, I wanted to ask again about the composition of the jury.

We've heard rumors it might include neighboring counties."

Joe's radar was up. "I suppose that's possible," he said. "There are bound to be so many people in this county who would know the parties involved."

"So, we know the mailing lists are generated down at the county clerk's office," Matt said. "Do you know the exact date of jury selection?"

"I'll be honest, you two." Joe's tone was serious. "This conversation makes me a little uncomfortable. Obviously, jury tampering would be a serious…"

"Oh, my lord," Aubrey cut in with a forced laugh. "Of course, we would never contemplate such a thing."

"Sorry, Joe," Matt added, "we surely didn't mean to alarm you. We're just curious about the process is all."

"Oh, I know," Joe said, returning their smiles. "We attorneys are just paranoid about these things."

After the couple had departed, Joe changed and went for a run, wondering how in the world the Ledbetters were planning to rig the jury.

CHAPTER 32

Day Four

"Okay, I want each of you to know that I respect your opinions. We've had good dialogue, and I really appreciate…"

"Can we just do this already?" Dirk cut in.

"Yes! Dirk, for once I agree with you," Sara chimed in.

"Okay." Jack sounded hurt. "Dirk?"

"Guilty."

"Frank?"

"Guilty."

"Quinn, ready to vote yet?" The group sat in silence for several seconds before Jack continued. "Sara?"

"Not guilty."

"Elston?"

"Not guilty."

"Priya?"

"Not Guilty."

"Ellen?"

"Guilty."

"Duncan?"

"Guilty."

"And I'm a guilty," Jack said, with a sigh. "It's still 5-3 with one abstention."

"Three and a half fucking days, and it's the same." Dirk groaned and rubbed his face with both hands. "All that worthless scribbling," he said, staring with disdain at the various lists on the whiteboard.

"I have to admit, I'm losing my patience with you three," Frank said, gesturing across the table. "We've got a guy running away from the scene with a gun and his DNA under the victim's fingernail."

"Not to mention the 'Hi, Carl' witness," Ellen chimed in.

"Totally agree," added Duncan, flashing a goofy smile at Ellen. "For me, he's a key witness."

Elston shook his head and loosened his tie. "I think the murderer is whoever scratched Justin's chest, and we know that wasn't Carl. The shot was at close range. It makes perfect sense."

"Yes, for me that's reasonable doubt," said Priya. "Do I think he did it? Maybe, but I'm far from certain."

"So, let me get this straight," grumbled Dirk. "You think he did it, but you're voting not guilty. Unbelievable." He shook his head.

"That's the law," snapped Sara.

Dirk jerked his head toward Sara and started to speak but stopped himself. "I need a break," he said, glaring down the table at her while he stood.

"Yeah, let's take fifteen," Jack said as others rose to file out of the small room.

Soon the room was empty except for Frank, who lingered at the water cooler at the back of the room. Jack re-entered the room and approached the retired military man.

"Hey, Frank, I'm with you on the verdict. I feel like Dirk is hurting our cause, though. He's alienating the not-guilty folks."

Frank eyed the foreperson warily. "We're not really supposed to be talking about the case without everyone present. The rules are pretty clear on that."

"Oh, of course. You're right," Jack said apologetically. "Well, hopefully, we can rein him in. It's up to us old-timers to get this done, I suppose," he added, with a pat on Frank's shoulder as he turned to leave.

CHAPTER 33

Joe was waiting outside the courtroom when his phone buzzed. "Hi, Chuck. What's up?"

"Clem Tettleton's alibi checks out. GPS puts him at home just before midnight. He wears an ankle monitor, and the PO verified his location."

Joe groaned into the phone. "So, down to one alternative killer."

"Maybe."

"Why maybe?"

"It just seems crazy to me there's not a way across that ravine. This generation is all about saving time and short attention spans, right?"

Joe shrugged. "You said Tettleton gave you the alibi before you asked. How did he know the time of death?"

"The Tettleton's tend to have their own network."

"Really?"

"Oh yeah, it's a high functioning hillbilly mafia."

"Fascinating."

"Also, I spoke to Doctor Death. He said checking the lab work will be easy, but he's not sure he can get the retesting done in time. He asked if you can push back the trial a few weeks?"

"Not a chance with this judge. Shit, Chuck. I need those tests. Can you ask again? Maybe bribe him with a fresh jug of formaldehyde."

Down the hall, Joe saw Pettigrew unlocking the courtroom and headed that way. "If we need to, we can throw some of that Ledbetter money at the problem," he said. "Whatever it takes. See ya, Chuck."

Inside the courtroom, the DA was sitting at the counsel table reading the paper. "Let me guess, a feature on the Steeler's back-up kicker on the front page?" Joe asked, setting his satchel on the counsel table.

"No," Pettigrew said, chuckling. "I think that was last week. So, what's the word? Do we have a deal or are we about to push football off the front pages with the trial of the century?"

"Deal?" Joe asked, as if the question were absurd. "Innocent client, Melissa." Just ask his parents, he wanted to add.

Pettigrew sat in silence, staring at Joe in disbelief.

"Afternoon, you two," Judge Boniface called from the doorway to his chambers. "C'mon back."

Joe dreaded what would come next. Admittedly, his client's position was unreasonable. Given the overwhelming evidence of guilt, his decision amounted to choosing life in prison rather than twenty years. Now, he would either be seen as incompetent for recommending trial for Carl or at least ineffectual in failing to persuade him to plead. Walking into chambers, he felt a tinge of guilt. It wasn't about him, after all.

"Looks like trial, Judge," Pettigrew said after they sat down.

Boniface looked at Joe with a pained expression. "You're kidding?"

"No, sir."

The judge scratched his chin. "How about a counteroffer then?" he asked. "Melissa, could you live with fifteen?"

This guy really hated trials, Joe thought to himself. From the look of his daily calendars, he figured the judge worked about three hours a day. A trial was bound to set his golf game back several months.

The DA turned to Joe. "If the defendant makes that offer, I'll consider it. But I won't negotiate against myself, so my official offer remains at twenty."

"That's reasonable," said Joe. "I'll run it by my client."

"One other thing," Boniface said, reclining in his chair. "Mr. Turner, I've heard reports of a defense investigator hounding the football team for interviews."

"I don't know about hounding, Judge. I would like to interview one particular member of the football team. I believe it's my right to ask."

"And I believe it's his right to say no," the Judge countered.

This guy was unbelievable. He wasn't even pretending to be unbiased. "Sure, Judge." Joe fumed. "I suppose if your golfing buddy's son has something to hide, then he has every right to say no."

Judge Boniface stared daggers, and Joe could tell the judge was weighing his options. He knew he didn't want to admit he was running interference for a friend. "Watch your step, counselor," he said quietly then spun his chair around, probably to curse him under his breath. "I'll see you two next Monday for motions in limine."

Pettigrew caught up to Joe outside the courthouse after he'd stormed out. "Hey, if you want any physical evidence brought to trial, let me know ahead of time. I have to get it from the evidence locker," she said, walking alongside him.

"Thanks, I would like to have the shirt Carl was arrested in." Joe had noted that the shirt was free of bloodstains.

"Sure thing."

"Also, a reminder about the Cabarton Ranch video."

"Yeah, there was a problem retrieving the video. Our office is working on it. And I understand you want to interview the Stuckey kid?" she asked.

"Yeah, all the other players have cooperated."

"I suppose he's got a lot…"

"Yeah, he's got a lot on his plate. I've heard," he said, disgustedly. "Holy shit, Melissa, he's a fucking high school quarterback in Bumfuck, Georgia."

"Wow, you're riled up about this. If you want, I can probably persuade him to come to our office. We can speak to him together."

The DA clearly wanted to know what he was up to. "No, thanks. I think I'll just subpoena his ass and see what he has to say at trial."

Pettigrew rolled her eyes. "Oh, simmer down, Joe. You think dragging Luke Stuckey into court is the move? You'd be tarred and feathered. Let me bring him in, and you can interview him. I'll just observe."

"Not happening," Joe snapped, turning to walk away.

"Suit yourself," she called after him. "But you best get your boy to plead."

"I'll try," Joe called back, knowing full well that wasn't happening either.

CHAPTER 34

August 24, 2025, Two Days Before the Murder
"Hi, Carl!" a young woman in a cheerleader outfit called from the kitchen. It was Karen Sarkliss, and Carl blushed.

"Hello, Karen. Why are you here? It's not Thursday."

"I know, Carl. I'm not here for calculus. Just saying hello," she said cheerfully.

"Hello," he said, turning back to the television.

Aubrey approached her son and removed his earbuds and ball cap. "Stanley Carl Ledbetter. You stand up like a gentleman and greet your guest."

Carl obliged. "Welcome, Karen," he said, walking to her. "Would you care for a beverage?"

"That's sweet of you to offer, Carl, but no thanks."

"I offered because social conventions are important to my mother, so I practice them scrupulously."

"Yes, I know that about you, Carl. So, I came today to invite you to the team party Friday at the Holts' place."

"I generally do not enjoy social gatherings."

"I know, but I really think this would be fun. I know the team wants you there."

"How do you know?" he asked.

"How do I know?" she repeated, confused.

"Yes, how do you know that the team wants me to attend? Did they say that?"

"Absolutely. The whole team said they really want you there."

"The Cubs have a day game, hon, so you're free that evening," Aubrey said on her way out of the room.

Carl thought for a moment. He was free after all, and apparently the entire team wanted him there. Also, Karen Sarkliss was quite a wonderful person. "Yes, I will come."

"Oh, that's great news, Carl. The team will be so pleased."

"Karen, would you like to be my girlfriend?" he asked, in a matter-of-fact tone.

"You are a persistent one, Carl," she said, smiling. "But we've been over this. You know I'm dating Justin. I don't think he would be very happy if I just started dating you, would he?"

Carl nodded. "I suppose not," he said then paused. "But perhaps he wouldn't care since I saw him kissing Sophia Montgomery recently."

Karen smiled with wide eyes. "Carl Ledbetter, you devil!" she said, playfully punching his shoulder. "Kissing Sophie Montgomery? The goth girl who smokes and wears black lipstick?" she said, laughing. "Carl, honey, you know it's not nice to lie, to your friend especially."

Carl grinned. Sometimes she said the most obvious things.

"Okay, Carl," Karen said turning to leave. "I'm off to cheer practice. I'll see you tomorrow night for calculus."

After she'd gone, Aubrey came back inside to find her son back in his chair, watching the game with his dad. She walked to him and removed one of his earbuds. "That was pretty nice of Karen to visit," she said, catching her husband's eye.

Carl smiled and felt himself blush again.

CHAPTER 35

Joe sat in the front room of the Victorian across from his client. "Carl, I'd like to talk to you about…"

Carl's audible groan interrupted him in mid-sentence, and Joe's client buried his face in his hands.

"What's wrong?" Joe asked. "I haven't even told you anything yet."

Carl looked up and sighed. *Now he's pretending like he doesn't know the code. Good God.*

"Okay, Joe Turner," he said, rolling his eyes. "What awesome news do you have for me? Of course, that was meant to be sarcastic as I said the opposite of what I meant. I can't say that I understand sarcasm, but my mother has taught me about it."

Joe smiled. "Very well executed sarcasm, Carl. Now, I'd like to talk to you again about the proposed plea deal."

This time, he didn't pause at all. Clearly, he knew nothing of the pause rules. And now, he was expounding on the dire prospects of a jury trial and the even more unique opportunity to spend fifteen years in prison.

As Joe droned on, Carl's mind went to the more pressing matter of the Cubs' depleted bullpen and tonight's game.

"I know it's an incredibly difficult decision, but what do you think?" Joe asked.

Noticing that Joe had stopped talking, Carl blinked back into focus. "Joe Turner—I'm saying your full name so as to impart the importance of my next statement, as my mother has told me it's an effective way to emphasize a point. I will not lie and say that I murdered my friend, Justin Holt. Period."

"I understand, Carl. And so, I will defend you. But Stanley Carl Ledbetter, you need to be honest with me."

"I am always honest. My parents are fond of saying that I am honest to a fault, although I've never understood their meaning."

"Carl, there was gunshot residue on your hands," Joe said, returning his client's frank tone. "Did you fire a gun on the day that Justin was shot?"

Carl searched his memory. "No, my father and I only go to the range on Sundays."

"So, the only way that you would have gunshot residue on your hands is if you shot Justin, touched a gun after it was fired, or touched Justin after he was shot."

Carl nodded. "I follow you, yes," he said, calmly. "I must have gotten the gunshot residue on my hands when I touched him after he was shot."

"I don't understand, Carl. You told me you saw nothing unusual when you went to thank Justin for the party."

"Yes, I told you that."

Joe sighed deeply. "Carl, please tell me what you saw when you said goodbye to Justin that night. Tell me exactly what you saw and what you did."

"I knocked on the door, but he didn't answer." Carl stared into space. "I went inside. He was lying on his back on the floor. I knelt down and shook him, trying to wake him up. It was pretty dark, so I didn't see the blood right away."

Joe sat quietly, trying to maintain his composure. "Carl, do you recall speaking with me about two weeks ago?"

"Yes."

"And telling me that when you saw Justin in his room, you didn't notice anything out of the ordinary."

"That was the case, yes."

"Carl!" Joe heard himself bark then caught himself. "Carl," he continued calmly, "wouldn't you agree that finding your friend's dead body was something out of the ordinary?"

"No."

"Excuse me?"

"At the time you inquired about whether I'd seen anything unusual, I was obviously aware that Justin had been murdered. So, at the time of your question, the presence of Justin's dead body seemed perfectly normal."

Joe absorbed his client's answer with a wry smile. "So Carl, just to be clear, when you arrived in Justin's room, he was lying on the floor, bleeding."

"Yes."

"Were you able to rouse him?"

Carl shook his head. "No."

"And you didn't see anybody around at that time?"

"No."

"While you were on your way to his room, you didn't see any of your teammates around?"

"No."

"Do you know who Clem Tettleton is?"

"Yes."

"Did you see him at any time that night?"

"No."

"You didn't see anything that"—he paused for emphasis—"at that time, you thought was usual?"

"No."

"And then you left?"

"Yes, as I've told you, I recalled that I needed to feed…"

"Yes, the fish," Joe interrupted. "So, when you left the room, did you see anything or hear anything that you believed was unusual at that time?"

"No."

"And did you see anyone as you were leaving?"

"No."

"So, Carl, your DNA was found under Justin Holt's fingernail. Did Justin ever touch you earlier that evening? Shake your hand, hug you, wrestle with you. Anything like that?"

Carl looked toward the ceiling. "Yes," he finally said and broke into a smile. "Justin and I had our special handshake. We did it after every touchdown he scored. That night, because social conventions are important to my mother and I practice them scrupulously, upon my arrival at the party, I sought out Justin to thank him for the invitation. Surprisingly, we did our handshake even though he hadn't scored a touchdown."

Eddy came in the front door, back from a run. She'd arrived from Tallahassee that morning. "You must be Carl," she said, approaching. "I'm Eddy."

Carl stood. "Hello," he said then stood silently for several seconds, taking her in.

"Odd name for a woman, right?" she said, smiling.

"It is uncommon, yes, but I've encountered many names that are androgenous."

"Well, Carl, I'll leave you two…"

"Part of your hair is purple," Carl said, cutting in.

"Excuse me?" Eddy asked, amused.

"There are some strands of your hair in the front that appear to be purple. This is very unusual. Typically, when people color their hair, the color is meant to replicate another color of hair. I'm curious as to its purpose."

"That's a very good question, Carl," she said, glancing at Joe, who was smiling at the interaction. "I'm not sure. I suppose I think it looks cool." She smiled then retreated to the kitchen.

After a few more questions, Carl's mom pulled up outside. Carl strode purposely toward the door then turned to face Joe. "Parenthetically, Justin only did that handshake with me," he said with pride in his voice. "I don't think he had a special handshake with anyone else on the team."

CHAPTER 36

"Thanks for agreeing to meet us, Coach." Arn Stuckey took a seat at a corner table at Nadine's across from Joe, Chuck, and Eddy. Joe was grateful for his girlfriend's presence. Despite his teasing, he appreciated her unique ability to read people.

Stuckey nodded. "Sorry it took me so long to arrange this. I own the Barton Feed Store," he said, gesturing across the street. "This time of year, I tend to neglect it, so this gave me a good excuse to check in on the place."

"We appreciate it. Will Luke be coming?" Joe asked as the waitress Joe recognized as the court reporter set down cups of coffee.

"Yeah, his mom's picking him up from weightlifting," he said, checking his watch. "He should be here soon. Damnedest thing. When I was his age, I couldn't wait to drive. Luke prefers to be carted around by his mom. About the only time he drives is on a date."

"I've heard the same thing about my nephew," Joe said, nodding.

"I blame the damn phones," the coach, said, shaking his head. "Why drive to visit your friends when you can have a conversation with your thumbs?"

"So, Coach, this is just a formality, but can we get the names and numbers of your poker buddies?"

"Uh, yeah. No problem."

Joe noticed a black Mercedes pull up outside the diner and soon heard heels on the diner linoleum behind him. He turned to find Monica Stuckey striding toward their booth with her son in tow. She wore designer jeans, a silver lamé "Football Mom" sweatshirt, and blingy designer sunglasses. "Hello, y'all," she said pleasantly as the men at the table stood. "My taxi service is up and running. Mr. Bigshot QB1 here has his private coach session at 5:00 p.m. back at the school."

"Hi, Monica, nice to see you again," Joe said.

"You too, Joe. And hello, Eddy." Her bright pink lips formed the familiar fake smile as her eyes scanned Eddy's clothing. "I just love your hair, by the way," Monica continued. "My college roommate had a purple streak like yours, and she was just the prettiest thing."

"Thanks," Eddy said awkwardly.

"This shouldn't take more than twenty minutes," Joe said, trying to hasten her departure.

"Okay then, I'll leave you to it," she said and bounced her way out of the diner, stopping twice to accept well wishes and revel in the glory of her status.

"Luke, can we get you something to eat or drink? A soda?"

"No thanks."

"He's on a strict diet," his father said, rolling his eyes. "Eats like a squirrel if you ask me."

Luke rolled his eyes. "There's lots of protein, Dad. It's just healthy is all."

"So," Chuck said, "we've just been asking all the players if they saw anything out of the ordinary on that terrible evening."

The young man thought for a moment. "No," he said, shaking his head. "Of course, I left the party around 8:00 p.m. At that time, everything seemed normal."

"Where did you go?" Chuck asked.

Luke stole a glance at his father to his left. "Me and Jen Scoggins—she's my girlfriend—we went over to her place. Her parents were away for the weekend," he said sheepishly.

Joe recalled reading Scoggins' statement to the police. She reported being at the party from 6:00 p.m. until the body was found but hadn't mentioned her trip home.

"And how long did you stay?"

"I'm not exactly sure. Until a little after midnight, I think."

"Then you and Jen went back to the party?"

"Yeah. When we pulled up, we saw all the cops there," he said solemnly.

"Did you happen to see anybody there that night who seemed out of place," asked Joe, thinking of Clem Tettleton.

"There weren't any football haters or anything like that," he said, "but before I left, I did see this goth girl there. She sort of kept to herself and seemed out of place."

After collecting contact information for Luke and his girlfriend, Joe and Chuck left father and son in the diner. "Thoughts?" Joe asked, once outside.

"I think the kid's a tough sell as the killer. Seemed genuinely sad about losing his teammate."

Eddy nodded. "I thought so, too. His mom's a piece of work, right?"

Chuck smirked. "I thought I noted some tension between you two. If her nose was any higher, she'd drown in a rainstorm."

"Well shit, Chuck," Joe said, considering the latest hit to the defense. "Can you check on alibis of father and son, just the same?"

"That's a Bingo," he said, walking away.

Joe knew it was a movie line but wasn't in the mood.

CHAPTER 37

Day Five

"I can't believe Ledbetter testified. The DA crucified his retarded ass," Dirk said, shaking his head.

"Dirk," Sara scolded from the end of the table, "you are literally the most offensive human on the planet." After four and a half days of deliberation, nerves were fraying.

"I'm just saying, if I were accused of murder, let alone murdering my friend, I'd show a little emotion."

"Were you listening? He has autism!"

"Yes," Priya added. "My cousin has Asperger's and has trouble showing emotion."

"Yum, ass burgers," Dirk said, laughing stupidly.

"Okay, let's remain focused," Jack said calmly with palms down. "Dirk, please be more respectful. And I think Carl's, um, condition, is something we should consider."

"So, if you're riding the short bus, it's okay to kill someone?" Dirk asked.

"Of course not," snapped Priya. "But his autism is highly relevant when you consider his testimony and his lack of ability to relate to people."

"He didn't relate well to one person, all right," Dirk said, with a snicker.

Exasperated, Frank dropped his notepad on the table. "Fine, let's focus on the evidence then. He had gunshot residue all over his hands," he began, tapping his large Naval Academy ring on the table to emphasize each point. "Was that an unlucky coincidence? Maybe. But was the DNA transferred too? Just more bad luck? Did the eyewitness just happen to identify this same unlucky suspect? At some point, you know the saying. If it looks like a duck and quacks like a duck, you can be pretty damn sure it's a duck."

Ellen, the anxious schoolteacher spoke up. "For me, the DNA is the most convincing evidence. I just don't buy the transfer theory," she said with a grimace. "Still, this is such a big deal." She rested her elbows on the table and massaged her temples.

"I agree," said Duncan, right on cue. "The DNA evidence has me convinced, but it's so stressful." Eyes rolled around the table.

"Duncan, I don't mean to offend you," Priya began tentatively, "but it seems like you're just agreeing with Ellen. We'd all like to know what Duncan thinks."

The paramedic blushed. "I'm just being honest. I thought the DNA evidence was persuasive," he mumbled.

"The DNA transfer theory is a load of crap," Dirk said with disgust. "That defense attorney is just casting lines out to see what idiots will bite."

"Dirk, I don't think that's productive," Jack said timidly.

"I'd believe him over the smarmy prosecutor," Elston countered.

"I agree," added Priya. "The whole Southern belle thing is a bit much. There's something I don't like about her."

"Maybe the fact that she's hot?" grumbled Dirk.

"Okay, we're getting way off track," Jack said, standing. "We're due for a break. Let's come back at 3:00 p.m."

Ellen remained in her seat, covering her face with both hands. Jack re-entered the room and sat across from her. "Stressful stuff, right?"

Ellen looked up, surprised by his presence. She nodded.

"I'm with you," Jack said, nodding. "My brain tells me there's enough evidence to convict. At least I think so. But I keep thinking if we get this wrong, we'll be responsible for an awful tragedy."

Ellen nodded. "Truly awful. So, what do we do?"

"I don't know," Jack said after several seconds of silence. "But I don't know if I can vote to convict and live with myself. I just don't know anymore." He got up and left, leaving Ellen alone with her thoughts.

CHAPTER 38

Joe knew a trial was a terrible idea, so he was surprised that Carl's adamant rejection of a plea bargain had brought a smile to his face, the plain words chiming a bell of clarity, the opening bell of a boxing match. Now, he sat at the counsel table, prepared and resolute.

Next to him sat Carl in a blue sport coat and tie. His Cubs cap lay on the table in front of him as he stared straight ahead with a poker face. His prescription glasses were tinted to combat the lights of the courtroom.

Although the judge hadn't required Carl's presence for the litigation of the pretrial motions, Joe had thought it better that he see the courtroom prior to the trial. As with the other pre-trial appearances, Judge Boniface had closed the courtroom to visitors.

The judge emerged from his chambers, buttoning his robe as he ascended the bench. "Okay, let's get this show on the road. Ready, Inez?" he asked the court reporter, who nodded. "Mr. Turner, I've reviewed your voluminous motions and the responses submitted by the DA. We'll start with your Motion for Change of Venue. Do you wish to be heard?"

Joe outlined his argument, preserving the issue for an appeal, but knowing the eventual outcome.

"Motion denied," the judge said firmly when he'd finished. "While the case has gotten its share of publicity, the jury pool will be drawn from the county at large. I'm confident we can find jurors who have not been prejudiced.

"Your motion to disqualify me in this case is denied as well. I did not know the victim personally, and although I know his parents, I do not socialize with them. Your claim that I'm close friends with coaches on the football team is patently false. I barely know Arn Stuckey."

The judge proceeded to hear arguments from Joe on each of his pretrial motions. He reclined in his chair and stared at the ceiling as Joe made his record, arguing again for a continuance, moving to suppress Carl's statement to the police, and requesting a limitation on the admission of autopsy photos designed to inflame the passions of the jury.

Every plea to the court met the same result. When Joe had finished each argument, the judge would sigh deeply into his microphone, as if bored to tears with the proceedings. "Motion denied," he'd mumble without making eye contact with Joe as the District Attorney sat silently.

Joe kept his composure, knowing his efforts were an exercise in futility. But he persevered, determined to make a record for the appellate courts. He only wished the transcript would reflect the judge's body language and tone of utter disdain.

"What's this?" the judge asked, flipping through one of Joe's motions, obviously for the first time. "A motion to exclude evidence of the victim's football career? On what basis?" the judge asked, bemused.

"On the basis that Justin Holt's ability to throw a football is irrelevant to the question of who murdered him," Joe answered, his tone pleasant but firm. "Your Honor, this town is obsessed with its high school football team. There should be no reason that the jury be made aware of his status as a football star. It would only serve to incentivize the jury to hold someone responsible for the crime."

The judge sat thinking for several seconds. Joe knew there was no basis whatsoever for denying the motion. "Let's take this on a case-by-case basis," he said, finally.

"Your Honor, what does that mean, exactly?" Joe asked, seething.

"It means if, during the trial, you find something objectionable, we'll take it up then."

"After the jury has already heard it? Your Honor, the whole point of an in limine motion is to…"

"Counsel, watch your tone."

"Okay," Joe continued, sarcastically, "just so everyone is aware, when Ms. Pettigrew cues the pep band in her closing argument, I'll be objecting."

"Ms. Pettigrew, you have a motion to exclude third-party culpability?" the judge asked, ignoring Joe's remark.

"Yes, Your Honor. The law prohibits the defense from theorizing about another party committing the murder without hard evidence. The state wishes to prevent the defense from engaging in baseless speculation."

Joe had read the motion and was prepared to vigorously object. It would preclude the defense from attempting to blame either Stuckey or Tettleton for the murder, which would be absurd. Luckily, the judge saw it his way for once.

"I'm not prepared to grant this motion," the judge said. "If the defense engages in speculation, you may object." Boniface spoke again, under his breath, but close enough to the microphone for all to hear. "Besides, granting that may well get the conviction reversed."

Joe was up out of his chair. "Excuse me?" He glared at the judge, scarcely believing his ears.

"I wasn't addressing you, Mr. Turner," the judge said, averting his eyes to shuffle papers on his desk.

"Judge, you basically just said you were certain my client would be convicted!"

Boniface stared down at him from his perch. "That's enough, counsel."

Joe shook his head in disgust. Finally, his frustration boiled over. "Judge, you're so bad at this!"

"Excuse me, counsel?" Boniface bellowed.

"You suck at your job," Joe said, matter-of-factly. "I mean, being unbiased is sort of your one job, right?"

"Mr. Turner, you're on thin ice. I will hold you in contempt."

Joe was shocked he hadn't already. Looking back, he figured the judge thought a contempt finding would draw more attention to his remark. Now, surely one more word and the judge would fine and jail him.

The judge rose. "That concludes our business today. I'll see you two for jury selection tomorrow. And Mr. Turner, I'll have no more impertinence in my courtroom."

Joe considered his options. Fuck it. "Impertinence. Impressive, Judge. Was that on your word-of-the-day calendar?"

"You…You're in contempt!" Boniface shouted, banging his gavel. "Alvin," he yelled, his face reddening. "Take Mr. Turner…Goddamnit, where's Alvin?" the judge called, looking around the courtroom for his bailiff. "Barbara, where the hell is he?"

The clerk turned to the judge. "He's at the restroom," she said without a hint of urgency. "I told him not to have the chili at that new diner." She shrugged.

Boniface slammed a file on his desk. "Well, he needs to be here, Goddamnit! I'm holding someone in contempt!" the judge railed, overcome with frustration. "You're in contempt!" he yelled, too close to his microphone as shrill feedback echoed throughout the courtroom.

Carl covered his ears at the noise and rested his head on the counsel table. Joe patted his shoulder, shaking his head at the chaotic scene. Presently, Alvin ambled into the courtroom, oblivious to the proceedings.

"Alvin! Take Mr. Turner into custody!" the judge demanded.

The judge's yell gave the bailiff a start. Wide-eyed, he trotted toward Joe, fumbling with his handcuffs. "Oh," he said, examining them closely. "I don't believe I have the keys to this pair. I'll just be a minute, Judge," he said, hustling back out of the courtroom.

Judge Boniface waved a hand in Joe's direction in disgust as he trudged down off the bench. "Enjoy our jail, Mr. Turner," he called on his way out of the courtroom.

Joe texted Eddy while waiting to be jailed, adding a grimacing emoji.

—*Hey. Will you bail me out?*

—*Of course. And you're incorrigible.*

Pettigrew, who'd been watching in stunned silence, offered to arrange for bail, but Joe declined. After she'd gone, Joe turned to Carl, who had remained stoic until the ear-splitting microphone feedback. "Carl, your mom should be outside to pick you up." Carl stood and turned to leave then hesitated. "Yes, Carl," Joe asked. "Is there something else?"

"Yes, I have two things to say," he said in his familiar, nasal tone. "Despite the judge's wishes, I do not believe you will enjoy the jail."

Joe smiled. "Carl, I totally agree. And what else?" he asked, hearing the approaching footsteps of the bailiff.

His client looked Joe in the eye. "Thank you for advocating for me," he said. Joe thought he saw a hint of a smile before he turned and walked away.

CHAPTER 39

"That was a fucking eternity," Joe said, settling into Eddy's rented sedan.

"Sorry. For a small-time jail, there was a surprising amount of red tape."

"No," Joe said, after a few minutes of silence.

"No what?"

"You always ask me if it was worth it? Not this time. That has to be the most disgusting jail cell in the world."

Eddy crinkled up her nose and rolled down the window. "Yeah, I think you brought some of its funk with you. Try not to touch anything until you've showered."

Joe's time in custody had been spent standing in the middle of a concrete cell, staring out its only window, a four-inch square of wire-enmeshed glass in the middle of the metal door. He'd declined the bench built out from the wall, stained as it was with what he assumed to be various bodily fluids. The stainless-steel toilet, rising starkly from the floor, had been out of the question.

Back in their temporary home, after a long hot shower for Joe, the couple grilled burgers, opened a bottle of Sancerre and sat on the porch while Joe highlighted his day in court.

"So, I take it 'Judge, have a wonderful day' never crossed your mind?"

Joe smiled into a grimace. "Sorry, Busier."

"How was the DA during all this?"

"She tried to sneak in some ridiculous motion that would have torpedoed the defense entirely."

"And what did your client make of the scene?"

"Carl was stoic, as usual."

"Uh, oh. Using your client's first name, again. Don't we have a rule against that?"

They talked about his autism, how he'd fare on the witness stand, and trial strategy. "The best evidence we have incriminates the Tettleton kid, right?" Joe asked.

"Yeah, that Instagram post was creepy. But didn't his alibi check out?"

"Yeah, unless he somehow got himself across that ravine, which is what Chuck suspects. Also, he's a Tettleton. Apparently, they're pretty much born to commit crime, or at least that's their reputation."

Eddy was pouring herself another glass of wine when her boyfriend sighed audibly. "What up, Turner?"

Joe had been thinking of Carl locked in that disgusting cell or, worse yet, trying to survive a state prison's general population. He shook away the images and quickly shifted his focus to the evidence. "A grudge against the football team and a suspicious social media post is not much," he said. "Not compared to gunshot residue on Carl's hands and his DNA under the victim's fingernail. Not to mention an eyewitness and his incriminating statement. It just seems like we're…" Joe paused, searching for the words.

"Rearranging deck chairs on the Titanic?" Eddy chimed in.

"Thanks, Busier. Ever helpful," he said, laughing. "It does seem like we're missing something, though."

"Well, there is the unknown person who apparently scratched Justin's chest. Do we know how long before his death that happened?"

"Dr. Death says superficial scratches usually heal within thirty minutes, so it could have happened when he was shot. Of course, if the killer made the scratch, that eliminates both Clem and Luke. The cops took DNA samples from everyone at the party, and you know Clem is already in the known-criminal database."

Joe sipped his wine and thought for a moment. "Busier, what is the most bizarre thing about Barton, Georgia?"

"Easy. The over-the-top, crazy obsession with its football team."

"Right? It's completely insane and unhealthy. I just think that if there's a motive for murder, it's more than likely wrapped up in that football hysteria."

Eddy nodded. "So, back to your theory, it was the second-string quarterback? The one with no evidence?"

"Yeah, I know. What did you think of Luke yesterday."

"Honestly, he seems as nice as pie, but it was obvious his parents put a ton of pressure on him. And his mom is a piece of work."

Joe nodded. "Anyway, I need to forget about that theory. There's literally no evidence to support it."

"Yeah, and you'd be blaming the murder on the current town hero."

Just then, Joe's phone buzzed with a text from Chuck. *—Guess whose cell phone pinged at the football party twenty minutes before the murder?*

CHAPTER 40

Walking to court the next morning, Joe called Carl's mom. "Aubrey, when Carl came home that night, did you notice anything different about him?" he asked. "Honestly, I'm just hoping there's a reason why he suddenly ran home from the party. I'm afraid the explanation about feeding his fish is not ideal."

"I get it. Well, Carl does have the ability to erase certain things from his memory that he finds upsetting. Once he had a dog named Banks who passed away. To this day, Carl doesn't remember the day he died. And it's more than just being in denial. It's like he's removed the event from his memory."

"That night, did he seem upset or unsettled?"

Aubrey paused again before answering. "No."

"Aubrey, if you noticed anything, even if it's incriminating, you need to tell me. I need to know what I'm up against."

Aubrey sighed into the phone. "Okay, here it is. After much debate, Carl picked out a blue and white striped shirt to wear to the party. I didn't love it, but he was dead set on it. Well, when he got home that night, he wasn't wearing it."

"Did you find it?"

Another pause. "It was in the washer."

"I see," Joe said awkwardly. "Well, good to know. I'll process this and get back to you."

He hung up and dialed Chuck.

"Hey, when did you get sprung?" the investigator asked.

Joe sighed. "I take it you heard."

"Oh, hell yes. Word at Nadine's this morning was that you called the judge every name in the book."

"This town is unbelievable. And that's not even accurate."

"Oh yeah," Chuck agreed. "A lie travels half-way around the world before the truth can get its pants on."

"Movie line?"

"Winston Churchill, I think."

"So, Chuck, it turns out our killer-QB1 theory just won't go away, huh?"

"Yeah, turns out Luke Stuckey and the truth ain't related. And not only does his cell phone put him there, none of the other players saw him after 8:00 p.m."

"Which means he was sneaking around the place," Joe said, nodding. "So, opening statements are either tomorrow or the day after. I'd kind of like to know who we're blaming."

"Motive, opportunity, and a fake alibi isn't exactly a smoking gun. I'd say stick with Tettleton. That defense has the added benefit of not having you run out of town on a rail."

"I guess so. Even though he has an alibi?" Joe asked.

"I'm working on that. Also, Coach Stuckey hasn't gotten back to me with numbers for his poker buddies."

"Interesting."

"Maybe it's better to hold off blaming anyone for now. Are you on your way to choose twelve angry men?"

"No, Chuck. You only get nine here in your home state. Any thoughts? Besides avoiding residents of Barton, football fans, redneck conservatives, churchgoers, and I don't know, people with children?"

Chuck laughed. "Go for the conspiracy theorists."

"Thanks. See ya."

"Have fun storming the castle."

The hallway outside Department One was crowded with prospective jurors. Joe walked to the side door of the courtroom and knocked. While he waited, he caught sight of a young man further down the hall talking on his cell phone. He looked familiar, but Joe couldn't place him.

"Morning, Mr. Turner. C'mon in," Alvin said, looking frazzled.

Inside, Joe sensed tension. Carl sat at the counsel table with perfect posture, rocking. The clerk and court reporter were already in place. Wearing his robe zipped to the top, Judge Boniface poked his head in the courtroom then disappeared.

"Glad to see you made bail," Pettigrew quipped, unpacking her file.

Joe glanced at her blue jacket and gray skirt. "What, did you leave your Steeler helmet in your office?"

Boniface took the bench. Joe wondered if there would be a further scolding. "Anything we need to take up before I let in the panel?" he asked.

Joe leaned to the microphone. "Yes, Your Honor. I neglected to mention one motion in limine. I would like an order that Ms. Pettigrew not inform the jury or refer to me being from out of town."

Boniface scowled and Joe could see his wheels turning. He was hoping the judge would grant the motion so as not to risk another of his blowups minutes before trial. "Ms.

Pettigrew, I'm inclined to grant this motion. Any objection?"

"No, Your Honor."

"Okay, that will be the order. Alvin, please let in the prospective jurors," the judge said, disappearing into his chambers.

After Barbara took roll, Boniface burst through the door to his chambers and strode into the courtroom with purpose. Alvin snapped to attention. "All rise," he boomed and belted out the introduction.

"Ladies and gentlemen," the judge said, reading from a script, "You have been summoned to serve in the case of the State of Georgia v. Stanley Carl Ledbetter. Mr. Ledbetter is charged with murder." Joe heard the inevitable murmurs throughout the courtroom.

After the judge covered the ground rules for jury selection, Barbara read the names of the first nine jurors. The clerk then handed Joe and the prosecutor each prospective juror's one-page questionnaire. They listed their ages, occupations, and one-sentence statements about their perceived role as jurors.

Whereas in most courts, attorneys could question the jurors, Judge Boniface had made clear he alone would conduct voir dire—the questioning of prospective jurors. As Joe had feared, the judge neglected to ask the most important question—in what city the jurors lived. That meant while Joe could unwittingly seat a jury of Barton residents, Pettigrew would have no trouble recognizing her fellow citizens.

Boniface's questioning was nearly useless. After eliciting the level of education and job title of prospective jurors and their spouses, he concluded by asking if there was any reason they couldn't be fair to both sides. A few jurors confessed to knowing the victim's family and were excused, but it was impossible to tell how many other biased jurors remained. Joe was forced to go almost entirely on feel.

Midway through the afternoon session, the defense had exercised 9 of its allotted ten juror challenges, the prosecution, only eight. "The State is satisfied, Your Honor," Pettigrew said. That meant if Joe was also satisfied, they had their jury. But if he excused another prospective juror, then Pettigrew could control the composition of the jury's final two seats.

Joe was generally pleased with the jury's composition, but there were definitely landmines. Although the construction foreman said all the right things, he had the smug look of someone who thought jury trials were a waste of everyone's time. Also, there was a retired ex-military man who was likely pro-prosecution. On the plus side, he'd been surprised that Pettigrew was willing to keep the progressive looking social worker who had referenced her partner.

The juror most concerning was a young man who looked to be painfully shy. He spoke in a monotone that reminded Joe of his client, and he thought he may be on the autistic spectrum as well. He wasn't sure, though, thanks to the judge's ineffectual questioning. What worried him was a prominent cross that hung from a chain around the young man's neck and a red, white, and blue watch band. When Joe started to stand to send the juror home, Carl touched his arm.

Surprised that he was paying attention, Joe covered the microphone in front of them and whispered, "Carl, this juror could be very conservative. I think he has to go."

"I think he should stay on the jury," Carl said in full voice, drawing chuckles throughout the courtroom.

"Your Honor, the defense is satisfied," Joe said, and the jury was sworn. Six men and three women would decide Carl's fate. Joe thought the foreperson would either be a retired tax attorney or an insurance salesman who seemed a tad too eager to serve. Two alternates were selected and advised that they would sit through the trial then be on telephone standby during the deliberations.

On his way out of the courthouse, Joe caught sight of the same familiar looking young man he'd seen in the morning talking on his cell phone down a courtroom hallway. Joe was nearly at his house when he recalled where he'd seen him before. He'd been behind the wheel of the golf cart that had whisked Carl to the guest house at the Ledbetter estate.

CHAPTER 41

August 25, 2025, One Day Before the Murder
"Hi Karen! Time for some calculus?" Aubrey Ledbetter asked, opening her front door for her guest.

"Hi Mrs. Ledbetter. Yes, and I don't know what I'd do without Carl. Thanks to him, I'm at least not failing."

"I'm glad. Come on in, Ms. Homecoming Queen. Congrats!"

"Thank you. It's been a busy week."

"I'll bet. You and Justin are such an adorable couple." She leaned in to whisper, "Even if Carl is insanely jealous."

"Oh, he's so sweet."

Later, while Carl was explaining an equation in the study, Aubrey poked her head in. "Would you two like a glass of tea or water?"

"Oh, no thank you, Mrs. Ledbetter," Karen said without looking up.

"Okay, dear, is any of it sinking in?"

"Carl's great, but I'm afraid I'm hopeless."

"Oh, I'm sure that's not true, is it, Carl?"

"No, it's mostly true. She doesn't understand some basics," Carl said in his matter-of-fact tone.

"Stanley Carl, that is rude," Aubrey scolded, trying to keep a straight face as Karen burst out laughing.

"No," Karen said, "it's totally true."

"That's my son. Never ask him if a dress makes you look fat. I'll leave you two alone."

Moments later, Karen looked up from her equation, her face suddenly awash with realization. "Carl, when did you see Justin kissing Sophie Montgomery?"

CHAPTER 42

"Good afternoon, folks. My name is Melissa Pettigrew. I'm a Daulton County Deputy District Attorney and the town prosecutor here in Barton." Pettigrew addressed the jury in her opening statement but spoke loud enough for the packed courtroom to hear. "Thank y'all for being here. I know jury service is not at the top of everyone's list, so I surely appreciate your time."

Joe had a feeling Pettigrew would be effective with the jury. Sure enough, she spoke with a confident, easy manner. Pleasant looking without trying, she charmed the men while earning women's admiration. Joe also thought he heard a bit more twang in her voice than usual.

"I'll get to the point. On the night of August 26th of this year," the DA said, pointing behind her at Carl, "that young man shot and killed Justin Cassady Holt, a seventeen-year-old native of Barton."

Glancing back at Carl, she turned to look at him. The jury followed her stare to find Carl, emotionless and intently trying to balance a pen upright on the counsel table. Pettigrew waited for several seconds then shook her head before continuing.

"What I can't tell you is why it happened. Justin Holt was, by all accounts, a fine young man—a football star, a good student, a wonderful son to his parents." Pettigrew clicked a remote device in her hand, and the victim appeared on the large video screen on a wall opposite the jury. Square-jawed, handsome, wearing his blue Steeler's jersey, Justin's smile lit up the courtroom as his mother in the gallery sobbed quietly.

While Pettigrew continued setting the scene for the murder, Joe slowly reached over and took Carl's pen from him and placed it on the table. He had spoken to Carl about how to behave in court, knowing it was useless. Carl was going to be Carl.

Joe had considered calling an expert witness to educate the jury about autism but decided it was better to let the jury get to know Carl first-hand. He hoped that if the jury noted his often-inappropriate affect in court, it would help explain the sudden run home to feed the fish and his lack of emotion when informed of his friend's death.

"But 'why' is the only question we don't know the answer to," the prosecutor continued. "Everything else about the crime will be obvious. We know that Justin was shot at close range. You'll hear the coroner tell you that gunshot particles were burned into the skin at the entry wound. We know that just before he was shot, Justin reached out and grabbed his killer, scratching him. We know the murder was premeditated because the killer used a gun with a silencer on it. That's why no one heard the shots.

"We know all this to a moral certainty," Pettigrew said, centering herself before the jury then pointing again. "We also know that Justin's murderer is sitting right there. The evidence will show that it is an absolute fact that

Justin Holt's murderer was Carl Ledbetter. We know this because the person identified running away from the body, just after the murder, is Carl Ledbetter. We know this because the only person at the scene of the murder who tested positive for gunshot residue is Carl Ledbetter."

Pettigrew smiled, savoring what was next. "Finally, we know this because of the work of a very thorough Daulton County evidence technician who took samples of Justin Holt's fingernail clippings, just in case he had managed to claw at his murderer moments before being shot at point blank range. And the person whose DNA was found under one of those fingernails," Pettigrew said, pausing for dramatic effect, "is Carl Ledbetter."

The Deputy District Attorney nodded a thank you to the jury and sat down. If the opening statement had been lost on Carl, Joe felt all its impact. It wasn't as if he'd expected mediocrity from Pettigrew, but this had been one of the best openings he'd ever witnessed. It had been aggressive, confident, and concise. In less than twenty minutes, the prosecutor had managed to summarize the devastating evidence against Carl, evoke sympathy for the victim and his family, and even point out Carl's inappropriate behavior in real time.

"Mr. Turner," Judge Boniface's voice boomed throughout the courtroom, "does the defense wish to make an opening statement?"

CHAPTER 43

Day Six

Ahead of him on the sidewalk, Jack saw Duncan cross the street, headed toward a coffee shop half a block from the courthouse. The morning had brought more bickering, and Jack had called a mid-morning break.

"Hey, Duncan. I know it's a bit early for our morning break. I just felt like we needed it."

"Totally agree. We weren't being productive."

Duncan got his coffee and was at the cream and sugar station when Jack approached him again. "So, on an unrelated topic," Jack said, "would you mind a piece of unsolicited advice from an old guy?"

Duncan looked confused. "Uh, sure, I guess."

"So, do you happen to know what trait women find the most attractive in a man?"

Duncan blushed. "Look, I know everyone thinks I'm totally into Ellen, but really..." He stopped in mid-sentence when Jack raised a hand.

"Hear me out. Women love men who listen. That's what they always complain to men about, right? 'You aren't listening to me.' Women go crazy for guys who listen. Also, more than anything, have an open mind." Jack shrugged. "Just something to think about," he said and walked away.

CHAPTER 44

"How's your jury?" Eddy asked over their morning coffee.

"No idea, but I'd love your opinion." Joe dug a stack of juror questionnaires out of his satchel and stood to leave.

Eddy glanced at the pages. "Name, age, occupation, and one sentence about being a juror? That's it?"

"Oh, c'mon Busier. That's more than enough for a psychology savant like you."

"I'll give it a shot. Did you get my email answering your random-ass Barton questions?"

"Yes, it was perfect," he said, pulling his case file toward the door on a hand trolley.

"Masquerading as a Georgia peach. Joseph Windgate Turner, you should be ashamed," she called after him.

"So sue me!" Joe called over his shoulder, laughing. He set off for the courthouse, resolved to make the second day of the trial better than the first. He hadn't been pleased with his opening statement. Given his indecision about whether to blame Stuckey or Tettleton, he'd been forced to be vague about the defense.

Hearing himself trot out the stale defense attorney axioms—innocent until proven guilty, beyond a reasonable doubt—had sounded like attorney double speak. Especially after Pettigrew's fact-intensive opening, his words rang hollow, floating to the jury box without effect.

On the trial's second day, he arrived at court to find a police officer sitting in the hallway, no doubt waiting to testify. He'd asked Pettigrew for her order of witnesses, but she had put him off, saying the situation was fluid or some such bullshit. At least admit it if you don't want to tell me, he'd thought to himself, continuing his pattern of finding things to dislike about his opponent. Frustrated, he had reminded her again about the Cabarton Ranch video footage.

"You'll have it when I have it," she said. "We're working on it."

Behind Joe, Carl's parents were seated in the front row of the gallery. After the jury filed in and Boniface had taken the bench to the usual fanfare, the judge turned to the prosecutor. "Ms. Pettigrew, call your first witness."

"Your Honor, the State calls Officer Darrell Billups." It was the officer who arrived first on the scene and later interviewed Carl.

After some introductory questions, the officer identified the victim. Next, Pettigrew began displaying a series of sobering photographs of Justin as he appeared after death—on the gurney at the hospital and at the coroner prior to the autopsy. As the photos told the story, the courtroom grew somber. On his back, arms akimbo, the victim's pale skin stained with blood, the photos displayed the savage violence and finality of his death.

Justin had been shot in his own bedroom on what was supposed to be a happy occasion, and a final photo captured the shocking suddenness of the attack. The close-up showed his body on the gurney, probably in the ambulance, just after he had died. Justin's head had lolled to the side, facing the camera. Mouth slightly open, eyes wide, he gazed to nowhere, as if pleading in disbelief.

Mercifully, the big screen went dark, and Pettigrew got to the substance of her examination. "Officer, you spoke to the defendant later that evening, correct?"

"Yes."

"Was the defendant a suspect in the murder at that time?"

"No. It was a routine interview."

"And when you asked him if he knew why you were there to see him, what did he tell you?"

"He told me, yes, he knew I was there to ask about the murder of Justin Holt." In unison, the jury bowed to make notes.

"Did you know of a relationship between Justin Holt and the defendant?" Pettigrew asked.

"I'd heard that the defendant and Justin were close."

"Can you describe the defendant's demeanor at the time you spoke to him?"

"He seemed very matter of fact. Not at all emotional."

"Did you ask the defendant if he could think of any reason anyone on the team would want to hurt Justin?"

"I did. He told me he couldn't think of any reason why anyone would want to shoot Justin Holt."

"The defendant specifically used those words, Officer?"

"Yes."

"Prior to that time, had you mentioned to the defendant how Justin Holt had been killed. Had you mentioned that Justin Holt had been shot?"

"No, ma'am, I had not."

Next, Officer Billups, also a ballistics expert, explained gunshot residue to the jury.

"So, these particles that are expelled from the gun when it's fired, how far can they travel?" Pettigrew asked, feigning genuine curiosity.

"Not far. Three to five feet."

"And can they linger in the air? In other words, if I fire a gun, could someone else walk through after the shooting and end up with residue on themselves?"

"No. The particles dissipate almost immediately. To have gunshot residue on your hands, you'd have to either be present in the immediate proximity of the shooter or be the shooter yourself."

Next, Pettigrew walked the officer through the protocol for the gunshot residue test then strolled from behind the podium to the jury rail. "Officer Billups, did you swab the hands of defendant Carl Ledbetter only hours after Justin Holt's murder for the purpose of testing them for gunshot residue?"

"I did."

"And what was the result?" the prosecutor asked, maintaining eye contact with the jury.

"Both hands tested positive for gunshot residue."

Pettigrew smiled at the jury. "No further questions, Your Honor."

On cross examination, Joe elicited that it was possible for gunshot residue to be transferred from one person to another.

"Officer, I take it that given his answers, Mr. Ledbetter became a suspect."

"Yes."

"And so, you were attentive during your administration of the gunshot residue test, correct?"

"Yes, obviously."

"And you were on alert for any other incriminating evidence?"

"Yes."

"Did you notice any scratch marks on Carl's face?"

"No."

"On his neck?"

"No."

"On his hands or arms?"

"No."

"How about his clothing, Officer? Did you see any blood on Carl Ledbetter's clothing?"

"No, sir."

"Officer, you mentioned that Carl seemed to know that Justin Holt had been shot. Did you…"

"Mr. Turner, please do not refer to your client by his first name," the judge said, interrupting him.

Joe blinked slowly and sighed. "May we approach, Your Honor?"

When the attorneys had arrived at the bench, Boniface covered the microphone. "Problem, Mr. Turner?"

"Yes, Judge, the prosecution has been referring to the victim as 'Justin' all morning. "

"That's different. Your client is a party to the action. Now let's get on with this."

"Judge…"

"Step back, Mr. Turner."

Joe stayed where he was for a full ten seconds, staring daggers at the judge before turning on his heel."

"So, Officer Billups," he said, getting his bearings. "Did you ask how Carl…" Joe paused, turning to the judge. "Excuse me. Did you ask how the defendant knew the victim had been shot?"

"No, sir. Sort of figured that was obvious."

"So, you assumed he knew because he was the murderer?"

"I figured that was a good possibility."

"And I take it you considered Carl's demeanor was inappropriate, given his friend had just been shot?"

"Yes, sir," the officer said, nodding.

"Tell me, Officer, prior to that night, had you ever observed Carl Ledbetter on a sad occasion?"

"No, sir."

"Had you ever spent any time with him to get to know him?"

"No."

"Did you know anything about him?"

"No."

"Did you know that Carl is autistic?" Joe asked, feeling awkward about the presence of his client.

"No."

"And are you aware that the syndrome affects the ability to effectively interact and communicate with people?"

"No."

"Are you aware that those with autism often display inappropriate emotions?"

"No."

Finally, Joe asked the officer about Clem Tettleton's ominous social media post. Pettigrew would later submit evidence of Clem's alibi. Still, though, Joe noted the buzz throughout the courtroom at the mere mention of the name Tettleton.

CHAPTER 45

Carl

August 25, 2025, One Day Before the Murder

I almost didn't push the 911 button. I really wanted to avoid the seizure, and my first thought was to just ignore it. Of course, this was illogical.

We have the 911 buttons in every room of our house. In rooms that I frequent—my bedroom and the family room, where I watch Cubs games—there are three. The rule is if I'm home alone, I push the button. I can usually feel the seizures coming on, and I did this time.

It's difficult to explain how I know they are coming, but I feel quite anxious for no reason. As a humorous aside, my family often thinks I'm going to have a seizure when I'm actually just feeling stressed about a close Cubs game.

The seizures—technically called generalized motor seizures—are apparently caused by a misfiring of electrical impulses, although the concept of electricity in my brain seems strange.

Anyway, sitting in the family room right next to one of the buttons on the wall, I began to feel anxious. The reason I hesitated was because of the party the following day. Frequently, I am confused for a time after the seizure while my brain sorts itself out. So, I was worried my mother would not allow me to attend the party.

Initially, I was very hesitant to attend the party, but the more I thought about it, the more positive I became. Karen Sarkliss told me the members of the team very much wanted me to attend. The Barton Steelers football team, as my parents will tell you, is very important to me. Therapists tend to dwell on that, but generally, they are correct.

Also, Karen Sarkliss asked me to attend, personally. Despite her unexplained inability to understand calculus, I consider her to be quite a wonderful person. She has rejected my offer to be her boyfriend on a number of occasions, but she is always polite about it.

Although I hesitated in pushing the button, I knew my mother would be very disappointed in me if I didn't. There have been occasions when the seizure resulted in me suffering some injuries, so I understand her concern. Once, I flopped off the couch and hit my face on the coffee table on the way to the floor.

So, this time, despite my reluctance on account of the party mentioned previously, I pushed the button, put cushions on the floor, and settled back on the couch to wait for my brain's electrical system to scramble.

CHAPTER 46

Joe took a seat on a park bench a block from the courthouse and crunched into an apple. After Officer Billups, the morning session had been filled with the morbid testimony of the county coroner, which included the unnecessary descriptions of two tattoos on Justin Holt's body—on one shoulder, a Steelers logo, on the other, a heart above his mother's name, Merrill. The witness confirmed the cause of death, which was obvious to everyone. Justin Holt had died of a single gunshot wound to his chest.

To Joe's surprise, the afternoon session brought the bright eyes and perky countenance of Jen Scoggins to the witness stand. The girlfriend of the current Steelers starting quarterback, the cheer squad member carried herself with the air of royalty.

Joe pulled up the witness's written statement on his laptop as she took the oath, scanning the two-page document. Although Scoggins hadn't mentioned leaving with Luke, her statement was otherwise unremarkable. She'd last seen Carl at the party, eating a cupcake by himself about 8:00 p.m. She didn't notice Justin acting strangely and didn't see Clem Tettleton that evening. So why did Pettigrew call her as a witness?

After some questions that covered the basics of her statement to the police, Joe had his answer. "Ms. Scoggins, you mentioned leaving the party about 8:00 p.m.? Did you leave with anyone?"

"Yes, I left with my boyfriend, Luke Stuckey."

Joe listened with interest. Pettigrew was clearly calling the witness to establish Luke Stuckey's alibi. The question was, why did she feel the need to do so?

"Where did you go?"

The witness hesitated. "We went to my parents' place," she said, lowering her voice. "They were away for the weekend, so we went there to make out."

"What's your address, Ms. Scoggins?"

"3372 Victoria Avenue."

"About a fifteen-minute drive from the Holts'?"

"Yes, ma'am."

"And was there a time when you returned to the party?"

"Yes, it would have been around midnight. Maybe a little later. By then, the police cars and ambulances were there."

"The entire time you were at your parents' house, was Luke Stuckey with you?"

"Yes."

"Did he leave your parents' house by himself for any reason?"

The teenager looked confused. "No, we were there together."

"Now, Ms. Scoggins, were you honest about your whereabouts that night with the police?"

"No, I wasn't. I didn't want my parents to find out that I'd been home alone with Luke, so I lied and said I was at the party the whole night."

As Pettigrew questioned Scoggins about her observations upon returning to the party, Joe tried to make sense of the testimony. How did Pettigrew even know that he viewed Stuckey as a possible suspect? Joe had interviewed all the football players, not just him.

He'd provided a copy of his phone records in a shared file, but Pettigrew had yet to open it. So, what did she know about Luke Stuckey?

"Ms. Scoggins, is there anything else you can think of that we should know about that evening?" Pettigrew asked, wrapping up her examination.

Scoggins was shaking her head and was about to answer when she hesitated.

Pettigrew looked up from her notes at the podium. "Ms. Scoggins?"

"Well, now that you mention it, you asked me earlier if there was anyone there who didn't belong at the party. I mean, not really, because everyone was welcome."

"So," prompted Pettigrew, clearly not prepared for the response, "was there someone there who didn't belong?"

"I wouldn't say didn't belong," the young woman said, wincing at the harsh-sounding words. "Everyone there was sort of a certain type. Like either into football or cheer or just had a lot of school spirit."

"Okay," said Pettigrew, trepidation in her voice. Joe knew the prosecutor's uneasy feeling of asking a question for which she didn't know the answer. "Was there someone there who maybe didn't fit that mold?"

"Yes, well," Scoggins began then hesitated again. "I mean, bless her heart. She's a goth. You know, black lipstick and all."

"And who was this person, Ms. Scoggins?"

"Sophie Montgomery."

CHAPTER 47

Day Seven

"You've got to be fucking kidding me!" Dirk had once again reached his limit. The big man abruptly stood, turned, and slammed a meaty forearm into the wall.

The other jurors fell silent, looking around the table at each other with raised eyebrows. They had gotten used to the construction foreman's daily rants, but this was the first time violence crossed their minds.

"As I was saying," Sara finally said, her chin in the air, "for me, Luke Stuckey just wasn't credible, and neither was his girlfriend."

Jack cleared his throat. "Maybe it's time for a break," he suggested, quietly.

"No," Sara said firmly. "We can't just stop the debate every time Dirk throws a tantrum."

"I agree with Sara," Priya chimed in. "Intimidation shouldn't be part of this. And I also agree about Luke. I think he was at the scene of the murder and lied about it. Not to mention he had motive."

"Motive?" countered Ellen. "Because he was second string quarterback and wanted to be first string? That's a bit of a stretch."

Sara was already shaking her head. "It really isn't. Not in this football-crazy town. As absurd as it seems—I can't even believe I'm saying this—but when it comes to the Barton Steelers, I actually think someone would kill to be QB1."

"You guys have no idea," Dirk said, sitting back down. "I was a Barton Steeler. It's a brotherhood. The idea that one teammate would kill another is ridiculous."

"I agree," said Duncan, subtly flexing his arms on the table. "I played some ball, too. It's hard to believe anyone would murder a teammate after going to war with your brothers on the field."

"You played?" asked Elston from down the table. "What year? I haven't missed a game in thirty years. What's your last name again?"

"Oh, I, I played, um, not here in Barton," Duncan stammered. "I played, back in, um, back where I grew up," he mumbled.

Dirk smirked from across the table, sensing weakness. "Yeah? What position?"

"Oh, I played um, some different ones," Duncan answered, obviously now thoroughly regretting his lie.

"I'm guessing some left bench," Dirk said, laughing at his own joke.

Jack stood up at the end of the table. "Okay, guys, we're getting off track, and we're past break time. Let's take ten." This time, everyone agreed and filed out of the jury room, most heading to the coffee shop.

On his way out of the courthouse, Jack caught up to Sara. "Hey, do you have a minute?" She shrugged and stopped walking. "So, I think Dirk is getting out of control."

"No kidding. Why are you telling me this?" she asked, sounding suspicious.

"Look, I know we're on different sides of this thing right now, but just hear me out on this." Sara shrugged again. "My cousin was on a jury once, and they had this super obnoxious juror. Apparently, the jury complained that the guy refused to deliberate with them, and the judge kicked him off. I'm not saying we're there yet, but his intimidation tactics are making it impossible to have a debate."

Sara was nodding. "It's becoming hostile."

"Exactly. Anyway, like I said, just something to think about," Jack said and walked away.

Sara watched him cross the street on his way to the coffee shop then muttered, "Yeah, Jack Painter, I don't trust you for a second."

When the group reconvened well caffeinated, the pro-conviction crowd took the offensive. Frank, the retired military man led off. "I have to say this theory that the backup quarterback was the killer is nothing but speculation. Seems clear to me the defense was just throwing stuff on the wall to see what sticks."

"And here's what I don't get," Dirk added, "and this is probably going to offend someone."

"Then don't say it," Sara shot back, drawing nervous laughter from the group. "Seriously, if you know you're about to offend us with some disrespectful comment about women or gays or who knows what, just save it for your neanderthal friends."

"Here's the thing," Dirk continued, ignoring her pleas, "It's obvious that old rock-and-roll Carl is at least a half a bubble off plumb. Which makes sense because, you know, most murderers are not exactly mentally stable. But that homo Turner has somehow tried to say that Carl is loopy, and that means he didn't commit the crime."

Sara glared at Dirk and slowly shook her head. "That's offensive on so many levels, I don't know where to begin. First of all, Carl isn't loopy. He has autism, and I guarantee he's more intelligent than you. Mr. Turner's point is that Carl's inability to show his emotions explains some of his statements and actions. And not that it matters, but I have no idea why you believe that Mr. Turner is gay, other than your chronic homophobia."

"That's actually interesting," said Duncan. "Don't get me wrong, I'm still voting to convict, but I hadn't really thought of it that way. It's good to keep his disability in mind when evaluating his testimony."

To his right, Ellen smiled. "That's a good point, Duncan," she said.

Duncan looked down the table toward Jack, who met his stare with a subtle nod.

CHAPTER 48

Joe met Chuck after court at the Bronze Cue, one of two bars in Barton. Three men sat at the horseshoe-shaped bar, looking like they'd been there all day. In the back, a couple played pool. Joe found a table in the corner while Chuck brought over beers.

Joe's cross examination of Jen Scoggins had been limited to reiterating her lie to the police. Even after learning that a murder had been committed, she'd stuck to her story about never leaving the party.

"Wonder what Pettigrew knows?" Chuck asked when told of Luke Stuckey's alibi witness. "Are we missing something?"

"No clue, but we need to figure it out fast. So far, we got motive, opportunity, and his lie about his alibi. It's thin."

Chuck nodded. "Yeah, especially compared to the prosecution's case against Carl."

"So, is Clem Tettleton's alibi airtight? I think his social media post still makes him more believable as the killer."

Chuck sipped his beer. "Working on that. I wouldn't be surprised if the Tettleton clan found a way to outsmart the ankle monitor. Lord knows they've had plenty of practice. I'm going to snoop around his place in Hell's

Holler. No Tettleton I ever knew threw away something as valuable as a gun."

They finished their beers and discussed the DA's witness list. Chuck left to draft a subpoena for Luke Stuckey and agreed to interview Sophie Montgomery. Joe ordered another beer and reviewed his notes on Stuckey's statement before packing up for the walk home.

Outside, darkness had fallen on the quiet streets of Barton. As he pulled his hand trolley behind him, the wheels beating a cadence across the lines in the sidewalk, Joe considered what was at the heart of his belief in his client's innocence. He smiled to himself, recalling Carl's question to Eddy about the purple streak in her hair. His unabashed honesty could be unnerving. Perhaps it was that simple. If Carl had murdered Justin Holt, Joe believed he would have told him so.

Emerging from his thought bubble, he heard a noise behind him. He turned and looked but saw no one there. Then, a half block back, he spied movement in the shadows cast by a streetlight.

Still five blocks from home, and with the memory of the Tettleton's shooting up a road sign still fresh in his mind, Joe quickened his pace. He lifted his trolley from the sidewalk for a few steps to stop its racket and now definitely heard footsteps. Stopping abruptly, he spun around again and glimpsed his follower darting into the shadows, a few hundred feet behind him.

"Fuck," he exhaled and started to jog. Pulling his trolley, he knew if his pursuer wanted to shoot him, it wouldn't be long. Still, he ran—a dead sprint now— cursing the second beer after an audible belch.

After a full minute of running for all he was worth, he staggered to a halt, the porch lights of his home in sight a block away. Doubled at the waist and gasping for breath, he turned behind him but saw nothing.

By the time Joe reached home, he'd caught his breath. "Hey there," Eddy called from the porch as he approached. "You look like you could use a beer."

Joe shook his head. "No, scotch please," he said, pulling the hand trolley up the steps of the Victorian.

Later, having recounted the eventful day over take-out fried chicken, Joe began to doubt that anyone had been following him home. They'd had plenty of opportunity to catch up to him, after all. Maybe all his thoughts of murder motives were to blame. It wouldn't be the first time his profession had warped his perception of reality.

Reclining on the porch, he heard a low rumble and turned to see headlights swing onto his street a block away. Peering through the darkness as the headlights slowly approached, Joe recognized the loud engine before the body of the truck came into view. Clem Tettleton's pale yellow pickup stopped to idle directly in front of the Victorian before roaring out of sight.

CHAPTER 49

In the morning, Eddy insisted she drive Joe to court. "So, what'd you think of those juror questionnaires?" Joe asked as they pulled out of the driveway.

"It's a pretty divergent group. You've got a construction foreman, a social worker…lot's of potential for discord. That's good for you, right?"

"Yep, the more conflict the better." Given that Joe's best hope was for a hung jury, the last thing he wanted was an agreeable jury.

"Also, the school teacher's comments might bode well. 'I hope I can,' and 'I'll strive to.' She might not be able to make a decision. And I think the engineer is a good defense juror."

Joe nodded. "They usually are. Engineers like proof to an absolute certainty."

"The construction foreman, on the other hand," Eddy added, cringing.

"Bad?" Joe asked.

"His comment was something like, 'My job is to keep this train on the tracks and not waste time.'"

"Meaning a quick conviction," Joe agreed. "What do you think about the insurance guy, Jack Painter?"

"Not sure but something seemed off about him."

"How so?"

Eddy thought for a moment. "His answer seemed too perfect. Like he really wanted to be on the jury."

Arriving at the courthouse, they were surprised to find plenty of parking right out front. Joe walked into the courtroom to find it empty, except for Barbara. "Morning, Mr. Turner," she said pleasantly, looking up from her desk in front of the bench. "I take it you didn't get the message."

"What message?"

"Turns out juror number four is sick. Rumor is it was the coleslaw at Bubba's Crab Shack. I think they leave it out too long."

"What?" Joe asked, confused.

"The coleslaw, hon. It's made with mayo. I think they overdress it myself. Anyway, my neighbor's daughter worked there last summer, and she says sometimes they left it out all day. I've always been taught that mayo needs to be kept cold. Of course, it could have been the seafood platter. My cousin Leanne could tell you about that. Anyway, the judge had me call and give the jury the day off. He and Melissa are in chambers if you want to go say, 'Hey.'"

Joe stood there, digesting the news, dumbfounded that the judge had made the decision without his input. Juror number four, the construction foreman, was his least favorite juror. Rather than take the entire day off, most judges would have at least considered substituting him with an alternate juror.

Joe noticed there was no sign of his client. "Barbara, did Carl show up this morning?"

"Oh, no," she said. "He surely would have heard about it."

Joe walked to the judge's chambers, wondering how in God's name everyone in town knew about this but him. He entered to find both DA and judge dressed casually in khakis and polo shirts. There were half-eaten sweet rolls in front of them on the judge's desk. "Mr. Turner, good morning," the judge said, "I didn't expect to see you here. Ms. Pettigrew and I were just going over last night's arrests."

"So, I'm told we're not in session today?"

"Oh, hell. I'd a thought you'd heard. Sorry about that. Turns out juror number four got a bad batch of coleslaw at Bubba's. That or the crab, I guess."

"So, Judge, did you consider using one of the alternates?"

"Naw, no reason to burn an alternate at this early stage," he said with a wave. "He should be fit as a fiddle tomorrow. Have a sweet roll," he said, gesturing to the pink box on his desk.

Joe decided against pressing the issue. Nothing could be done now, and he needed to choose his battles. "Okay then," he said, turning to leave.

"Oh, Mr. Turner, I hear you served a subpoena on Luke Stuckey?" Boniface asked.

Of course, Joe thought. You heard from his dad, your golfing buddy. "Yes, Judge. I plan to call him as a witness. Is there a problem?"

"Of course, you're free to try your case the way you see fit. I'd just say that putting a fine young man like Luke in your crosshairs might not be the way to go."

"You mean a fine young quarterback, Judge? Because you wouldn't know whether or not he was a fine young man, would you? Since you barely know the family. Isn't that what you said on the record last week?" Joe turned and walked out.

With a free day in front of him, Joe texted Eddy and made plans for a hike. The heat wave had passed, and they enjoyed time away from the case on a perfect fall day. On their way home, Joe's phone buzzed.

"Hi, Chuck, I imagine you heard."

"About the coleslaw? Of course. I had breakfast at Nadine's."

"I heard it could have been the crab."

Chuck laughed. "I heard the same. Imagine that. Bad seafood in Barton."

"I take it you served Luke Stuckey with the subpoena?"

"Served his mom. You can do that in Georgia. Caught her at the hair salon. She was madder than a wet hen. Hey, have you, by chance, heard from the Tettleton clan?"

"Matter of fact, yes. Followed me home last night. Sort of has me spooked. Why?"

"I think the kid, Clem, got wind of me snooping around his place yesterday. Bastard left a dead possum on the seat of my truck."

Joe groaned. "Tell me that's not some sort of hillbilly warning, like a dead fish."

"Not that I know of, but keep your head on a swivel. I'm off to get a haircut."

"I thought you'd be solving the case today."

"I am. Like I said, I'm getting a haircut."

CHAPTER 50

Day Eight

Frank bowed his head and rubbed his crew cut with both hands. The military veteran was losing his patience and his back was acting up. "Elston, you're an attorney. I can't believe you're falling for this fingernail transfer BS."

"I'm not falling for anything," Elston said calmly. "Again, I'm not saying the transfer definitely happened. I'm saying, for me, the possibility that it happened constitutes reasonable doubt."

"Totally agree," added Priya. "Frank, you're forgetting that it's not up to the defense to prove innocence. The prosecution has the burden of proof."

"And the prosecution has put forth a lot of evidence," countered Ellen. "The eyewitness, the DNA, the gunshot residue. That just seems like a lot of evidence to me," she added, as if trying to convince herself.

"What do we make of the defense theory that it was the Stuckey kid?" Jack asked from the head of the table.

"Total bullshit, that's what," Dirk said, crushing a paper cup in his hands.

"Don't be so dismissive, Dirk," Sara scolded.

"I agree," Duncan added. "It's worth considering."

"Whose side are you on, Mr. Football superstar?" Dirk chided. "I thought you're voting guilty."

"I am. I just think it's good to have an open mind," he said.

To Duncan's right, Ellen nodded her approval. "I agree. Speaking of hearing from everyone, Quinn," she called in her schoolteacher voice, "we're all still waiting to hear what you think."

At the end of the table, Quinn recoiled in his chair and bowed his head. Dirk looked down at him and shook his head. "That dog won't hunt," he said, belly laughing as the group cringed.

"As I was saying," said Priya, "I wouldn't necessarily rule out Luke as the killer. There's a reason why he lied about being at the party at the time of the murder."

"I don't think he lied," Frank countered. "He said he left his phone there."

"Oh please." Sara exhaled on her way to the water cooler. "Ellen, you're a teacher. When was the last time a teenager left their phone behind?"

Frank stood to stretch his back. "Tell me this, then. If Luke Stuckey was the murderer, why wasn't there gunshot residue on his hands?"

"Oh c'mon, Frank. Whoever the killer was had plenty of time to wash his hands afterwards. And he would have. Carl had no reason to wash it off because he wasn't hiding anything."

"Oh, wow, that's genius," Dirk said sarcastically. "The gunshot residue is actually evidence that Carl *didn't* commit the crime."

"Dirk, really, the sarcasm isn't productive," Priya said from across the table.

"Look," Dirk said, ignoring the comment, "the DNA transfer theory is straight up bullshit. If any of y'all had played football," he said, leering across the table at Duncan, "you'd know that you can't play with long fingernails. Since Justin didn't have long nails, he would need to really scratch someone to get DNA under them."

Frank nodded his approval. "That's right. You especially can't play quarterback with long fingernails. And it's not like DNA just makes its way under short fingernails. Carl's DNA was under that short nail because Justin scratched him. Only way it could have gotten there."

"I don't recall any testimony on that point. You guys are just making stuff up," countered Sara.

"Also, if Justin scratched Carl's face or neck, why didn't the officer notice it when he interviewed him?" asked Elston.

"I think whoever scratched Justin probably killed him," Sara said. "We all heard that creepy doctor say it likely happened within thirty minutes of his death."

Dirk laughed to himself. "That Carl is a piece of work. Did y'all see that retard on the stand?" he asked, drawing groans around the table. He continued, mimicking Carl's nasal monotone. "We were acquaintances and enjoyed each other's company. So naturally, I had to kill him."

Sara stood, slamming her notepad on the table, glowering at Dirk.

"Easy darlin'," the big man said, with a laugh, "your panties are in a bunch. Or should I say boxers?"

"Dirk, I have to ask you again not to be so offensive," Jack pleaded as the other jurors shook their heads in disgust. "You're really making it impossible to deliberate."

Jack's eyes met Sara's, and she slowly nodded.

CHAPTER 51

On Friday morning, Joe was reviewing his notes at the counsel table when his client took his seat next to him. "Good morning, Mr. Turner."

"Carl, call me…" He stopped in mid-sentence at the sight of his client's face. His left eye was blackened, and his bottom lip appeared split. "Carl, what happened to you?" he asked, resting a hand on his shoulder.

"There was a misunderstanding," he said. "My mother said she hopes my tinted prescription glasses partially obscure my injuries, although I do not know why that's necessary."

Joe turned to Aubrey and Matt, seated behind him in the front row of the gallery. Aubrey mouthed the words, "Tell you later," as the jury filed in.

The first witness of the morning was a ballistics expert who testified how striations left on the expended shell casing found at the scene indicated the use of a silencer.

After the morning break, Pettigrew stood at the podium. "Your Honor, the State calls Sinclair Lewis to the stand." The prosecutor clearly wanted to end the week with a bang.

Lewis' newly polished boots slowly made their way up the center aisle of the packed courtroom. Smiling proudly, he took in the scene as he went, scanning the gallery for familiar faces. Clean-shaven and sporting a fresh buzz cut, he wore a new pair of dark blue denim overalls over a red plaid flannel shirt. To Joe's left, Carl was rocking again.

"Good afternoon, Mr. Lewis," Pettigrew began after Barbara swore in the witness. "Can I ask where you live, sir?"

"I live at 971 Chance Avenue, here in Barton."

"And were you living there on Friday, August 26th of this year?"

"Been living there since 1968. So, yeah," Lewis deadpanned, drawing laughter throughout the courtroom.

Joe sighed quietly. Great, a charmer.

"Were you home that night a few minutes before midnight?"

"I was. I had gotten up to visit the washroom." The witness turned to the jury. "These trips take longer than they used to," he added as the jurors chuckled. "Anyhow, I keep the front windows open at night. As I walked back to my bedroom, I heard heavy footsteps out on the street."

"Mr. Lewis, is Chance Avenue a paved road?"

"No, ma'am. It's gravel."

"Did you eventually look out your front window?"

"I did. I saw this young fella running down the middle of the road."

"Are there any streetlights in front of your home?" Pettigrew asked.

"No, but I have a light on my porch, and it was one of those full Georgia moons. I could see him well."

"Do you wear glasses, sir?" Pettigrew asked.

Joe watched the witness closely. His eyes darted away from Pettigrew for an instant. "No," he said, shaking his head. "I have reading spectacles for reading or whittling but not for seeing distance. I've been blessed with perfect vision."

"Mr. Lewis, was this person you saw running down the street carrying anything?"

"Yes, ma'am. He had a handgun in his hand."

As the courtroom stirred, Joe sat wondering if he'd heard the witness correctly. He quickly scanned the witness' written statement. There was no mention of a gun. And yet Pettigrew hadn't seemed surprised by Lewis' answer.

"Finally, Mr. Lewis, I'd like you to look around the courtroom and see if you recognize the person you saw running down the road that evening."

"Yes, ma'am, I will," the witness said, nodding earnestly. Then he looked directly at Carl, who had increased his rocking pace. "He's sitting over there next to his attorney," Lewis said, leaning into the microphone.

"Your Honor, may the record reflect that the witness has identified the defendant, Stanley Carl Ledbetter?"

"The record will so reflect," Boniface said.

"No further questions, Your Honor."

The judge looked over his glasses at Joe. "Mr. Turner, cross examination?" he asked with the hint of a smirk on his face.

Joe placed a hand on Carl's rocking shoulder as he rose. "Good afternoon, Mr. Lewis," he said, reaching the podium. "We've not spoken before, correct?"

"No, sir."

"How about Ms. Pettigrew? Have you spoken to her prior to today?"

"Well, yes. Once on the phone and once in her office earlier this week."

"And presumably, that was to review your testimony in preparation for today's hearing?"

"Yes," Lewis said, smiling again toward the jury. "Understandably, Ms. Pettigrew was quite interested in my eyewitness testimony. People have told me that I sort of cracked the case." The old man shrugged. "I don't know about all that."

"Mr. Lewis, on one side of your property sits the Jessup's hay field, correct?"

"Yes."

"And on the other, that's about where the turnoff is to County Route 9 that goes on up to Lindsay, right?"

In her seat, Pettigrew sported a wry smile. She knew Joe was sprinkling in facts so the jury would think he was a local attorney. And with his in limine motion granted, she couldn't tell them otherwise.

"Nice, peaceful place, right?"

"Yes, sir."

"So, you'd agree that seeing someone running down the middle of the road at midnight is very unusual."

"Yes."

"But Mr. Lewis, the most unusual part about what you saw was the fact that the man was carrying a handgun, right?"

The witness was leery of a trap. "I suppose so," he said, without conviction.

"Then, Mr. Lewis, when you first told the police what you saw, why was it you didn't mention that the person running down the middle of the street was carrying a gun?"

Lewis paused, looking confused. "I don't think, I, um…" He stopped, looking to the prosecutor for guidance.

"Well, I'd say it's about time for our lunch recess," Boniface, said, ruining the moment for Joe. He looked at the clock. It was 11:54 a.m.

"Your Honor, may the witness be permitted to answer?" he asked, quietly seething.

"Absolutely, Mr. Turner. After our lunch recess. We'll see everyone back at 1:30 p.m.," he said and banged his gavel.

After the jury filed out, Pettigrew sidled over to Joe. "Pretty slick, Joe. But you might want to work on your Southern drawl."

"Just trying to level the playing field, Pettigrew," he said, still livid with the judge. "Now, go ahead, and coach up your witness. You know what to tell him. Personally, I'd go with the nerves and confusion, being late at night and all," he said, walking out of the courtroom. "And I need that Cabarton Ranch video!"

CHAPTER 52

Clyde Epperson's barbershop on Main Street looked out on the gazebo in the town square. Opened in 1975, Chuck had been there once a month until he left town for college at eighteen and every time he came back to Barton. Sometimes, he'd get a haircut or a shave. Mainly, he went to catch up on town news.

The rules in Clyde's were simple. No personal gossip—it wasn't a damn beauty salon, after all—and no politics other than local elections. Other than that, it was a safe place to cuss, complain, chew tobacco, needle your friends, and speak your mind on any number of topics without fear of them ever leaving the barbershop.

"Holy shit, look what the cat dragged in." The proprietor spotted Chuck through the mirrors as he entered.

"Howdy, Clyde." Chuck nodded to the five other men in the shop and took a seat. Chuck listened for several minutes as the men talked about the weather, football, and their late-summer vegetable gardens.

Presently, Red Alpers, who ran the antique shop next door with his wife, came in and took his customary seat in the empty barber chair. He greeted Chuck with a nod. "I heard you were in town. You still out West?"

"Yeah. Just in town for the trial."

"I heard that, too," Red said, unfolding the newspaper. "I know you got a job to do an all, but I'll be happy when it's over. Team's bound to be distracted."

Next to Chuck, Bubba Pickler put in a fresh chew. "So, you work for Ledbetter's attorney? I met him recently. Heard he's giving old Judge Boniface what for."

Chuck smiled. "He's a hard dog to keep on the porch, that's for sure."

An older man with a white beard in the corner chimed in. "Figured the Ledbetters would hire a good one."

"Course I don't know first-hand," Clyde said, sharpening his razor blade, "but I heard the case was pretty cut and dried."

Chuck shrugged. "Course I'm a little biased, being on the defense team and all, but I think there's some secrets people aren't telling. Not sure the Ledbetter kid has it in him."

"He's sort of a half bubble off plumb, ain't he?" Red asked.

"I wouldn't exactly put it that way," Chuck said. "He's definitely different, though. Has some difficulty dealing with people."

"Apparently so," Clyde said, and the men had a laugh. "So, Chuck, I'm not sure you can tell us, but what's the defense strategy?"

"What else?" Chuck said, already chuckling. "Blame a Tettleton." The room erupted in laughter.

The conversation returned to football, and the lunch crowd cleared out, leaving Clyde, Chuck and Red alone. "So, Chuck, how does it really look for the Ledbetter kid?" the barber asked.

"It's lookin' bleak. Why?"

"My niece is a classmate of Carl's. Says he's a sweet kid. Says he's definitely a little off but would never hurt a fly."

Chuck nodded. "That's my impression too, but the Tettleton suspect has an alibi. He was home at midnight. Couldn't have committed the murder at 11:50 p.m. and made it home in time. Back in the day, he would have taken the rail car across that holler."

There was silence as Clyde and Red looked at each other then turned to look at Chuck with knowing smiles.

The investigator returned their stares. "What, guys? Am I missing something?"

CHAPTER 53

Walking into the courtroom after lunch, Joe knew the minute he saw the paper at his place on the counsel table. "Let me guess," he said, addressing Pettigrew, the only other person in the courtroom. That's a supplemental report saying Lewis later told the police he saw a gun."

"I'm so sorry, Joe," she said, sounding sincere. "I just got that report myself."

"Bullshit," he snapped. "And save the Southern belle routine." Joe shook his head. Normally, he would ask the judge to strike Lewis' testimony from the record, but with Boniface on the bench, it'd be useless.

"Excuse me?" Pettigrew fumed. "I'll have you know that I've been busting my ass with Barton P.D., which, if you haven't guessed, isn't exactly Scotland Yard. That report just showed up on my desk this morning, so quit being a big-city prick about this!"

"Well, here's a crazy idea, Melissa." Joe's voice quivered with anger. "Why don't you mosey on over to that there police station and use that Southern charm to collect every last police report in this here murder case. And when those good ole cops ask which murder case," he said, his voice rising to a crescendo, "you tell them the only fucking murder case they've investigated in the past fifty years!"

Joe hadn't noticed that Carl had taken his seat to his left. His tirade complete, he sat down next to his client as Pettigrew slammed a file on the counsel table. "Mr. Turner," Carl said, "why would that be a crazy idea to ask the police for the reports?"

Joe sighed, collecting himself. "Carl, what's usually the answer when you think I've said something that makes no sense?"

Carl's eyes flashed with recognition, and he smiled. "Sarcasm."

"Yes! Well done, Carl Ledbetter."

When the proceedings resumed, Lewis took the stand with a ready explanation. "I s'pose I was a bit rattled the first time I spoke to the police," he said apologetically. "I surely didn't mean to keep the information about the gun from anybody. I hadn't had much sleep that night and was still not myself by the time the police showed up."

"So, Mr. Lewis, when you first saw this fellow running down the middle of the street with a gun, you didn't call the police, did you?"

"No, sir. It was odd, but I didn't figure it was a crime."

"When the police first contacted you, they told you there'd been a shooting up at the Holts', didn't they?"

"Yes."

"So, at that point, surely your mind went straight to that fellow you'd seen running away from the Holts' with a gun, right?"

"Well, it's been a while now. I don't rightly know."

Joe walked to the clerk's desk and retrieved a one-page document. "May I approach, Your Honor?"

"You may." Boniface grumbled as Joe walked toward the witness stand.

"Mr. Lewis, I'm showing you what's been marked as defense Exhibit C. Do you recognize that?"

The witness took out his reading glasses and balanced them on his nose. "Looks like my statement to the police," he said, holding the document away from himself with an outstretched hand.

"And nowhere in your statement does it say that the man you saw running was holding a gun, does it?"

"No, sir," he said, without looking at the document.

"Mr. Lewis," Joe said, walking away from the podium, "you testified that you have perfect vision."

"Yes, sir. Perfect for distance," the witness said, sitting up in his chair.

Joe picked up his satchel and walked up the aisle toward the back of the courtroom. "And the man in the street was about forty feet away from you, right?"

"Pert near," Lewis said. Facing away from him as he reached the back of the courtroom, Joe didn't see the confident smile spread across the witness's face.

"Mr. Lewis, that's about the same distance as I am to you now, right?"

"Yes, sir."

Joe produced a green apple from his satchel and held it in front of him.

"So, Mr. Lewis, would you mind telling the jury what it is I'm holding?"

The witness hesitated. "I'm not sure," he said, squinting across the courtroom.

"Sir, that's because you can't see what I'm holding, correct?"

Lewis nodded. "Yeah," he said, smiling wide. "From here I can't tell if it's a Granny Smith or a Gravenstein."

Laughter spread throughout the courtroom, and Joe blushed. Furious with himself, he walked back up the aisle and dropped his satchel at the counsel table. "No further questions, Your Honor."

Judge Boniface beamed at the witness. "Well, Mr. Lewis, we greatly appreciate your testimony. You may step down. Also, ladies and gentlemen, it's Friday, and some of us have a football game to get to. We'll take the afternoon recess a little early. Y'all have a pleasant weekend."

After the jury had gone, Joe was packing up his file when he felt Carl's stare heating up his face. He turned to face his client, who sat with perfect posture, arms hanging awkwardly to his sides. "Yes, Carl?"

"I don't understand why you asked Mr. Sinclair Lewis to identify an apple."

"Well, Carl. I mistakenly thought that he wouldn't be able to see it, and that would help establish that he didn't see you. At least not with a gun."

Carl considered his answer for a moment. "Why did you think he couldn't see it? If I recall, Mr. Sinclair Lewis testified that his vision was perfect."

"Carl," Joe said harshly then caught himself. He took a deep breath and blinked slowly. "Based on some other information I had, I didn't believe he could see it."

Carl nodded. "Well, that was suboptimal," he said, standing. "It was suboptimal because Sinclair Lewis was shown to have excellent vision."

"Yes, Carl, I'm aware."

"Perhaps next week you'll be able to show that his vision was not excellent at all."

Joe smiled, recalling Carl's mom's words. His client could definitely be a challenge. "I hope so, Carl," he said. "C'mon, your parents will be waiting for you."

Outside the courthouse, Eddy's rental was idling at the curb. On the ride back to the house, Joe told of the apple gambit that backfired.

"Yikes," Eddy said, cringing. "Sorry, babe."

"Chuck is usually right about this stuff. I feel like I'm missing something."

"Maybe he wore contact lenses," Eddy suggested.

"Maybe, but there's no way to prove it. Shit! I should have anticipated it."

"Turner, that's nuts. Anticipate that a witness would lie and wear contacts lenses?"

"Did you put my random facts about Barton to good use, by the way?"

Joe nodded, happy to change the subject. "Yeah, thanks. There's some chance that they think I'm local."

"Well, how about you let me actually help, Turner. I'll be here for another week, and since I'm here in the middle of nowhere, I might as well contribute. Have Chuck send me on an errand. Anything."

"Okay," Joe mumbled, "I'll think of something." Eddy took her eyes off the road and glanced at Joe with a smirk. She knew her lover well and could tell that the last thing Joe wanted was her stumbling into harm's way. She found the sentiment sweet but a little annoying.

Later, after a regrettable takeout decision from Uncle Yu's, Joe was reading on the porch when Eddy sat down next to him with two glasses of wine and tried a French accent. "Appellation Sancerre?"

"Thanks, babe, but please don't say apples."

Eddy laughed. "I was thinking about that. So, Lewis' testimony obviously hurts because he says he saw Carl running away from the murder scene with a gun, right?"

"Yes."

"And you're going to try to convince the jury that not only didn't he see a gun, but that it wasn't Carl that he saw, right?"

"Correct."

Eddy paused and smiled. "Hmm."

"And you're wondering how I can sleep at night knowing that he actually saw Carl running home?"

Eddy laughed. "I wouldn't go that far, but it does seem a little tricky."

"It's no doubt a little tricky but not unethical. If I was going to put Carl on the stand to deny that he ran home, that would be a different story. But if he doesn't testify, I'm obligated to argue that it wasn't him."

"How so, Mr. fancy talker?"

"Because I'm ethically bound to put the best spin on the evidence for the jury. I don't think trying to convince the jury that Carl was running home to feed the fish would fly."

"I see your point. So, you've decided he's not testifying?"

Joe stood and sighed. "Yeah. For now, anyway. Come on, Busier. How about you sleep with someone who can't sleep with himself."

"Now you're talking."

CHAPTER 54

Carl

My mother is fond of saying, "Sticks and stones can break your bones, but words can never hurt you." She is correct, of course. Over the course of my life, owing mostly to my special way of looking at the world—that's the way my mother describes it—I've often endured the unpleasant experience of having people call me certain names.

Some are immediately recognizable as unflattering. Others are entirely inscrutable or make no sense. Generally, the names fall in one of two categories, either identifying me as unintelligent or mentally imbalanced. Sometimes, like today, it is both.

Most often, people will call me these names because of something I've said. On those occasions, it can usually be ascribed to my mother's claim that I am honest to a fault, which I admit to not understanding completely. If, for example, someone asks my opinion about something, my initial inclination is to believe that they have asked my opinion because they want me to share my opinion with them. So, I share my opinion. However, I have learned that this is not always the purpose of their inquiry.

I've often thought it would be helpful if a code were used so as to inform me whether they actually want me to share my opinion. For example, they could ask my opinion then wink, thus communicating to me they had no real interest in my opinion but instead preferred me to lie and compliment them.

But I digress, because today, it hadn't been anything I said that triggered the name calling. I was walking home from the library. I very much enjoy the quiet there. The lights are not too bright, and it's a nice place for me to rest or read after a day in court, which is very taxing. As I walked by Madigan's, two men stumbled out the front door. One bumped into me on the sidewalk. He said, "Watch yourself," in an angry tone.

Because his command made no sense to me, I asked for clarification, responding, "What do you mean, watch myself?" For some unknown reason, this made him even more angry, so he shoved me. Then the other man told the angry man that I was the crazy half-wit who killed our star quarterback. Then the angry man hit me in the face with his fist at least twice. I'm not certain how many times, but I have two distinct injuries to my face.

"Half-wit" is something I've heard before and do not understand as I believe I am of above-average intelligence. "Crazy" I've heard more frequently and is no less confusing since I don't believe I display any outward signs of hysteria or insanity.

The most unsettling remark identified me as my friend Justin Cassady Holt's murderer. Parenthetically, I only recently learned his middle name during the trial, which is a shame because, as he is now deceased, the information is less useful. Anyway, while I realize the men were not part of the trial, the concept of innocent until proven guilty is a well-known tenet of our criminal justice system. Also, the thought that a segment of the community believes I killed my friend and teammate, Justin Cassady Holt, is quite upsetting.

My mother has emphasized her belief that the men involved had likely been drinking. I have learned that, used in this context, "drinking" actually means drinking alcohol. My mother's theory is buttressed by the fact that, apparently, Madigan's is an establishment that serves alcohol.

In the hours since the attack, it has occurred to me that my mother's assurance that words can never hurt me may be only true in the literal sense. Parenthetically, I have recently become exposed to the concept of irony, and it is not lost on me that I, of all people, should not complain about a strictly literal interpretation.

Anyway, as the wounds to my face heal, I better understand the nuanced meanings of my attackers' words. While my mother is correct that the words will never physically hurt me, they do linger unpleasantly on my mind.

CHAPTER 55

"Watch out for ornery judges," Eddy called from the porch as Joe set off on a run. She knew he half-hoped to cross paths with Boniface again. Embracing Southern cuisine, she fried eggs, made biscuits from scratch, and brewed strong coffee.

While Joe was still on his run, Chuck stopped by to share his barbershop revelations. Immediately, Eddy knew what lay ahead. She quickly changed into some workout clothes and hiking boots and was off before her partner's return.

Within a few minutes, Eddy was guiding her rented sedan through the quiet streets of Barton and across the Mulberry River to the edge of the hollers west of town. With the windows down and the sunroof open, excitement surged through her.

Eddy hadn't mentioned that she, too, found Carl very likeable and was emotionally invested in the trial. While helping with the jury was nice, she wanted to do more.

Turning on Chance Avenue, she drove past a crumbling home on the left—from Joe's description, she knew it had to be the Lewis' place. To her right, the landscape gently sloped downward into the maze of thickly forested hollers. Eddy made a U-turn and headed back past the house. She slowed her sedan to a crawl, her eyes trained on the roadside, looking for her landmark. Adrenaline coursed through her as it came into view. It was a thick oak tree, its trunk split and blackened by a lightning strike.

She parked on the shoulder and walked to the tree. Beyond it a few steps, the hillside fell away quickly, a fifty-foot drop before a more gradual descent into the forest below. Stepping over Chuck's rusted rail tracks, Eddy walked around the tree. Above her, she saw the handle, a makeshift rig made from bicycle handlebars. She stared down at the valley below, for the first time questioning her decision. She'd never tried a zipline.

CHAPTER 56

August 25, 2025, One Day Before the Murder
Aubrey Ledbetter hated to see her son like this, so helpless and vulnerable. Alerted by Carl's push-button emergency call, she'd arrived home just in time to see him loaded into the ambulance.

By now, the worst of the seizure was over, but he still occasionally thrashed about in its aftershocks. He lay on his back, strapped to the gurney for his protection, his head and neck held fast by inflatable cushions.

As Aubrey climbed into the back of the ambulance, she nodded to a paramedic. "Afternoon, Ms. Ledbetter." All the EMTs serving the area were well-familiar with the routine. Despite rules to the contrary, Aubrey would ride in the ambulance with her son, holding his hand, careful to keep the pulse oximeter on his finger and the oxygen mask on his face. She would remain with him at the hospital until it was over, stroking his forehead and whispering words of comfort.

Above the mask, Carl's eyes bulged, looking plaintively to his mother as the tremors began anew. "My sweet boy," Aubrey whispered, holding her son's chest as tears filled her eyes.

No matter how many times the scene repeated itself, feeling Carl's quaking body always brought the tears and with them unanswerable questions. Why was her first son taken from her? Why did Carl have to endure all this? Was it to make up for how easy life was for the rest of her family? If so, she would gladly give it all up.

Later in the hospital, exhausted by the seizures, Carl would nap, then awake to find his mother still with him. "Mama," he would say. He only called her mama after seizures.

"Yes, Carl, I'm here," she would answer, and he would doze off again.

This day, he stirred again, still half asleep. "Mama," he mumbled, with his eyes still closed. "May I still go to the party tomorrow?"

CHAPTER 57

Eddy looked up at the makeshift rig. "Fucking death trap," she said aloud. A heavy chain extended from the pulley to the bicycle handlebars, welded in place by an amateur. Three feet of heavy rope hung from the handlebars and passed through a wooden disk the size of a dinner plate, presumably the seat. No harness, no spotter, and no helmet.

Her eyes followed the cable that angled steeply down as the hillside fell away then disappeared beneath the canopy in the distance. You're an idiot, Eddy, said a voice in her head. On the other hand, according to Chuck, the holler-dwellers used it all the time.

More importantly, she knew it was important to Carl's defense, which made it important to Joe. If the contraption worked, then Clem Tettleton could have committed the murder and made it home for his probation check-in. Besides, Chuck wasn't up for this. Even if he caught someone careening down the hill, he wouldn't know where it led or how long it took.

Eddy set the stopwatch on her phone and tucked it away then lifted the handlebar off a tree limb. Suspended from the cable before her, the apparatus seemed even less stable. With a deep breath, she straddled the rope and settled her backside onto the disk. She grasped the handlebar and stared down the hill.

The feat would require a plunge from a point a few steps ahead where the terrain began to slope. Depending on how far the cable sagged under her weight—another unknown—she'd be about fifteen feet above ground for the first fifty yards before the hillside fell away, leaving her suspended some fifty feet in the air, racing over the ravine. From there, it was anyone's guess, as the cable disappeared under the tree line.

Eddy breathed deeply, shuffling to the takeoff spot with the rope between her legs. "Now or never, Eddy," she whispered. With one more pleading glance up at the pulley, she re-gripped the handlebar and stepped forward into air, leaning back on her seat as she plunged downhill. The speed of the dive took her breath away as the ground raced beneath her. In no time, she was hurtling over the ravine, the cool fall air filling her lungs and stinging her face. Not risking a peak below, she stared straight ahead, her body clenched in fear.

Suddenly, her world dimmed as she dipped below a dark green blanket of oak, ash, and loblolly pines. The forest floor raced past, much closer now, the scent of rotting leaves and campfires flooding in. As the grade of the slope decreased, her airspeed slowed considerably. Easing her death grip on the handlebars, she adjusted her seat and reclined a bit, enjoying the glide through the dark woodland.

The thought of when and how she would disembark had just crossed her mind when the cable dipped ever closer to the ground. Now, her feet were dragging over tall ferns and underbrush as she weaved between the low hanging branches of trees. Although her speed had decreased considerably, the prospect of a crash landing at twenty miles per hour seemed like a terrible idea.

Ahead, Eddy saw her answer at the end of the zipline where the cable attached to the white trunk of a massive gum tree. Before it lay masses of leaves piled ten feet off the forest floor. Of course, she laughed to herself, as she hurtled toward the tree. Reaching the edge of the leaf pile, she curled her knees to her chest and released the grip on the handlebars, plunging into the mound and sinking into musty, dark dampness.

She hadn't reached the ground, so standing was impossible. Instead, she rolled her way out of the pile, emerging disoriented, seated on the forest floor. Recalling the stopwatch, she dug her phone from her pocket and clicked: Three minutes, thirty-six seconds. "Yes!" she whispered to herself. Assuming the Tettleton place was close, it was more than enough time to make it home for his probation check-in.

Getting her bearings, she stood, shaking the leaves from her hair as she took in her dark, lush surroundings. She stood in a grove of majestic gum trees, their gray and white peeling bark stretching high above, where narrow shafts of sunlight filtered through the olive canopy. The forest floor was spongy underfoot, layered with mulch and detritus that perfumed the air with the pungency of fall.

Eddy stood still for a full minute, taking in the tranquility, the dim light and heavy air lending a soothing stillness. A few feet to her left, a rustling of leaves on the edge of the leaf pile broke the silence. Then from the pile trotted a skunk, pausing to eye its visitor. Eddy froze then relaxed as the critter turned and moved away from her.

She smiled as the cute critter walked away, its paws silent on the leafy ground. Now ten feet from her, still facing away from her, the animal's head bowed to the ground. Then, to Eddy's amazement, the skunk performed a handstand and looked back at her from between its legs.

Eddy did not know—but was about to learn—that Spilogale putorius, the eastern spotted skunk, having had its peaceful afternoon nap in the leaves disturbed, was taking dead aim. She heard a hissing and was about to run when she felt the warm oily liquid streak across her neck as the nauseating smell engulfed her. She doubled over at the waist, frantically wiping her neck with her sleeve, as the odor overwhelmed her. Groaning, she crumpled to her knees, desperately rubbing leaves against her to escape the stench.

Then she heard laughing from the other side of the leaf pile.

CHAPTER 58

Day Nine

"You've got to be shitting me." Dirk propped his elbows on the table and buried his face in both hands.

Sara snorted in disgust. "Why? Because he listens to reason?"

"Listens to reason? Is that what you call it?" Dirk asked, chuckling.

"Yeah, what would you call it?"

"Falling for the defense bullshit, that's what."

"Look, let's be productive, folks," Jack cautioned. "Sara, Priya, and Elston all made good points, but last night I had time to reflect. I'm changing my vote to not guilty. It's as simple as that."

"Well, it's complete horseshit," Dirk grumbled, shaking his head.

"Well, I, for one, think your open-mindedness is commendable," Priya said. "And I'm not just saying that because you agree with me."

"Thank you, Priya. In the end, I just thought about the finality of this decision. We all know what a guilty verdict would mean for Carl," Jack said, with a glance toward Ellen, who sat massaging her temples. "I just have a lingering doubt, and I couldn't live with myself if I was wrong."

Frank sat with arms crossed, staring daggers at Jack. "I smell a rat."

Jack shrugged, palms up. "What's that supposed to mean?"

"It means I've been watching you—sidling up to people, playing your games."

"Look, Frank," Jack said smiling nervously, "we're all under a lot of pressure here. I can assure you that I…"

"Who owns Echo Insurance?" Frank demanded.

"What?"

"Your insurance company? Don't the Ledbetters own it?"

"No, it's…I don't know," Jack stammered. "It's a national company," he said, smiling again, looking around the room for support. "This is ridiculous."

Frank stood and stalked to the water cooler. "Well, something's fishy, and I intend to find out what."

"If we could please return to our task," Priya said calmly. "If I'm correct, it's now four for guilty—Dirk, Frank, Ellen and Duncan, and four not guilty—me, Sara, Elston, and now Jack."

"Last I checked, four and four is eight," Dirk muttered. "Is rain man down there ever going to vote?"

"You're such an asshole," Sara said.

Ignoring her, Dirk leaned forward to look down the table at Quinn. "I mean, c'mon, dude. Do you even have a pulse? Time to activate that retard brain."

"That's enough!" Sara said as Quinn turned toward the wall and others chimed in, shouting down Dirk.

Dirk shrugged. "At least he has an excuse. I just can't figure how the rest of you can't see through Mr. Turner's bullshit. Trying to make us think he's from around here with the little local references. I looked him up."

Sara shook her head, making eye contact with Jack at the other end of the table. "Which, according to the jury instructions," she said, "we are not supposed to do."

"Yeah, turns out Turner's from San Francisco," Dirk continued, turning to Sara. "Your kind of place, right," he said, laughing. "No wonder you like him."

"Dirk…" Jack began but just shook his head. Then he looked at Sara, and they exchanged subtle nods.

CHAPTER 59

Eddy scrambled to her feet, her senses inflamed with the overpowering odor. Through watery eyes, across the leaf pile twenty feet away, she could make out a slender teenage boy leaning against a tree, laughing and covering his nose.

"There's no cause to worry, miss," he said, still chuckling. "Trust me. I don't aim to come any closer than this." As her vision cleared, Eddy could see he wore coveralls over a dingy white thermal shirt.

"Name's Clem Tettleton. I'm the guy y'all want to frame for the murder," he said casually. "It don't bother me, though. I reckon you figured I shot him then high-tailed it back here on the zipper. Could have happened that way. Except for one thing."

A wave of nausea washed over Eddy, and she doubled over at the waist. "Look, sorry if I'm intruding," she said, after a dry heave, "but is there any way to…I mean, this is so bad."

"You need to get your face in the crick. C'mon," he said and turned to walk away.

Eddy's fear of the stranger was far outweighed by the caldron of bile that raged in her nostrils. After a short walk, she clambered down a steep bank. Kneeling beside a stream, she plunged her face into the cold water, feeling immediate relief.

"Better?" Clem asked from up the bank after several dips in the water. Eddy nodded and hiked up the bank. Near the top, Clem offered a hand while covering his nose with his shirt. Eddy took it, and he pulled her up.

"Thanks," she said. "I do feel better. I suppose I should start hiking out."

Clem rolled his eyes. "That'll take all day. I'll give you a lift. My truck's just up the hill."

Eddy hesitated. Accepting a ride with a suspected killer definitely seemed like a bad idea. But then she was already in the middle of nowhere with him. "Thank you," she said. "That's very kind."

On the hike up the hill, Eddy noticed for the first time that her escort was barefoot; it was incredible, given the terrain. He also seemed to climb silently, his feet barely disturbing the leaf-covered hillside.

"So, I saw your cannonball into the leaves," he said as they neared a pickup parked on a dirt road that followed a ridgeline. "We call that our hillbilly hydraulics."

Eddy laughed. "It was fun."

Her thoughts returned to Clem's comments about his alibi. "So, Clem, earlier you said the zipline could have been your alibi but for one thing."

"Oh, that. I didn't know you were paying attention at that point," he said, smiling.

"Well?" she asked, after several seconds passed.

He stopped and turned to face her. "You just rode that zipline, so you know the timing of the fall into the leaves is important."

"Yes."

"Fall too early, you miss the leaves, and too late and you slam into the tree."

"Agreed," Eddy said, nodding.

"If you haven't noticed, there ain't a lot of streetlights in this holler. Can you imagine trying that in the pitch dark?"

"I see your point, Clem."

Reaching the pickup, Tettleton gestured toward its bed. "Sorry. You ride back here. Can't have you stinking up my ride."

"Understood," Eddy said, climbing over the tailgate.

Riding out of the holler in a maze of dirt roads, Eddy was certain she couldn't have found her way back to town. Forty minutes later, they pulled up outside the Victorian. Eddy climbed out of the pickup and walked to the driver's window. "Thanks, Clem," she said earnestly. "Really. Thanks."

He nodded and pulled his shirt over his nose. "Tomato juice," he said. "And burn your clothes," he yelled as he pulled away.

CHAPTER 60

"It was like someone dropped a rotten egg in a smelly sock and cracked me in the face with it."

Joe smiled across the kitchen table at his girlfriend on Monday morning. "Was? You're still not exactly a bouquet of roses, babe." They'd spent the weekend recovering from the ordeal. Joe had burned Eddy's clothing in the backyard, and Eddy had spent much of Sunday bathing in tomato juice.

"You should have seen the little asshole," Eddy said, recalling the event. "He totally targeted my face. I thought he was so cute with his handstand, like he was showing off for me. Then wham!"

"Showing off for you?" Joe raised his eyebrows. "Busier, I'm no Jane Goodall, but I'm fairly sure that impressing humans with their athleticism is not a top priority for most wild animals."

"Well then, he was just being vindictive. He could have just walked away."

"How do you know it was a 'he'?"

Eddy shrugged. "Just a feeling I got. I know the type. Impulsive and narcissistic," she said, laughing.

Although a nightmare, Eddy's skunk encounter had given them both a welcome distraction from the trial. It had also nullified Clem's alibi. Although Eddy was convinced Clem was no murderer, his social media threat still made him a better suspect than Luke Stuckey.

On his way to court, Joe called Chuck. "Hey, have you confirmed Coach Stuckey's poker alibi?"

"Yes and no. You were right. The poker alibi was bullshit. Coach Stuckey now says he was with another woman. Confirmed that last night."

"Well, having met Mrs. Stuckey, I can't say I blame him."

"Good luck in court."

Back in Department One, Pettigrew called a series of witnesses that revealed a shrewd strategy. Owing to their concern about drunk driving, the Holts had diligently documented the comings and goings of the partygoers. The hosts had collected car keys and only returned them after their owners had taken a breath test borrowed from the police department.

After calling three football players and two cheer squad members to the stand to testify where they were at the time of the murder, Joe recognized the DA's plan. Rather than relying on the affirmative evidence of Carl's guilt, she would also plug up any leaks in the case by eliminating all other potential suspects. Presumably, Carl would be the only person unaccounted for.

After the jury had left the courtroom for the lunch recess, Carl turned to Joe. "Mr. Turner, Sinclair Lewis' testimony was unfortunate."

Joe blinked slowly and took a deep breath, controlling his frustration with his client. "Yes, it was, Carl. As you've pointed out more than once."

"Perhaps…"

"Sorry, Carl. The DA wants us to meet with the judge. Have a nice lunch."

In chambers, Boniface spoke while eyeing the brown sack lunch on his desk. "Make this quick, Melissa."

"Sure, Judge. I have a simple request. Sinclair Lewis contacted me this morning. He'd like to attend the rest of the trial." It was standard practice to prohibit witnesses from attending trial to prevent them from altering their testimony in light of other evidence. Since Lewis had already testified, Joe didn't see the harm.

The judge snickered. "Old Sinclair wants to bask in his fame. Mr. Turner, any objection?"

Joe shook his head. "Not so long as Ms. Pettigrew doesn't plan on calling him back to the stand."

"Really?" the judge asked, sounding surprised. "What a welcome change. I've become conditioned to your objecting to everything."

"Choosing my battles, Your Honor."

"Good. Tell Sinclair he may attend but no signing autographs. I'll see you two after lunch."

Joe met with Chuck at Nadine's for an update. Dr. Death needed another week to retest the DNA sample. Jen Scoggins' cell phone records had been subpoenaed, but they likely wouldn't arrive until after the trial. Unless something else shook loose, Joe would present Luke Stuckey as a suspect but concentrate his efforts on convincing the jury that Clem Tettleton was the murderer. That would mean calling Eddy as a witness to her zipline heroics.

"I feel like I'm missing something," Joe said, standing to leave. "It seems like the answer is here, right in front of us. If I could just see it."

"If all the ifs and buts were candy and nuts," said Chuck, "every day would be Christmas."

CHAPTER 61

Back in court, after some uneventful testimony by two members of the cheer squad, Pettigrew announced her last witness of the day. "Your Honor, the State calls Luke Stuckey."

The courtroom buzzed as the star quarterback strode confidently up the center aisle of the courtroom. A blue blazer fit snugly over his athletic frame. His dark eyes scanned the courtroom on the way to the witness stand.

"Good afternoon, Mr. Stuckey," Pettigrew began, after Barbara had administered the oath.

"High bar, ma'am," the witness replied as Joe rolled his eyes.

Pettigrew got straight to the point. "Mr. Stuckey, where were you at about 11:50 p.m. on the night of Friday, August 26 of this year?"

"I was with my girlfriend, Jen Scoggins, at her home on Sheldon Avenue. We drove there from a party at the Holts'."

"Did you make any stops on the way to the Scoggins residence?"

The witness thought for a minute, running a hand over his black buzz cut. "Yes, ma'am. I believe we stopped for gas at the station across from the grocery there on Elm. Then we went on to the Scoggins'."

"And how long were you two at the Scoggins' home?"

"We arrived around 9:15 p.m.," he said. "Left around midnight."

"Once you arrived there at about 9:15 p.m., did you leave that location at any time prior to midnight?"

"No, ma'am."

"Now, Mr. Stuckey, I understand your cell phone wasn't with you that evening." Joe had expected this. Pettigrew was preemptively addressing the issue to lessen its impact.

Stuckey smiled sheepishly. "Naw," he said, shaking his head. "I ended up leaving my phone in someone's car that night. I reckon I had other things on my mind."

Laughter rippled through the courtroom. Boniface, grinning himself, half-heartedly tapped his gavel. "Order, ladies and gentlemen."

"Mr. Stuckey, I understand you and Justin Holt were close?" she asked, her tone now solemn.

The witness nodded then started to speak but stopped. "He, uh…" Another pause. "Sorry," he said, with a wan smile.

"Take your time, Mr. Stuckey," Pettigrew said from the podium. "I know this is difficult."

The witness breathed deeply. "Justin was a good friend." His voice was quaking. "We competed on the football field," he said quietly. "He couldn't have been a better teammate. He was my brother."

A hush fell over the courtroom. Pettigrew let the moment resonate, pausing before concluding her examination. "No further questions."

On cross examination, Joe knew he had to tread lightly. Luke had the jury in the palm of his hand, and now the prospect of blaming him for the murder of his best friend seemed absurd. Still, he only needed to convince one juror.

"Mr. Stuckey, you competed with Justin Holt for the quarterback position at Barton High?"

"Yes, sir."

"And heading into the season, he was the starter, and you were second string?"

"Yes, sir."

"And since you and Justin were both seniors, this was your last chance to earn a college scholarship."

"Yes."

"Before the season, you didn't have any scholarship offers because no one had seen you play, correct?"

"Correct, sir."

"And since becoming the starting quarterback after Justin's murder, you have interest from several colleges, right?"

"That's right."

"Mr. Stuckey, you now know that GPS shows your cell phone at the Holt residence at the time of the murder."

"Yes, sir."

"If you're like most high school students, your phone is important to you, correct?"

"Yes, sir."

"But you were okay to spend the night without it?"

"Yes, sir. Jen had her phone, if we needed it."

"Did she make any calls that you are aware of?"

"No."

"Besides your girlfriend, do you know anyone who can verify your presence at the Scoggins' home?"

"No."

"Did you two order a pizza or anything while you were there?"

"No, sir."

"And about this trip to the gas station, Mr. Stuckey? Did you pay with a credit card?"

"Cash."

"Cash, really?" Joe asked, eyebrows raised. "That's unusual."

Pettigrew stood. "Objection, Your Honor. Counsel is testifying."

"Sustained. Mr. Turner, please stick to questions."

"The Scoggins live in a gated community, correct?" Joe continued.

"Yes, sir."

"So, a guard at the gate could verify your presence there, right?"

"We, uh, parked outside the gate and walked in," Stuckey said. "I guess Jen didn't want her folks to know we were there alone."

"Mr. Stuckey, are you aware that Jen Scoggins initially told the police that she never left the party that night?"

"Yes."

"And would it surprise you to know that when I asked Jen to account for her whereabouts that night, she didn't mention the trip to the gas station?"

The witness thought for a minute and shifted in his chair. "Not really," he mumbled, staring at the floor.

"Really, why is that?"

Even before the question was out of his mouth, Joe saw the answer coming and regretted asking. For the first time, he saw anger in the young man's eyes as he stared back at him. Then Luke Stuckey breathed deeply, his shoulders slumping. "Probably because I had, uh, also purchased some condoms there."

Joe cursed himself. In a single question, he had probably undone an effective cross-examination. Unless

Luke Stuckey was an actor worthy of an Oscar nomination, everyone in the courtroom knew he had just told the absolute truth. "No further questions, Your Honor," he said, trying not to show his disappointment.

A beaming Boniface dismissed the jurors for the day.

On Joe's way out of the court, Chuck called. "That girlfriend of yours is nuttier than a squirrel turd."

Joe laughed. "She doesn't smell much better, either."

"How'd it go with the quarterback? Is our hair-brained theory still alive?"

"Alive but it's running on fumes. Luke claims he stopped at a gas station on Elm Street that night. Can you check for video surveillance?"

"Sure. And sorry about the Sinclair Lewis fiasco. I'd still bet dollars to donuts he's blind as a bat. I'm not giving up on this. This time, it's personal."

Joe laughed. "'This time, it's personal?' Must be a movie line."

"Yep. In every sequel ever made."

CHAPTER 62

The following morning before court, Joe met with Carl's parents on a park bench across the street from the courthouse. The stress of the trial was wearing on them, but they were staying strong for their son.

As usual, Aubrey did the talking while Matt stood stoically by her side. "We were pleased with your cross examination of Mr. Lewis," Aubrey said, hopefully. "He definitely seemed a little too eager to be the star witness. But the eyesight thing didn't really work out."

"It was a disaster," Joe agreed. "Poor judgment on my part, but I've got Chuck on it."

"And I thought there was something fishy about that Luke Stuckey," Aubrey said. "They were so close. I'd hate to think he had something to do with it, but his story didn't sit right."

Joe told them about Eddy's zipline discovery and the DNA retesting before Aubrey stood to excuse herself. "I'm going to get Carl ready for court," she said. "That child ties his own fly-fishing flies but refuses to learn how to tie a necktie."

Joe told Aubrey he'd like to meet with Carl after court to discuss his direct examination. The strength of the prosecution's case had made Carl's testimony a necessary risk. "Sure, Joe. Just come on out to the house any time." Aubrey walked away, leaving Joe with her husband.

Matt stared across the town square at the jail. Joe could read his mind. He had to be thinking of Carl, alone in a sterile prison cell. They both knew Carl would suffer more than most in custody.

Matt shook himself. "Mr. Turner," Matt said after his wife was out of earshot, "I appreciate all you're doing, but I hate to see Aubrey get her hopes up." He paused, searching for words. "Don't get me wrong, I believe—no, I know—that Carl didn't do this. But with the gunshot residue and DNA evidence… It's bad, isn't it?" His eyes pled with Joe to disagree.

"I'm afraid it is." Matt bowed his head. "But there are two reasons why we need to stay positive. First, every one of those jurors is looking at Carl, me, and probably you, too, in the courtroom. If there's doubt in our eyes, they'll see it. Also, I don't want to give you false hope, but I believe in your son's innocence. This jury system isn't perfect, but most of the time, it has a way of getting it right."

"Thank you," Matt said solemnly and walked away, leaving Joe alone with his thoughts. Part of him regretted saying that last bit and admitted that he was probably guilty of wishful thinking.

Back in court, Pettigrew called Butch Ford to the witness stand. The stocky young man in a letterman's jacket walked up the center aisle, his wide eyes taking in the packed courtroom.

The prosecutor began with some introductory questions. Ford was a senior co-captain of the team and a straight-A student. He'd been to the party but had consumed no alcohol, a fact that drew an approving nod from juror number three, the insurance salesman. Along with the construction foreman, Joe now figured him to be a problem for the defense. He seemed conservative and had been smiling throughout the prosecution's case.

"Mr. Ford, I understand you made a trip into the Holts' backyard that evening?" Pettigrew asked.

The witness looked sheepishly at the jury. "Yes, the bathrooms inside were pretty busy all evening, so I walked out the back door and around to the side of the house to, um, relieve myself in some bushes."

"Do you recall what time that was, approximately?"

"It was about 11:45 p.m. I remember because I was thinking I had planned to be home by midnight. I had the SAT the next morning."

"And Mr. Ford, prior to that time, when was the last time you'd seen Justin Holt?"

"Around 11:00 p.m. Justin was taking the test in the morning too, so he said his goodbyes to his friends and went out to his bedroom."

"Can you describe where Justin's bedroom is in relation to the house?"

"Yes. His bedroom is a one-room building in the backyard."

"So, it's a free-standing structure?"

"Yes, ma'am."

"Mr. Ford, on your way to relieve yourself, did you hear something that stuck with you?"

"Yes. As I walked by Justin's bedroom, just past an open window, I heard a voice from inside."

"Did you recognize that voice?"

"Yes," Ford said, nodding as the memory reached him, "it was definitely Justin's voice." Joe exhaled silently. This kid was obviously telling the truth. Shit!

"And, to remind the jury, at this time, it was approximately 11:45 p.m.?" Pettigrew asked, strolling from behind the podium.

"Yes, ma'am."

"And Mr. Ford," Pettigrew said, signaling importance to the jury with a pause, "please tell the jury what you heard Justin Holt say from inside his bedroom at approximately 11:45 p.m."

"He said, 'Hi, Carl.'"

A low din of conversation swept over the courtroom. "Order," Boniface said gruffly into the microphone. "Order in the Court."

As the murmurs died down, Pettigrew paused again, milking the moment. "Thank you very much, Mr. Ford. Your Honor, I have no more questions."

Outside the courthouse, Joe heard a call from behind him and turned to find Pettigrew jogging to him. "I almost forgot," the DA said, reaching into her jacket pocket and handing over a thumb drive. "The long-awaited surveillance video from the Cabarton Ranch sign."

The prosecutor could hardly contain her glee.

CHAPTER 63

"How long has he been out there?" Joe asked, popping open a beer as he stared out the open kitchen window. Directly across the street, Clem Tettleton sat in his rusted-out pickup, the beat of rap music pulsating from within.

Eddy poured herself a glass of wine. "I noticed him just before you got home. Normally, I'd be freaked out, but he was really kind to me."

"Your knight in shining armor," Joe said, smiling.

"Not exactly shining, Turner."

"I think he must be sweet on you, Ms. Eddy. And I wouldn't have pegged him for a rap fan."

"He's a renaissance man."

"Clearly." Joe sipped his beer. "You know, I was thinking about how Chuck and the whole town talk about 'the Tettletons,'" Joe said, using air quotes, "as if they're an inferior race of criminals. It can't be easy being born into that clan."

The two walked out on the porch, and Tettleton promptly drove away, the deafening rumble of his jalopy echoing throughout the quiet neighborhood. "Ah, he's shy, Busier. He was probably getting up the nerve to bring you flowers. Or maybe a pot of possum stew."

"Very funny. But I think fresh roadkill is the hillbilly tradition on the first date. So, how was court?"

Joe shook his head. "Horrible. Lots of fresh-faced, square-jawed young men who would never tell a lie. Today, one of them put Carl at the scene minutes before the murder."

Joe's phone buzzed in his pocket. "Hi Chuck." As Joe listened, Eddy watched his face. It would betray nothing to a stranger, but she noticed her lover's sad eyes. "Thanks, Chuck. See ya."

The two sat quietly for several minutes as a cricket's rhythmic whistle pierced the soft air. "DNA tests confirmed," Joe finally said, quietly. "Carl's DNA was under the victim's fingernail."

"Well, you've got the handshake explanation, right?" Eddy asked with a grimace. Joe rolled his eyes. Although Carl's revelation about his handshake with Justin was at least something, it seemed like a stretch.

"So, Joseph," Eddy said after a time then hesitated.

"Yes, Edna? Out with it."

"Okay, I'm not saying I buy this, but is there a possibility that Carl…" Another pause.

"No chance. He's innocent."

"I mean, maybe he had a seizure and somehow lost control of himself? I don't know."

Joe sighed. "Obviously, I've thought of that. And I realize that at some point, the evidence becomes overwhelming."

"But?" Eddy prompted.

"It's hard to explain, but I just sort of know he didn't do it. You remember when you said you didn't believe Clem Tettleton was guilty? It's just a feeling, right?"

"Well, then, counselor, you'd better get to work. Meanwhile, I'm making mac 'n cheese," she said and went inside.

Despite his unshakable belief in his client's innocence, deep down, Joe knew more bad news was on the way. Back at his desk, he plugged in the thumb drive and watched a spinning icon as the video file loaded on his laptop.

The footage was of good quality and not as dark as he'd expected. The camera on the Cabarton Ranch sign angled downward, perfectly capturing a thirty-foot stretch of Chance Avenue. Joe recognized the huge oak that marked the spot of Chuck's old rail tracks and Eddy's zipline. He and Chuck had missed the zipline in the gloaming of their twilight visit.

Joe fast-forwarded the video until there was movement on the street. The timer on the screen read 11:56 p.m. when the solitary figure bounded into the frame from the left, jogging down the middle of the street. Carl's silhouette was clear, outlined in the moonlight beneath his familiar Cubs cap. Joe also recognized his odd jogging style—a quicker version of his rigid, forward-leaning gait.

He backed up the tape to 11:45 p.m. and played it again in real time, watching for another twenty minutes. There was no sign of Clem Tettleton near the zipline, and yet another defense escape route was blocked.

Joe thought about what Carl's mom had told him. Carl had the ability to erase unpleasant events from his memory. Shooting his good friend would certainly qualify as unpleasant.

He returned to the footage of Carl, slowing the speed of the video and leaning to the screen. Something was in his right hand, the moonlight glancing off its metallic form. Angling the screen this way and that, Joe peered at the object, desperate for a better view. In the end, he couldn't tell.

Was it Aubrey Ledbetter's phone that he held, swinging back and forth with his stride? Or had Sinclair Lewis been right after all?

CHAPTER 64

The following day's morning session was filled with the depressing and creepy testimony of Daulton County's Chief Forensic Pathologist Nicholas Piper. Smartly dressed in a tweed suit and bow tie, the frail doctor had apparently lost touch with how disgusting his work seemed to the average person. Either that or he had a sadistic side that took pleasure in the discomfort of others.

When asked about the gunpowder burns found at the gunshot wound, Piper's fingers rattled on his laptop that was linked to the flat screen on the wall opposite the jury. "I think this image best suits our purposes," he said, smiling, as a grotesque image of the dead victim's partially decomposed face and bare torso filled the screen. In the photo, taken at the autopsy, Justin's Holt's face and chest were ghostly white and accented with purple where damaged blood cells had settled. His eyes, long since deprived of blood, had grayed and sunken back into their sockets.

Audible gasps escaped from the Holt family seated near the front right of the courtroom behind the prosecutor. A few got up and headed for the exit, one man covering his mouth on the way.

Joe was out of his seat. "Objection, Your Honor."

"Doctor, um, Doctor Piper," stammered Pettigrew. "Please take down the photo."

"If you'll just allow me," the oblivious witness said, his eyes wide with excitement, "the photo is truly a textbook…"

"Doctor, take down the photo!" thundered Judge Boniface as the courtroom began to empty. The judge, looking sickly himself, shaded his eyes from the ghastly image. The jury averted their eyes as well.

Belatedly, Piper began fumbling with his laptop. "Let's see, I can't seem to exit," the doctor said, now rattled as he realized the urgency of the matter. But after thirty seconds, the gruesome image remained. The judge beckoned Alvin to the bench. "Unplug the fucking…" he said into his hot microphone before turning it off.

Alvin jogged toward a bank of outlets with a look of worry on his face. Joe's laptop went black, then the lights on the counsel table, but the face remained.

"Apologies, ladies and gentlemen," a flustered Boniface said, addressing the jury. "Let's take a recess. Ten minutes," he said, glancing up at the screen. "No, make it twenty."

After the break, with the coroner's laptop taken away, the testimony went smoothly. "I observed sear marks around the chest wound," Piper said. "Also, there was tearing of the skin around the entrance. Both indicate that the muzzle of the gun was in contact with the victim's chest when the gun was fired."

"Doctor, is the fact that the suspect's DNA was found under the fingernails of the victim surprising to you?" Pettigrew asked.

"Not at all. It's likely that once the victim realized he was about to be shot, he lashed out with his right hand, desperately clawing at the gunman."

"Given all your findings, doctor, do you have a theory how Justin Holt was murdered?"

"Objection, calls for speculation," Joe said, knowing it was futile.

"Overruled," mumbled Boniface. "You may answer, Doctor."

"Yes, indeed," the doctor said, smiling inappropriately. "It's likely the suspect was a surprise visitor since the victim was shirtless when found. I believe the murderer approached the victim without altercation as there were no signs of injuries secondary to a fight or struggle," he said as if describing the benefits of an insurance policy.

"Next, the suspect pushed the gun against the left side of the victim's chest where we see the entry wound and stippling. Caught unawares, the victim—who I understand was right-handed, scratched at the suspect, depositing the suspect's skin cells under the victim's right middle fingernail. The suspect fired his weapon once. The cause of death was the gunshot wound to the chest, which caused massive hemorrhaging."

Piper's testimony concluded with an analysis of the time of death. Using the body's temperature and rate of cooling, the doctor calculated that Justin Holt was shot between 11:45 p.m. and 11:55 p.m. The jury trudged out of the courtroom at lunch time looking shaken and exhausted.

In line at the hot dog cart outside the courthouse, Joe's phone buzzed. "Chuck, tell me something good," he said, checking the area for jurors.

"I got the video from the gas station. I went to school with the owner."

"And?"

"Luke Stuckey was there all right."

Joe covered his mouth and cursed.

"Video shows him there, pumping gas and picking out condoms at 8:20 p.m., which is really 9:20 p.m. The owner says the time is accurate, but it's off by an hour."

"Damn. Looks like we're left with Tettleton and his zipline."

"I got the first copy of the video, so the DA won't have it yet."

"Thanks, Chuck."

Joe digested Chuck's last comment as he ate his hot dog, sitting on the park bench. Technically, since he didn't plan on playing the video at trial, he didn't have to disclose it to the prosecution. Then again, Pettigrew would likely visit the gas station as well and get the surveillance footage herself. Joe smiled as a rather devious thought entered his mind. He downloaded the video and forwarded it to the prosecutor.

Joe knew the afternoon session would be rough for the defense. Pettigrew's DNA expert would testify, and his conclusions would go unchallenged. Joe stared across the park to the ominous county jail, its ivy-covered gray stone recalling medieval times. The top of the three-story fortress was lined with small square windows crisscrossed with black wrought iron. The relic still housed inmates serving short sentences and the county's psychiatric ward.

From his own short stay inside, Joe recalled the chilling dampness and chaotic noise of the place. The cracks of the deputies' radios, shrieks from unstable inmates, and the constant clanging of the metal doors all made for a non-stop racket. Inevitably, Joe thought of Carl, sitting alone on a cold metal bench, covering his ears with both hands, alone and afraid.

CHAPTER 65

Carl

In our meeting after court today, Joe Turner expressed his belief that things had gone poorly this afternoon, and I have to agree. Ms. Pettigrew and her expert witness had gone on and on about the DNA, proving that my skin cells were under Justin Cassady Holt's middle fingernail. The odds it was someone else's DNA was one in 4.8 quadrillion.

Humorously, I noted to myself that at least it wasn't one in 4.8 quadrillion and one. Thanks to Mr. Turner, I've been working on sarcasm as a form of humor but so far have kept the jokes to myself until my understanding is more complete.

Mr. Turner pointed out to the jury that no trace amounts of blood were under Justin's fingernails, as one would expect if he had scratched me immediately prior to the shooting. Although a fair point, I am forced to concede that my DNA under Justin's fingernails is powerful evidence of my guilt.

The purpose of the meeting with Joe Turner was to help me prepare for my testimony in court. I'm quite glad the meeting is over. Mr. Turner's advice was to relax and tell the truth. For a fairly intelligent person, Joe Turner says some extremely unintelligent things. I consider his advice to be flawed on both fronts.

Relaxed is something you either are or you aren't. It's like telling someone with a cold to feel better, which, by the way, I have actually heard on more than one occasion. The level of my relaxation is not something I can control. I've read about relaxation techniques, but they involve things like closing your eyes and thinking of peaceful settings, and other strategies that are impossible to undertake while on a witness stand.

And even if I could employ these techniques, I doubt I could achieve relaxation, given the circumstances. I'll be answering questions into a microphone that will amplify my words to an intolerable volume. The jurors will be there judging me, evaluating my answers in silence.

As an aside, I find it odd that during the trial, the jurors are not allowed to speak. It would certainly assist the attorneys if they could blurt out, "That doesn't sound right to me," or, "I find this witness very credible." Instead, they sit there with poker faces, thinking their secret thoughts. If nothing else, hearing from them might clear up misunderstandings. "Oh, I must have misheard. Four point eight quadrillion and one makes all the difference." More sarcasm. I believe I'm actually getting the hang of it.

But I digress. I will be unlikely capable of relaxing when I testify, facing the silent faces who will judge me. I will be quite desperate that they believe my testimony, given that if they do not, I will be imprisoned for the duration of my life.

Other than the obvious lack of freedom, prison would bring other concerns like being away from my mother and father and missing Cubs games, but enough of that for now. I have avoided these thoughts thus far and intend to continue to do so. Still, relaxation on the witness stand will not be possible.

Mr. Turner means well, but his advice that I tell the truth is also quite unnecessary. As my mother will tell you, I always tell the truth. She often remarks that I do so to a fault. She has explained that this means that, in speaking the truth, I often fail to account for the feelings of others.

While I understand that theory, its premise is flawed because I have no way of knowing the unspoken feelings of others. Given that it's impossible for me to account for these mystery feelings, I intend to continue with my blanket policy of always telling the truth. I will no doubt offend people along the way, but at least people will know where I stand on a particular topic. I would know the jury's thoughts, by the way, were they allowed to speak, as previously mentioned.

So, to sum up, Joe Turner's advice that I relax and tell the truth is, on one hand, impossible to execute, and on the other, wholly unnecessary.

For reasons I will never understand, Mr. Turner insisted we practice my direct examination. Presumably, he already knows the questions he will propound, and given my aforementioned policy on truthfulness, I already know my answers.

Perhaps my truthful answers would offend the jurors. It seems odd that since the trial is a search for the truth, Mr. Turner would have me shade or varnish my answers to account for the emotions of others.

In the end, though, I went along with Joe Turner's wishes and dutifully practiced my direct examination. After all, Mr. Turner has proven to be quite a nice person, and it seems important to him.

CHAPTER 66

On Friday morning, Joe was grateful to hear Judge Boniface inform the jury that due to a prior commitment—Joe had little doubt it was a golf match—they would be adjourning for the day at noon.

It had been a long and difficult week for the defense. By the time Pettigrew had finished with the DNA evidence the day before, Joe knew the jury had already seen more than enough to convict.

After his meeting with Carl, freshly motivated to find a way to help his client, Joe had made coffee and stayed up late, poring over the case file well into the night. Then, just past 1:00 a.m., somewhere deep within his mind, the tiniest of synapses had fired. However fleeting, a spark had flickered. He couldn't identify the thought—it was more of a feeling, really—but the key to Carl's defense was there. Somewhere.

This morning's session began with the testimony of more partygoers. They provided their whereabouts around the time of the murder, often corroborating each other's accounts of the evening. Then came the prosecution's two closing acts. As expected, Pettigrew played Carl's taped statement for the jury.

"Carl, do you know why we're here early on this Saturday morning?"

"I assume it's about what happened to Justin." Amplified through the courtroom's sound system, every part of his statement seemed even more incriminating than Joe had recalled.

"Can you think of any reason you would want to harm Justin?" The thirty seconds of silence that followed seemed like ten minutes. The second hand on the courtroom clock clicked in unrelenting monotony. "Sir, did you hear the question?"

Joe saw some of the jurors exchange glances in the further silence that followed. However expressionless, their meaning was obvious. "Can you believe this guy?" "Is he actually thinking about revealing his motive?" To his left, Carl sat, expressionless. Joe knew that if interviewed again, he would give exactly the same answers.

There was momentary relief when the officer moved on until Joe recalled the next series of questions. "Of course, I am familiar with silencers, as they are important for ear protection…" Carl's adenoidal tones, expounding on his knowledge of firearms, seemed to last an eternity.

Finally, Pettigrew directed the jury's attention to the video screen. The entire courtroom watched the elevated view from the sign on Chance Avenue. Soon, Carl came bounding into the frame. Pettigrew paused the tape with him centered, perfectly capturing his profile.

"Your Honor," Pettigrew began as Joe held his breath. The DA had yet to play the gas station video that proved Luke Stuckey's alibi. "The State of Georgia rests," the prosecutor said, and Joe exhaled.

Outside the courtroom, Chuck approached him. "Hey, I caught the last thirty minutes. What gives?" he whispered, checking the area for jurors. "You gave Pettigrew the video, right?"

"Of course! And shame on you for thinking otherwise!" he said in mock indignation. Then he added after a pause. "I may or may not have told her the time stamp was an hour off."

Despite the rough morning in court, Joe walked home with a bounce in his step, owing to yesterday's fleeting ray of hope. Part of him wondered if he'd manufactured the feeling, but deep down, he knew. After two weeks of being buried under an avalanche of prosecution evidence, a slender shaft of light had appeared from above, and he was determined to follow it to its source.

Arriving at home, Joe spotted Clem Tettleton's pickup parked across the street. He sighed heavily and dropped his satchel on the porch in disgust. He intended to spend the afternoon immersed in the case and didn't need the constant worry of this creepy hick. Besides, he thought, striding confidently across the street toward the pickup, the Cabarton footage had been proof that Tettleton wasn't the murderer.

From the middle of the street, Joe smelled the pungent aroma of pot wafting from the pickup. Arriving at the darkly tinted driver's side window, he knocked then stepped back, anticipating the billowing smoke that came when the window lowered.

"Howdy," came the voice through the smoke. Soon a face appeared beneath a ball cap.

"Clem, I'm Joe."

"Hey, Joe," he said pleasantly, smiling in a far-away stare.

After an awkward silence, Joe spoke up again. "So, Clem, Eddy and I have seen you out here. You should know that we've abandoned the theory that you're the murderer. Not that anyone would have believed it."

Clem nodded. "Okay, Joe, I appreciate you telling me that." He sounded genuine, and Joe knew what Eddy meant when she'd called him appealing.

Another moment passed. "So, Clem, feel free to sit here and smoke out or whatever, but is there anything we can do for you?"

"Actually, I thought I'd ask you about your career. I'm thinking about law school," he said.

Taken aback, Joe paused before Clem dissolved into laughter. "Very well done," Joe said, laughing.

"Actually," Clem said after their laughter had died down, "there is something I thought I should tell you."

"What's that?"

"So, your client, Carl. You may already know this, but he didn't kill that football player."

Joe stepped closer to the open window. "I'm listening."

"I've seen how them football players treat him, by the way. They're good to him when he's around, but they all have their impressions of him. Anyway, I was there that night. Not at the party but sneaking around it. I'd planned to slash some tires, set off a cherry bomb. Harmless shit."

He paused to take a drag on a joint and offered it to Joe, who declined.

"I reckon I got there around 11:30 p.m.," Clem continued. "I sat up on the hill behind the property scoping it out. The light was on in that little building in the back where the body was found. Someone went in there around 11:45 p.m. and walked out a few minutes later. Then a minute or so later, Carl shows up then leaves."

Joe stood, riveted to his words. "Could you see who went in before Carl?"

"No, it was dark. I just recognized Carl on account of his walk."

"Did you see where the other person went?"

"Disappeared around the main house. Then a few seconds later, I heard a car door close and a car drive away. The car was coughing and sputtering like it had a bad engine. Backfired a few times."

Joe surged with adrenaline as he digested the words. "Clem, this is obviously huge for Carl, but only if you testify."

He smiled and shook his head. "Naw, you may have heard. We Tettletons don't participate in the court system. Family wouldn't allow it. Besides, admitting I was there along with my threat the day before? Not to mention I'm a Tettleton. Probably would get my ass thrown in jail." He turned the key and the pickup gurgled to life.

Joe started to protest but knew it wouldn't make a difference. And he had a point about being prosecuted. "So, Clem, I understand you didn't take the zipline. So, how'd you make curfew?"

"Hell no, I didn't take the zipline," he said, with a smirk. "Not in the dark. Your crazy girlfriend might, but not me. It's been a pleasure."

"So, how'd you make curfew on your GPS?" Joe called again over the sputtering engine.

"You expect me to tell you all my secrets?"

Joe shrugged. "No, just curious."

Clem put his pickup in gear. "Let's just say we Tettletons aren't as dumb as we look." And with a polite nod, he was off.

As he drove away, it occurred to Joe that this last admission meant Clem didn't have an alibi for the Justin Holt murder after all.

CHAPTER 67

After a Saturday away from the case hiking with Eddy, Joe spent Sunday holed up in his home office. Energized by Clem Tettleton's observations, he re-read the entire file. His experiences in Barton added context to the witness statements and reports. The town's obsession with their high school football team permeated every aspect of the case, and Joe sensed, like before, that it was the key to the mystery. Desperate for the epiphany that he knew was close, he sat silently in concentration.

He thought about Tettleton and his blood feud with the football team. Having met both parties, Joe knew which side he would choose. Among the players and cheerleaders who had testified, he detected a subtle air of superiority and entitlement. He could well imagine them mocking Carl when he wasn't looking. But how did it all tie into the murder of the star quarterback?

At 4:00 p.m., a frustrated Joe closed the file. It was nearly time for another prep session with Carl. Eddy dropped him off at the Ledbetter's guest house with plans for a late dinner.

Sitting across from his client, Joe questioned Carl again about his observations both before and after discovering Justin's body. He'd asked about this before, but now it seemed possible that on the way to Justin's bedroom, he may have seen the person Clem described as leaving shortly before Carl's arrival. "Of course, if I made any observations that were important, I would tell you," Carl answered evasively.

By now, Joe was well-acquainted with his client's inability to lie. Instead, he relied on word games and an adherence to literal meaning to obscure the truth. Now, he suspected he was hiding something, and it was maddening.

"Joe, I've been thinking about Sinclair Lewis again."

"I think you're trying to change the subject."

Carl looked confused. "Of course I am. I believe we have covered this many times, and I wish to return to the Sinclair Lewis issue."

"Carl, listen. I know you weren't surprised that Sinclair Lewis could see the apple because he said his vision was perfect." He paused to laugh at himself for using Lewis' full name. His client was obviously rubbing off on him. "But, Carl, I didn't believe him when he said his vision was perfect. Believe it or not, sometimes people do not tell the truth. But obviously, I was wrong. I screwed up."

"I only bring this up because of Sinclair Lewis' damaging testimony that he saw me with a gun."

Joe sighed, exasperated. "Carl, I know his testimony was damaging. I'm just not sure what can be done now. I've apologized. We need to move on. In fact," he said, pulling another file from his satchel, "we only have another fifteen minutes before Eddy picks me up. It's been a long day. I think I'll just review some of your medical reports."

Joe had ordered a copy of Carl's medical records in order to better understand his mental condition. Given the ever-increasing likelihood of a conviction, he planned to advocate for a prison close to his family with special accommodations for his mental health needs.

As he flipped through the records, Joe felt Carl's relentless stare boring holes in his head from across the table.

"Yes, Carl?" He knew he would not give up the Sinclair Lewis topic until he'd said his piece.

"I know that people sometimes do not tell the truth, Joe. Often, they are unaware of the truth, like when people said the earth was flat for hundreds of years. Other times, I realize that individuals intentionally prevaricate, although this is rare."

Joe continued reading the medical records, only half-listening as Carl continued, expounding on different forms of falsehoods. "Of course, it wasn't just Mr. Sinclair Lewis' words that made me suspect he would be able to see the apple," he said. "It was the fact that I believe he wore contact lenses."

Joe froze in mid page-turn, then slowly looked up at his client. "Carl, how did you know he wore contact lenses?"

"I don't *know*," Carl corrected. "I believe it to be true."

"And why is that?" Joe asked, summoning patience.

"I recall when you approached Mr. Sinclair Lewis on the witness stand and showed him his written statement. Naturally, because he had previously testified that he used glasses for reading and whittling, he put them on so he could read his statement. But then…"

"He needed to hold it away from him to read it!" Joe interrupted, excitedly.

"Precisely. Because he was wearing contact lenses for seeing distance, his reading glasses were no longer powerful enough for him to see up close."

"Well done, Carl!" Joe said. "And I apologize for not listening to you sooner. You really notice things."

"Thank you, Joe. I'm glad my observation was useful." Then, true to form, he rose and walked out of the building. "Carl Ledbetter," Joe whispered to himself, "you are one of a kind."

CHAPTER 68

"Carl had a seizure late last night." Aubrey's voice trembled in Joe's ear as he walked to court on Monday. "He'll be at court, but I wanted to let you know…" Her voice trailed off and Joe knew she was barely holding it together. "All this is just too much for him. It's so far from his routine," she said, her voice cracking. "He's so anxious."

They discussed requesting to delay the proceedings, but Aubrey decided against it. "My son needs this nightmare to be over as soon as possible."

As Joe approached the courthouse, he felt the pressure to win like never before. Eddy had been right, of course. He cared about Carl. In the criminal justice world where everyone—attorneys, cops, defendants, and even judges—was looking for an edge, Carl's utter guilelessness was endearing.

Also, Joe knew the stakes could not be higher. Although the prosecution wasn't seeking the death penalty, a guilty verdict may well have the same result. He'd read how prison inmates with autism were more vulnerable to being bullied, exploited, and sexually abused. Carl's sensitivity to bright lights and loud noises would have his anxiety through the roof. Worse yet, Joe knew it was only a matter of time before Carl offended someone—with fatal results.

As Joe unpacked his satchel at the counsel table, a text from Chuck nudged him from his thoughts. —*Operation four eyes is a go.*

On the first day of the defense's case, Joe had planned to call Carl to the witness stand but was about to change course. Joe had shared Carl's revelation about Lewis' contact lenses with Chuck. They agreed that getting him back on the stand was a priority. The witness's sighting of Carl on Chance Avenue had been confirmed by the video, but his insistence that Carl carried a gun was not. For this, the jury would have to rely on Lewis' testimony.

Last night, Chuck had snuck through the woods to the edge of the old man's property. Soon, Lewis pulled in, driving his pickup. A pair of thick glasses never left his face.

This morning, Chuck's text confirmed that he'd arrived at the courthouse wearing glasses. That meant no contact lenses. Joe turned and briefly scanned the gallery. There was Lewis, halfway back, smiling proudly and soaking up his star witness status. After his testimony, he couldn't risk being seen wearing glasses in court.

The jury filed in, looking refreshed after the weekend, and Boniface took the bench to his typical fanfare. "Ladies and gentlemen, the prosecution has rested. Since the prosecution has the burden of proof, the defense may call witnesses or simply rest on the state of the evidence. Mr. Turner, does the defense wish to call a witness?"

Joe rose. "Thank you, Your Honor. The defense calls Sinclair Lewis."

Pettigrew stood, looking confused. "Your Honor, may we approach?"

Boniface shrugged. "Approach."

"Your Honor, counsel had an opportunity to cross-examine Mr. Lewis. Given that the witness has been in court listening to the testimony, I don't think this is appropriate."

Joe was shaking his head while Pettigrew spoke. "I agreed that he be allowed to attend. I wasn't forfeiting my right to call him as a witness."

"Your Honor, this is highly unusual."

Boniface placed his hand on his microphone. "Everything about this trial is unusual, Ms. Pettigrew. I'm curious to find out what Mr. Turner has in mind."

Walking back to the counsel table, Pettigrew whispered to Joe. "A glutton for more punishment?"

He smirked. "The defense calls Sinclair Lewis," he announced again and turned to see a very confused-looking Lewis still sitting in his seat.

Boniface scanned the gallery from his bench. "Mr. Lewis, there you are. Sir, please take the witness stand." Lewis remained seated for another few seconds before slowly rising and making his way to the witness stand, where he paused. "Your Honor, I've already said my piece. Is this necessary?" Joe heard the hint of desperation in his voice.

"Yes, Mr. Lewis. And I'll remind you that you're still under oath. Mr. Turner, proceed."

"Thank you, Your Honor. Good morning, Mr. Lewis."

"Morning," the witness grumbled.

"Mr. Lewis, I know you're probably tired of this, but I'm going to have to ask your indulgence once again. Sir, as I recall, you testified you do not wear glasses for distance, correct?" Joe leaned in to whisper to Carl, who reached into his pants pocket.

There was a mumble from the witness stand. "I'm sorry, Mr. Lewis, I didn't catch that."

"Yes, that's correct," the witness said.

"So, naturally, on August 26, you weren't wearing glasses when you saw Carl Ledbetter jogging down the street in front of your house."

"No, sir."

"And I'm correct that when you whittle, you wear glasses for seeing up close."

"Yes," came the timid answer. Joe sensed that Lewis knew what was coming. He also knew the vengeful side of him didn't mind prolonging his agony.

Joe asked to approach the witness. "Mr. Lewis, I'm showing you Exhibit C. You've seen this before. I'd ask you to read the last line of that statement."

Pettigrew spoke up, sensing impending disaster. "Your Honor, I have to object. This ground has been well-plowed."

"Overruled. The witness may answer."

Lewis removed reading glasses from the breast pocket of his blazer. "It says, 'This is a true and correct statement.'"

Joe took back the report. "Well done, Mr. Lewis. I happened to notice that when I asked you to read from the statement last week, even though you wore reading glasses, you had to extend your arm far out away from you. Today, you didn't have to."

"I need a stronger prescription for my readers," Lewis said, smiling nervously. "Just now, I didn't see it well, but I remembered it was the last line. Was just looking at it this morning." The witness smirked, satisfied with his answer.

"Oh," said Joe. "That was lucky then. Mr. Lewis, I'm going to walk back to my position, about forty feet from you, where I previously embarrassed myself, I might add." Joe was relieved to hear laughter throughout the courtroom.

Arriving at his location in the back of the courtroom, he pulled Carl's baseball from his pocket and held it in front of him, then tossed it playfully in the air. On the witness stand, Lewis leaned forward, squinting at him.

"Mr. Lewis, you didn't plan on testifying in court today, correct?"

"What's that?" he asked, placing a hand to his ear.

"You didn't plan on testifying today in court, did you, sir?"

"No, and I feel like you're pulling a fast one."

"If you would have known you'd be testifying, you would have put in your contact lenses, correct?"

"I've already testified," Lewis growled, still squinting down the aisle. "I shouldn't have to do this again!"

"You wore contact lenses the first time you testified, didn't you, Mr. Lewis?"

"I don't have to answer that!" he spat.

Joe smiled, knowing his answer had been enough for the jury. "Mr. Lewis, I'd like you to tell the jury what I have in my hand."

Lewis leaned further forward, still squinting futilely toward him. "Granny Smith?" he asked feebly.

"Sir, I'll ask you to please put on your glasses." Lewis crossed his arms and sat still, glaring at Joe for several seconds. "Mr. Lewis, your glasses, please. The ones you wear for distance. I believe you'll find them in the pocket of your overalls."

The witness looked helplessly at the judge. "Mr. Lewis, if you have glasses in your pocket, please put them on." Lewis grumbled something under his breath and complied.

"You wore those when you drove to court this morning, didn't you, Mr. Lewis."

"I'm tired of your questions, and I'm not answering anymore!" the old man yelled.

"That's fine, Mr. Lewis," Joe said, not wanting to appear a bully. "No further questions, Your Honor."

CHAPTER 69

For Joe, the direct examination of his client, fraught with potential disaster at every turn, was always the most stressful part of the trial. It was like rolling a baby carriage out onto a busy street. After lunch, it was time. "The defense calls Carl Ledbetter."

"Relax and tell the truth," Joe whispered to his client as he rose to take the oath. Carl appeared to be slightly smiling.

"My name is Stanley Carl Ledbetter," he said, beginning to rock even before he spoke.

As always, he sat with perfect posture. Aubrey had chosen a blue tie with yellow horizontal stripes, a white shirt, and blue blazer.

"Carl, I understand that you have been diagnosed with autism."

"Is that a question?" Carl asked. Joe's wording had been intentional since he wanted the jury to understand how Carl's mind worked.

"Yes, Carl. Is that true? And can you tell the jury about that?"

"It is true," he said, the microphone accentuating his nasal tone. "Autism is a neurodevelopment condition that affects the ability to interact and communicate with people."

Joe continued with some introductory questions designed to relax his client, but his rocking was constant, and he knew he had a death grip on his baseball under the podium.

"Carl, taking you back to August 26 of this year, do you have a memory of the events of that evening?"

"As I've said many times, I do not recall all the events of the evening. I'm sure there are things I've forgotten—how many glasses of punch I had at the party, how many teammates I spoke to. However, I have a memory of major events."

"You mentioned your teammates. What is your position with the Barton High School Football Team?"

"I am the team equipment manager. Coach Burgess insists I'm a teammate even though I do not play on the field."

"Is that position important to you?"

"Yes." Joe was hoping he would expand.

"Why is that, Carl?"

"I don't understand the question."

"Okay, I'll move on. You attended the football party on August 26 at the Holt residence?"

"Yes."

"Was that unusual for you to attend a party?"

"Yes. I rarely enjoy social gatherings, but I was made aware that the team very much wanted me to attend."

"What time did you arrive?"

"I arrived at 7:01 p.m. My mother drove me there. It is very important for me to be prompt. I was told the party began at 7:00 p.m., but unfortunately, no one else arrived until nearly 7:45 p.m."

"Did you speak to Justin Holt at the party?"

"Oh yes. He told me he was glad I was there."

"I understand you two have a special handshake."

"Yes. We had," he corrected. "As you know, Justin is unfortunately deceased."

"That night, did you two do your handshake?"

"Yes, which was surprising to me because the handshake was usually reserved for Justin's touchdown celebrations."

"Did you socialize with others at the party?"

"I tried to say hello to Karen Sarkliss, but she was busy speaking to her friends. Other than that, no. I very much dislike socializing."

"What time did you leave the party, Carl?"

"I left the party at approximately midnight. I sought out Mr. and Mrs. Holt in order to thank them for hosting. Social conventions are important to my mother, so I practice them scrupulously. I could not locate the Holts, so I went to thank Justin instead."

"Did you go to Justin's bedroom behind the main house?"

"Yes."

"And what did you find?"

"Justin was on the floor of his bedroom. He appeared deceased, or at least unconscious. There was a chest wound. He was bleeding profusely," Carl answered. His tone remained flat.

"What did you do, Carl?"

He paused, searching his memory. "I crouched beside him. I remember kneeling awkwardly to avoid the pooling blood. I checked his pulse on his neck at the carotid artery. I did not feel a pulse."

"What did you do next, Carl?"

"I left."

"Carl, did it occur to you to alert someone or call for help."

"It did occur to me. However, Justin appeared to me to be already deceased. Also, informing people would have meant an extensive amount of interaction with people who were extremely emotional. So, I declined."

"How do you feel about that now, Carl?" Joe smiled at his client. They'd worked hard on this answer.

Carl breathed deeply. "I realize now that was a mistake. It has been explained to me that I acted selfishly."

"What did you do next?"

"I ran home."

"Can you tell me why you ran home, Carl?" Joe held his breath. He had managed to talk Carl out of his answer about leaving to feed his fish.

"I wanted to leave the area to avoid interactions with people, as I mentioned." Joe exhaled, but too soon. "Also," Carl continued, "I needed to get home to feed my fish. It was my responsibility, and I had neglected to ask my father to do it." Behind him, murmurs spread throughout the gallery.

"Carl, did you have any reason to wish harm to Justin Holt?"

"No, I didn't."

"Did you have an argument with him that night?"

"No."

"Did you ever have a gun with you that night at the party?"

"No."

"Carl, did Justin Holt ever intentionally scratch you that night?"

"No, he didn't."

Joe walked from behind the podium. "Carl Ledbetter, did you kill Justin Holt?"

"No, I didn't."

"He was your friend, wasn't he?"

Carl paused and stared toward the ceiling then nodded slowly. "Yes. I believe so. As I mentioned, we had a handshake. I do not recall seeing him doing a special handshake with anyone else." It was very subtle, but Joe thought he heard a hint of pride in his client's voice.

CHAPTER 70

August 26, 2025, The Night of the Murder
Sophia Wentworth Montgomery knew that her socialite stepmom, Tracy, hated her goth look. Although powerless to stop it, Tracy couldn't help herself with the not-so-subtle comments. "Honey, that's just a lot of black," or, "I think your skin tone would look so beautiful with some earth tones." Sophie enjoyed watching her squirm when they went out together. "How about a booth over in the corner?" she'd said last week at a crowded restaurant.

Tonight, Tracy had been so thrilled that Sophie was attending the annual pre-season football bash. As she'd reminded Sophie for the hundredth time, her tiny blonde self had been on the cheer squad at Barton High and then at LSU. Overall, Tracy wasn't a horrible stepmom. So tonight, Sophie wouldn't burst her bubble. She'd stashed the black lipstick and her combat boots in her car and had left for the party in heels.

Sophie hadn't mentioned that she wasn't exactly attending the event as an honored guest. In fact, although the Holt residence was her destination, she had no intention of partying with those rock head jocks or their stuck-up glitter bitches—Sophie and her goth friends' nickname for the cheer squad and their hangers on.

No, she was going to the Holts' for the same reason she'd been there twice before—to visit the bedroom of the star quarterback. Justin had said that after the party had died down would be the perfect time. His parents would be busy with other partiers and wouldn't disturb him the night before the SAT. Also, he didn't say it, but she suspected that by then, his girlfriend would have gone home to study for the test as well.

It didn't bother Sophie much that Justin didn't want to be seen with her. After all, dating the prom king wouldn't have gone over well with her goth friends either. And it hadn't been purely physical with Justin. They'd had some laughs and some interesting conversations about their English readings. Of course, his quarterback body and good looks didn't hurt either. But in private moments, she admitted the real reason for her late-night rendezvous. It was the ultimate gut punch to her nemesis, Justin's girlfriend, and queen of the glitter-bitches, Karen Sarkliss.

Sophie was pretty sure Karen didn't harbor the least bit of hatred toward her. What with her life as a prom queen and all it entailed, she didn't give Sophie a second thought. At most, Sophie was an unsightly, lesser being in her world of white teeth, pearls, and perfect skin. None of that bothered Sophie. She was happy to let the popular kids frolic in the limelight, content in the shadows with her like-minded friends.

The reason for her hatred of Karen Sarkliss, in particular, was quite specific. It had been two years ago, during her freshman year, at the high school awards ceremony. Students and parents filled the school theatre to honor athletic and academic achievements. Sophie was to receive an award for poetry and was happy to see her friend, Esther Richins, there to receive an award in mathematics. Esther was a large girl who suffered from depression, and Sophie was excited for her award.

Karen, as class president, and another cheer squad member were taking turns presenting the awards on the raised dais. Karen announced the math award, and Esther made her way to the front. On the last of three stairs to the stage, Esther tripped and stumbled toward Karen but caught herself. Esther collected her award amid enthusiastic applause and began making her way back to her seat. Mistakenly believing the microphone had been turned off, Karen addressed her co-presenter on the dais. "God, I thought she was going to trample me," she said, her whisper carrying in crystal clarity throughout the theatre.

Karen covered her mouth theatrically then dissolved into laughter and ran off-stage, managing to make the moment all about her. Meanwhile, Sophie watched as Esther left the theatre in tears, never returning to her seat. By the time Sophie made it outside, her friend was nowhere to be seen.

Esther didn't commit suicide that night. That happened a year later, but Sophie always held Karen Sarkliss responsible.

CHAPTER 71

"What'd you do with the gun, Mr. Ledbetter?" snapped Pettigrew before she reached the podium.

Carl looked genuinely confused. "What gun?"

"Mr. Ledbetter, I'm going to show you a photograph of Justin Holt's right middle finger on the night he died," said Pettigrew, as the photo appeared on the big screen. "You would agree that Justin's middle fingernail is well trimmed, wouldn't you?"

"Yes."

"And so, you would agree it would be very unlikely that someone else's DNA could get under that fingernail from incidental contact?"

"Objection," Joe said firmly. "Calls for speculation."

"Overruled. You may answer, Mr. Ledbetter."

Carl nodded. "Yes."

"Now, Mr. Ledbetter, about this handshake you had with Justin Holt. I'm guessing it didn't involve scratching each other, did it?"

"No, ma'am."

"So, Mr. Ledbetter, you would have to agree that it seems impossible your DNA got under Justin Holt's skin from a handshake, right?"

"I agree," he said. "I don't know about impossible, but it does seem extremely unlikely."

Joe sighed. Jesus, Carl. He'd expected his client to tell the absolute truth, and Pettigrew was taking full advantage.

"Extremely unlikely," Pettigrew repeated, nodding.

"Mr. Ledbetter, Mr. Turner just asked you whether you had any reason to want harm to come to Justin Holt. Do you recall that?"

"Yes."

"And actually, a police officer asked you this very question the morning after the murder, didn't he?"

Carl nodded. "He asked me a similar question, yes."

"And you didn't answer for a very long time, did you?"

"No, I didn't."

"And that's because you didn't want to say it, but you actually very much wanted harm to come to Justin Holt, didn't you?"

"No."

"Then why the delay, Mr. Ledbetter?"

Carl cleared his throat. "The question the officer asked me specifically was whether I could think of any reason. I wanted to give myself ample time to think of a reason," Carl said calmly. "I could not."

"So, you were in the presence of Justin Holt around midnight, correct?"

"Yes."

"And then afterwards, you just happened to recall that you had to feed your fish?"

"Yes."

"And that was so urgent that you had to run home?"

"My mother wasn't scheduled to pick me up for another hour, so yes," Carl answered earnestly. "I take my responsibilities at home quite seriously."

"Mr. Ledbetter, you live up on Buena Vista Avenue, right?"

"Yes."

"What's that, four or five miles from the Holts'?"

"Yes."

Pettigrew shook her head. "Mr. Ledbetter, can you explain why Mr. Lewis would lie about seeing you with a gun?"

"As I believe my attorney, Mr. Joe Turner, illustrated in his cross examination, Mr. Sinclair Lewis appears to suffer from myopia. That is the scientific name for near-sightedness. As for Mr. Sinclair Lewis' motivation for saying that he saw me with a gun, I wouldn't know."

"Mr. Ledbetter, you say that Justin Holt and you were friends, correct?"

"Yes."

Pettigrew looked incredulous. "Mr. Ledbetter, are you the least bit sad that your friend is gone?"

Carl considered the question for several seconds then answered in a matter-of-fact tone. "Justin's Holt's passing is extremely unfortunate, both for himself and for his family."

Pettigrew nodded. "I see. And, Mr. Ledbetter, I heard you say a few times during your direct examination, 'as I've said before.' I take it you and Mr. Turner practiced that direct examination that we heard today several times." Joe cringed.

"Oh, yes," Carl said, nodding. "For reasons I do not understand, Mr. Joe Turner insisted that we go over the questions and answers many times."

Pettigrew smiled, reveling in Carl's answer.

"Your Honor, I have no more questions."

Boniface peered over his glasses at Joe. "Mr. Turner, re-direct examination?"

Joe rose. "Thank you, You Honor. Just briefly."

"Carl, why did I tell you I wanted to practice your direct examination?"

"You said because I'm not always good with people, you didn't want me to give the wrong impression."

"And why did you believe it was silly for us to practice."

"Because I planned to tell the truth. It seemed to me that practicing telling the truth is not at all necessary."

Joe considered his options and decided to take a chance. "Carl, one last question. Ms. Pettigrew asked you if you were the least bit sad that your friend, Justin Holt, was no longer with us."

Joe had not previously attempted to elicit emotion from Carl, wanting to save it for this moment. Now, Carl's rocking increased its rate, and Joe knew he was not happy to revisit the topic. "Carl has emotions inside him like everyone else," his mother had told him, "but he doesn't know how to let them out."

"Carl, can you tell the jury how you feel about losing your friend?"

Carl breathed deeply and stared straight ahead, his face betraying nothing. Then he bowed his head and was silent for several seconds. When he looked up, his face was streaked with tears. "Justin Holt's death was extremely unfortunate, both for himself and his family," he said again, his voice cracking. Another deep breath. "As I mentioned previously," he continued, now whispering into the microphone, "I do not believe that Justin Holt had a handshake with any of the other players."

CHAPTER 72

Back in his home office, Joe sat in quiet concentration. On balance, Carl's testimony had gone as well as he could have expected. He'd allowed the jury a peek inside his client's unique perspective. Hopefully, Carl's charmingly odd affect had convinced the jury that he was, in the words of his mother, exactly the person who would run from the crime scene to feed his fish.

Carl's emotion on the stand had been a bonus. But, as Eddy had bluntly pointed out, the jury may well think Carl was sad about committing the murder. Given the state of the evidence, it was the most likely scenario.

Sinclair Lewis' testimony that he'd seen a gun had been discredited by the exposure of his myopia. Joe smiled at Carl's word choice. The gunshot residue could have been transferred to Carl when Carl checked the victim's pulse. His expert witness would make that clear. But Butch Ford's "Hi, Carl" testimony was damning, proving that Justin was alive at the time of Carl's visit.

More importantly, Carl's DNA under the victim's fingernail loomed as insurmountable evidence. Joe was sure the jury had swallowed the prosecution's theory hook, line, and sinker. Carl had walked up close to the victim, as he posed no threat. When he pushed the gun to

Justin's chest, the victim had clawed at Carl in defense, imparting Carl's DNA under his right middle fingernail before Carl shot him at point blank range. The boys' handshake as a means of the DNA transfer was, at best, a stretch.

Joe sighed. Just a few days ago, he'd thought himself on the verge of a breakthrough. He didn't think he'd imagined it, as the feeling was familiar. It started with the slightest of inklings, deep in the recesses of his mind. Unrecognizable at first, it would inevitably take shape and bubble to the surface. The moment of clarity often took him by surprise, when his thoughts had wandered elsewhere. But this time, days had passed, and he feared the spark had fizzled and was lost forever.

Joe's sad eyes fell on the six-inch stack of Carl's medical reports resting on the far corner of his desk. He'd procrastinated his review of the documents as it signaled surrender. If he used the reports to Carl's advantage, it would only be to advocate for a more suitable prison.

He began flipping through the stack, beginning with the most recent adjustment to his medications. Next came the hospital records and ambulance reports documenting Carl's seizure the day before the murder.

As Joe pictured Carl in his home, thrashing about helplessly, something flickered in his mind. It was unmistakable this time. He closed his eyes and concentrated. Quickly, he opened his laptop and pulled up a police report. His heart began to pound as puzzle pieces jostled into place. Joe's eyes raced over the report then stopped cold as a ping of recognition chimed in his brain. "Yes!" he said aloud, punching the air. He fumbled for his phone, frantically thumbing out a text.

—*Chuck, I need a subpoena served!*

CHAPTER 73

August 26, 2025, The Night of the Murder
Parked just down the street from the Holt residence, Sophie adjusted the vanity mirror on the visor and raised the clove cigarette to her black lips. Up ahead, the house reminded her of a frat house at Ole Miss where she'd visited her sister. She'd never been inside the Holts' main house—a grand, three-story colonial with pillars that supported a front balcony.

Sophie heard the pulsating beat of the music and the occasional yell of a partier. Small groups had gathered on the vast front lawn and front porch. The front door of the house was open, and she could make out shadows of dancing figures through the large bay windows.

Sophie had to admit it looked like fun. She'd heard the Holts were supplying beer and collecting car keys, which was cool. Otherwise, kids would just smuggle in alcohol. Of course, she'd hate the company, but the idea of the party seemed fun.

Behind her through the mirror, she saw glimpses of blonde hair and sweaters approaching on the sidewalk, their pearls shining in the moonlight. Reaching her car, a tall girl wearing a letterman's jacket over a sundress leaned down to peer in at Sophie through the passenger window then walked on. After a few steps, the group broke into laughter.

"Oh my God," one of them said, laughing, "I thought I smelled cloves." What was it about these glitter bitches? Why did they think no one could hear their insults? More likely they didn't care.

"That's so random!" said another. "What is she doing here?" More indistinct chatter followed then another explosion of laughter as they walked out of earshot.

Sophie sat in her car, seething. Still with an hour to kill before her rendezvous with Justin, she snuffed out the stub of her cigarette and lit another. Reclining in her seat, she imagined approaching the tall blonde in the letterman's jacket, or better yet, that princess, Karen Sarkliss. "Do you know who likes the smell of cloves, sugar?" she'd ask sweetly? "Why, Justin does. I mean, he hasn't told me so exactly, but I just have a feeling about it." Sophie would smile, pleased with herself. Then she'd tell that bitch exactly what she was doing there tonight.

CHAPTER 74

On Tuesday morning at Nadine's, several heads turned as Dr. Curtis Berrian walked in and joined Joe and Chuck at a booth.

A suit, black and wrinkled, hung on his tall bony frame. His skin was ghostly white and sagged from sharp cheekbones below bulging eyes. Long wisps of white hair grew in a ring around the top of his bald head and hung to his shoulders, where his suit jacket was speckled with dandruff. The former Alameda County Coroner and now expert witness assumed, incorrectly, that his "Dr. Death" moniker referenced his occupation and not his appearance.

The doctor's enthusiasm for his morbid profession was unmatched. Joe and Chuck often bet on how long it would take for him to request a copy of the autopsy photographs, even if wholly unrelated to his analysis. Berrian also happened to be one of the nation's leading experts in forensic pathology, and he had testified for Joe in more than a dozen cases. The Ledbetters had immediately agreed to his hefty fee and had flown him in on their private jet the previous night.

"Interesting case," the doctor said with a smile of yellowed teeth as the server arrived. "Coffee please and two glazed donuts." He was prepared to testify how gunshot residue could have been transferred to Carl's hands when he checked the victim's pulse. As for Joe's latest revelation, he had briefed him on the phone during his flight.

"In preparation for my testimony," Berrian said as the donuts arrived, "although I will not be rendering an opinion on the cause of death, if it's no trouble, I should probably have a look at the autopsy photos."

"Of course," Joe said as he and Chuck exchanged glances.

Joe asked the doctor the questions outlined in his direct examination.

"It seems your epiphany came not a moment too soon," Berrian said when they'd finished, popping the last of the donuts into his mouth. "Is the prosecutor aware of your theory?"

Joe stood, failing to suppress a smile. "I have no reason to believe so, Doctor. I'm heading over to court. See you there this afternoon."

On the way to the courthouse, Joe cautioned himself against overconfidence. Although he now had a plausible defense, the victim had been a town hero.

Arriving in the courtroom, he found Pettigrew unpacking her file at the counsel table and a uniformed paramedic seated in the front row. Joe judged him to be in his mid-twenties. His blond hair was neatly tied in a ponytail, his two-day stubble accentuating his rakish good looks.

"You're calling a paramedic?" asked Pettigrew when Joe reached the conference table. "I don't recall seeing any listed on your witness list."

Joe said good morning to Alvin before addressing the prosecutor. "Ah, but he was on yours, Melissa. Along with everyone else remotely related to the case. Sort of a bush league move, but now I appreciate it. Thanks."

Joe approached the paramedic and introduced himself. "Thanks for coming. Sorry about the short notice."

"Aw, that's okay, but I'm not sure how I can help you."

"Let's talk in the hallway," Joe said, knowing Pettigrew was seething as they walked out of the courtroom.

After a brief but productive chat, Joe was back in court as the jury filed in. "Well, ladies and gentlemen," said Boniface, addressing the jury after his grand introduction, "we've made it to the last day of evidence. Tomorrow, the attorneys will argue, and you will begin your deliberation. Mr. Turner, your next witness?"

"The defense calls Sebastian Delucchi." Joe had noted the unusual name in the police reports, and it jumped off the page when it appeared again in Carl's medical records.

"Mr. Delucchi, please tell the jury how you are employed," Joe asked after the paramedic had taken the oath.

"I'm an EMT," he said with a lazy drawl. "I work for Bel-Air Medical. Our company has the contract for ambulances that serve Daulton County."

"Mr. Delucchi, how many ambulances does your company own?"

"Three rigs, but only two are in service at a time. Three crews are assigned to each ambulance."

"So, each day of work, you use the same ambulance?"

"Yes, sir. I'm assigned to Ambulance Number Two."

"And were you assigned to Ambulance Number Two on Thursday, August 25 of this year?"

"Yes."

"On that day, did you respond to the Ledbetter Estate on Lawton Ave. in Barton?"

"Yes, sir. Carl Ledbetter had suffered a seizure, and we were dispatched there by the 911 operator."

"Do you recognize Mr. Ledbetter in the courtroom?"

"Yes, sir. I know Carl. He's seated at the counsel table wearing a tan blazer and blue tie."

"Let the record reflect that the witness has identified the defendant," said Boniface.

Joe continued. "Mr. Delucchi, the next evening, August 26 of this year, were you dispatched to 1071 Chance Avenue?" To his left, at the counsel table, Pettigrew began digging through her file with urgency.

"Yes, sir. My partner and I were dispatched to a reported shooting at that location?"

"At that location, what did you find?"

"The victim, Justin Holt, had suffered a gunshot wound to his chest."

"Was Mr. Holt alive?"

"Only technically. We found a faint pulse, but he was unresponsive. Given the amount of blood loss, his death was a foregone conclusion. Still, we instituted live-saving procedures and transported him to Daulton General Hospital."

"Did you transport Mr. Holt in the same ambulance that you had transported Mr. Ledbetter the previous day?"

"Yes, sir. Ambulance Number Two."

"Returning to the previous day, when you transported Carl Ledbetter in your ambulance, did you attach a pulse oximeter to him?"

"Objection. Relevance, Your Honor," said a flustered Pettigrew.

"Seems relevant to me, Ms. Pettigrew," said Boniface. "Overruled."

"Yes, we did. The device measures oxygen levels in blood."

"And Mr. Delucchi, did I ask you to bring a pulse oximeter to court this morning?"

"Yes. I have one here," the paramedic said, reaching into his pocket and retrieving the device that resembled a small clothes pin. "It's totally non-invasive. It just clips onto your finger," he said, inserting his finger inside the clip. "It works using small beams of light that pass through the finger."

Joe had the device marked as an exhibit.

"Does the pulse oximeter for Ambulance Number Two stay with that ambulance?"

"Yes. It's part of the ambulance's standard equipment. It never leaves the rig."

"Mr. Delucchi, I assume there are sanitary measures in place to keep your ambulance clean?"

"Yes, sir. We change out the pillows and blankets after every callout. Those get washed. Syringes are replaced. If blood or bodily fluids are involved, then everything is wiped down and sanitized."

"Were there any blood or bodily fluids involved in your treatment of Carl Ledbetter on August 25?"

"No, sir."

"Are pulse oximeters cleaned after each use?"

"No. Non-invasive devices—pulse oxes, blood pressure cuffs, immobilization straps—they undergo a maintenance cleaning at the end of every week."

"So, the pulse oximeter used on Carl Ledbetter was not wiped down or cleaned at any time prior to your callout to the Holts' the next day?"

"No sir. Not to my knowledge."

"Mr. Delucchi, when you transported Justin Holt to the hospital, did you place Ambulance Number Two's pulse oximeter on his finger?"

"Yes. That's standard procedure," he said as a low hum of conversation swept over the courtroom.

"Order, ladies and gentlemen," said Boniface.

"And was that the same pulse oximeter that had been placed on Carl Ledbetter's finger the previous day?"

"Yes, sir."

"Mr. Delucchi, is there a particular finger that is commonly used with the pulse oximeter?"

"Yes. The most accurate readings are taken from the middle finger of the right hand. That's the finger we always use."

Now, full throated conversation spread throughout the courtroom and Boniface banged his gavel. Joe couldn't resist a smile. "No further questions, Your Honor."

CHAPTER 75

At lunch, Joe grabbed a hot dog from the street vendor and sat on the park bench, outlining his closing argument. Reeling from the pulse oximeter evidence, Pettigrew had composed herself for a decent cross examination of the paramedic. The paramedic conceded that, ideally, the device would be wiped clean after each use and that it was at least possible that another paramedic had done so. Still, Joe had presented a believable explanation for the DNA evidence.

Dr. Death took the stand after the break, his eccentric appearance drawing lots of raised eyebrows from the gallery and jury. After listing his impeccable credentials, he testified confidently about the characteristics of gunshot residue.

"It has the consistency and viscosity similar to flour," he told the jury. "When a gun is fired, gunshot residue is expelled into the air. Picture dipping two hands into a bag of flour then clapping them together. The victim in this case was shot at close range, so I would absolutely expect the residue to be on his face, neck, and shoulders.

"As is the case with flour, it is entirely possible that the gunshot residue found on Mr. Ledbetter was deposited when he checked the victim's pulse at the carotid artery on his neck."

The doctor also addressed the plausibility that Carl's DNA was left inside the pulse oximeter then transferred to Justin Holt. "Human beings shed microscopic skin cells constantly. Each skin cell has a full complement of DNA. The transfer of these skin cells from one surface to another happens frequently. Here, records indicate that both Mr. Ledbetter and Mr. Holt's right middle fingers were in the pulse oximeter for approximately thirty minutes. Given that period of time, I would certainly expect that Mr. Ledbetter shed a significant amount of skin cells into the oximeter. Not only would I not be surprised by a transfer, I would expect it."

Next, Joe addressed the scratch mark on the victim's chest, showing a closeup of the scratch on the flatscreen. DNA evidence proved it had been left by someone other than Carl.

"Dr. Berrian, do you have an opinion as to whether the killer left the scratch on the body?"

"I cannot say conclusively. However, I've reviewed the photograph of the scratch in some detail. The scratch did not penetrate past the epidermis, which does not contain blood vessels. Barring an unusual skin condition, this type of mark would usually disappear within thirty minutes. So I believe the victim was scratched within thirty minutes of his death."

On cross examination, Pettigrew wisely did not challenge the science behind the doctor's testimony. Instead, she challenged its factual premise. "Doctor, what is the source of your information that Carl Ledbetter checked the pulse of Justin Holt?"

"The statement of Mr. Ledbetter himself."

"And you realize that this is the only source of this information? There is no other evidence that this happened."

"I am aware of that."

"No further questions, Your Honor."

After Pettigrew sat down, the judge spoke up. "Mr. Turner, any further witnesses or evidence?"

"Yes, Your Honor, the defense intends…"

"May I be heard outside the presence of the jury, Your Honor?" Pettigrew cut in. Joe shot the prosecutor a sideways look. What was she up to?

"Certainly, Ms. Pettigrew. Ladies and gentlemen of the jury, we are in the home stretch. Let's take our afternoon recess. We'll see you in fifteen minutes."

After the courtroom was cleared, the prosecutor addressed the Court. "Your Honor, it is my understanding that Mr. Turner intends to play a video of a football awards banquet in which the victim speaks about his relationship with the defendant. I object to the video as it is more prejudicial than probative. It is a blatant attempt to sway the jury with emotion."

Joe rolled his eyes at the DA's baseless argument. "Your Honor, my client is accused of murdering the victim. This video goes directly to his lack of motive."

The judge was shaking his head even before Joe finished. "I've seen the video, and I agree with Ms. Pettigrew. I'm excluding the video."

Joe could scarcely believe his ears. "Your Honor, this is direct evidence that the victim and my client cared for each other. It is absolutely, without question, directly relevant to whether or not he had a motive to kill."

"Mr. Turner, I've made my ruling."

"This is unbelievable!" Joe heard himself yell. "There is no logical reason to exclude this evidence!"

"Mr. Turner, I'm warning you, I will not stand for much more of this."

Joe glanced at Carl, looking helpless and worried. He heard Eddy's voice saying, "Judge, have a wonderful day." "Judge," he said, pausing slightly, "this trial is a joke, and you're an embarrassment to the State of Georgia! I have never in…"

"You're in contempt!" the judge yelled, talking over him, but Joe just carried on, even louder. "…my life seen such a travesty of a mockery of a sham of a trial. My client's due process is being violated at every turn, mainly because of your abject incompetence."

"Alvin, throw this New York fancy-pants in jail!"

"And for the last time, I'm from California!" Joe yelled.

Boniface's face twisted in hatred as he pounded his gavel, and Joe knew he was imagining smashing his face. "Bail is $10,000, no, $50,000!" the judge growled, red-faced. "Send the jury home, Barbara," he said, stomping down off the bench. "And Mr. Turner, we're having closing arguments in the morning. And if I hear any more from you tomorrow, you'll be giving your closing from custody!"

After the judge was gone, Alvin began fumbling with his handcuffs again. "Sorry, Joe, you know I hate to do this."

"No worries, Alvin," he said, pleasantly. "I know you're just doing your job. Let me help you. I think they go this way," he said, slipping the cuffs over his wrists.

"Thanks," the bailiff said. "Let's just pretend they're latched. I'm not sure I have the right key on me."

Joe smiled and turned to his client. "Carl, I'll see you tomorrow. Keep your spirits up. Today was a good day."

Carl nodded silently, still looking frightened.

On his way out of the courtroom, escorted by Alvin, Joe texted with Eddy. —*Hey. On my way to jail. Again.*

—*Want me to bail you out now or wait a while? I know you were disappointed to miss dinner last time.*

—*Hilarious.*

CHAPTER 76

The next morning, Joe sat in Boniface's chambers having been summoned by the clerk. "Coffee?" the judge asked, gesturing for him to sit.

"No thank you, Your Honor. Shouldn't Ms. Pettigrew be here?"

"Mr. Turner, I don't suppose you've ever heard of a feller named Joseph Lamar?" Joe shook his head, bewildered. "Was raised up in Ruckersville. His family were pig farmers. Went to UGA. I'll be damned if he didn't become a member of the U.S. Supreme Court. Probably impossible for you to believe that."

"Judge, it was never my intention…"

"How about William Woods?" Boniface asked, ignoring him. "Ring a bell, Mr. Turner? My great granddaddy was his neighbor over in Covington. Valedictorian at Yale. Another Supreme Court Justice from right here in backwards-ass Georgia."

"Judge, I know I haven't been as respectful…"

"Respectful?" Boniface asked, cutting in. "From the first day you set foot in my courtroom, you've been insolent and condescending to me and my staff. We all see you rolling your eyes, wondering how in the hell you found yourself in a courtroom full of idiots. Mr. Turner, that stops today."

Joe paused, letting the judge's criticism sink in. Part of him knew it was true. "I apologize, Judge. I'm a guest here, and I should be more respectful."

The judge nodded, acknowledging his apology. "You're a good lawyer. You can rail all you want against me, my rulings, and the prosecutor, but I must demand respect for this court."

"Understood." Joe stood to leave.

"One more thing," the judge said. "And this is not an accusation, just a word of caution. There's been holler whispers about jury tampering by the Ledbetters. I've seen those green Bellcrest shirts snooping around the courthouse, same as you. I don't have to tell you that turning a blind eye is unethical."

"Yes, Judge," Joe said. He kept a poker face but felt his stomach lurch.

Out in the courtroom, he found a plastic bag resting on the defense end of the counsel table. Its top was sealed with a sticker that read "Daulton County Evidence Locker, Item #34875."

"I remember you requested the defendant's shirt," Pettigrew said. "I'll stipulate to its admissibility if you'd like."

Joe's mind raced. Shit. He'd forgotten about his request. He'd wanted to show the shirt to the jury since the reports had indicated there wasn't a spot of blood on it. But that was before he'd learned from Aubrey that the shirt would be different than the one that appeared in the video. Obviously, Pettigrew hadn't seen the shirt.

"Oh, thanks, but that's okay. I asked the cop about the shirt. That's good enough for me," he said, trying to sound casual.

Pettigrew frowned his way and held her stare when he looked away. Finally, she shrugged. "Okay, suit yourself," she said as Joe breathed a sigh of relief.

Boniface began the morning session by reading the jury instructions then addressed the prosecutor. "Ms. Pettigrew? Closing argument?"

"Thank you, Your Honor."

"Ladies and gentlemen," the prosecutor began, "I'd first like to thank you for your jury service. I know this doesn't make anyone's bucket list, so I surely appreciate you." Joe rolled his eyes. During the trial, Pettigrew's down-home, Southern belle routine had gone from tolerable to nauseating.

"I'll be brief today because this case is about as straightforward as it gets."

Like most attorneys, Pettigrew was brief, like Polonius, reviewing every piece of evidence and highlighting the important jury instructions. After an hour, Pettigrew casually strolled to the rail of the jury box.

"One way y'all can look at this is to ask, if Carl Ledbetter didn't commit this murder, then who in God's name did? Your options would be fairly limited because you heard every one of those partygoers tell you they didn't see anyone there that didn't belong. So, if it wasn't Carl, who? A teammate? A cheerleader? A family member? Are any of those viable alternatives?" Pettigrew paused to smile. "Of course not."

"For a while there, it seemed like Mr. Turner was trying to convince you that Clem Tettleton had committed the murder. But then we heard about Tettleton's airtight alibi. Then he told us it was Luke Stuckey, Justin's Holt's best friend, as absurd as that sounds.

"You might ask why the defense would even suggest such crazy theories. Maybe it was Luke Stuckey, maybe it was Clem Tettleton, maybe the DNA got transferred from a handshake or from a pulse oximeter. Why the scattershot approach?

"The answer, ladies and gentlemen, is because the defense knows he only needs one of you. What's that P.T. Barnum said? There's a sucker born every minute. He only needs one of you to buy into one of his crazy theories. It's called throwing as much you-know-what against the wall and seeing what sticks." Pettigrew scanned the jurors' faces. "Don't be that one juror.

"Y'all know that usually the simplest explanation is the best. So how about this? The killer is the person who Justin Holt said, 'Hi, Carl,' to right before he died. Carl Ledbetter. The killer is the person with gunshot residue on his hands. Carl Ledbetter. The killer is the person who Justin Holt scratched just before he was shot, leaving DNA under his fingernail. Carl Ledbetter."

Pettigrew walked to her laptop, and a photo of Justin Holt filled the courtroom's flatscreen. Clutching a football, sitting on the tailgate of a truck, he was handsome, carefree, and full of life. "Unfortunately, we can't ask Justin who committed his murder. Justice for Justin Holt is up to you."

The closing had been well organized, thorough, and powerful.

After a ten-minute break for the jury, it was Joe's turn. "Ladies and gentlemen, good morning. In your jury instructions, you'll find the definition of reasonable doubt. It is having an abiding conviction for the truth. An abiding conviction," he repeated. "Something that stays with you.

"Last spring, I planted some flowers in my backyard. The very next day, my gardener pulled them up, mistaking them for weeds. It was a mistake, but it was okay. I forgot about it the next day. Convicting Carl Ledbetter of murder would be a different sort of mistake. That would be something that would stay with you."

Joe talked about how much the football team meant to Carl. "And Carl is not the sort of person who develops close relationships with people," he told the jury, "But I think we all saw what his handshake with Justin Holt meant to him. Certainly, he had no motive to kill his friend."

Joe argued that Luke Stuckey's motive made him a likely suspect and questioned his alibi. "He told us he left his cell phone in someone's car that evening. But how many teenagers do you know who could go an entire evening without their cell phone?"

Next, Joe reviewed the prosecution's evidence and pointed out its flaws. Sinclair Lewis' near-sightedness prevented him from seeing a gun in Carl's hands. The gunshot residue was transferred when Carl checked Justin's pulse. The DNA was transferred via the pulse oximeter. Carl's unique inability to deal with emotion caused him to flee. He ran away not to escape capture but to avoid the emotional outpouring that was sure to follow. "And what was Carl's escape plan?" Joe asked rhetorically. "Running down the middle of the street waving the gun around?"

Joe didn't have an explanation for Butch Ford's "Hi, Carl," testimony. For all the scientific evidence, it was ironic that this testimony could be the most damning. He was left to hope the jury assumed Ford had simply been mistaken.

After forty-five minutes, Joe walked to the counsel table where Carl was rocking away, staring straight ahead. Joe sipped water from a paper cup then walked back, centering himself before the jury.

"There once was a small boy and a wise old man who lived in a village," he began. "The boy was constantly trying to outsmart the wise old man. One day, the boy found a small bird that had fallen out of its nest. He brought the bird to the old man, hiding it in his hands. He planned to ask him if the bird was alive or dead. If the old man said dead, he would open his hands to reveal that the bird was alive. If he said, alive, he planned to crush the bird in his hands then open them to reveal the dead bird.

"'Old man,' said the boy, 'is the bird in my hands alive, or is it dead?'

"The old man looked at the boy and smiled. 'My son,' he said, 'the bird is in your hands.'"

Joe scanned the poker-faced jury, looking each of the nine in the eye. "Ladies and gentlemen, Carl Ledbetter is in your hands."

CHAPTER 77

Outside the courthouse, Carl went off to find his parents, and Eddy greeted Joe with a kiss. "Nice job."

"Thanks. Not too cheesy?"

"Not at all. Might as well pull out all the stops, right?"

Aubrey and Matt Ledbetter approached, looking exhausted. After introducing Eddy, Joe fielded all the usual questions as Carl stood nearby listening to a Cubs ball game on his earbuds. No, Joe didn't know how long the jury would deliberate or who would be the foreperson. He didn't know which way the jury was leaning and didn't know whether they should hope for a quick or lengthy deliberation. "Sorry," he said, "from here on out, I'm afraid I'm as useless as a screen door on a sub."

The Ledbetters smiled, appreciating the attempt at levity. "Okay, thanks again. Obviously, we'll be waiting by our phones," they said, walking away.

"A screen door on a sub, Turner?" Eddy said, smirking. "What's next? You gonna whittle?"

Joe smiled. "Overheard it at Nadine's."

"Can I buy you lunch?" Eddy asked.

"Okay, but how about later? I feel like walking home."

"Sure. See you there."

Walking back past the courthouse, Joe glanced up to spy a man slinking out a back entrance. His face was obscured in the building's shadow, but he looked like the same employee of the Ledbetters he'd seen at the courthouse during jury selection. At least he was dressed in the same green polo shirt.

"Damn," Joe said, aloud. He'd successfully put aside his concerns about the prospect of the Ledbetters' jury tampering, but now that the trial was over, the judge's words of warning echoed in his head. He didn't have solid evidence, so there was no ethical obligation to report it. The question was, should he ask Chuck to turn over some rocks?

Soon, Joe's thoughts returned to the trial, the jury deliberation, and his client. Another trip inside the jail had brought renewed fears for Carl. Thinking back to his last blow-up in court, part of him wondered if he hadn't wanted to see the inside of the jail one more time for motivation.

This time, knowing what to expect inside, he'd been able to concentrate on the nuances of his captivity. He'd taken in the musty smells, the cool dampness of his cell, and the jarring clangs of metal, committing them all to memory. He recalled a glimpse of the water tower from one of the narrow windows, high on the wall of his cell. How cruel for the prisoners to get a glimpse of sky and an iconic symbol of life on the outside.

Now, passing the town square, he looked up at the water tower, reading the words painted in blue, "Steeler Pride" and "High Bar." Over the last month, Joe had heard the latter uttered as a greeting countless times. He took several steps before stopping in his tracks. High Bar. Hi, Carl. "Shit!"

CHAPTER 78

August 26, 2025, The Night of the Murder
Even as Sophie walked toward the party, she wasn't sure why. She still had an hour before her scheduled rendezvous with Justin. Part of it was curiosity, to be sure. The entire football crowd all seemed so fake at school. She couldn't imagine the time and energy it took, always worrying about what they said, what they wore, and with whom they were seen. It made for good people watching. Sometimes at school, she would just observe them from afar, marveling at their capacity for feckless drama.

Although she would never admit it, part of it was jealousy. Not that she envied them, but a party would be nice. Why should she and her friends be banished from the fun? After all, technically, everyone in the school had been invited. "Y'all come launch the football season at the Holts'," Karen Sarkliss had said into the microphone at the school assembly.

And it wasn't that she despised every member of the football crowd, she told herself, as the Holts' home came into view. Justin was much more interesting than she would have guessed, and she was willing to keep an open mind. She was hopeful that, off school grounds, the rigid social structure that had her at the bottom of the food chain might relax a bit.

Sophie made her way up the long stone path that led to the grand entrance of the home, drawing a few stares from the porch crowded with teenagers but at least no rude comments. So far, so good.

A tan woman in her forties greeted her on the front steps. "Hi there, I'm Merrill, Justin's mom." Sophie saw her eyes travel from her jet-black hair to her combat boots and back.

"Hello, I'm Sophie."

"Did you drive, honey?" Mrs. Holt asked, handing her a clipboard. "If so, I'll need your keys."

"No, ma'am," she lied and printed her name on the roster.

There was an awkward pause as her host flashed a smile that never reached her eyes. "Well, then, I suppose, just enjoy yourself."

Good God, Sophie thought, Mrs. Holt couldn't have been more uncomfortable. She'd be just thrilled to know about Justin and me. Sophie grabbed a can of beer from a cooler and retreated to a quiet corner of the porch. She sat alone at a table decorated with the blue and silver of the Steelers and watched the animated conversations set to the pulsating beat of the music.

Presently, a boy named Carl sat at the next table. Sophie recognized him from physics class. Obviously, something was different about Carl. He reminded her of her cousin who was autistic. Sophie recalled Carl being a high achiever in physics but completely lacking in social awareness. Now, looking a bit overwhelmed, Carl sat facing away from the crowd on the porch with his ball cap pulled down low.

Soon, two football players approached him wearing Steeler jerseys. "Carl! High bar!" one exclaimed, slurring his words. "We got something for ya, Carl!"

"Yeah, Carl," said the other, stifling a laugh. "Knowing you don't drink beer, we brought you a soda." As he placed a can of soda on the table in front of Carl, Sophie noticed several more football players lurking nearby.

Carl looked up at the two boys, surprised. "Thank you. That's very kind," he said, beaming. He opened the can to an explosion of soda that sprayed Carl's face and soaked his shirt. The football players staggered away, their hateful laughs piercing Carl's ears. Sophie gathered napkins from surrounding tables and began mopping Carl's face as he sat motionless and more confused than ever.

"Those guys are assholes," she said, dabbing his forehead. "Carl, let's go see if the Holts have a dry shirt for you, okay?"

Carl stared down at the can of soda on the table and began rocking in his seat. "No," he said finally, as if noticing Sophie for the first time. "Thank you for your assistance," he said earnestly, looking her in the eye. "I think it's best that I thank the host and go home."

CHAPTER 79

"I can't believe I didn't think of this until after closing arguments," Joe said, burying his face in his hands. It had been two days, and he hadn't gotten over it.

Next to him on the couch, Eddy patted his shoulder. "Hey, I knew about the 'Hi, Carl' witness, too, and God knows I've heard 'high bar' ten times a day for the past month. It never occurred to me either. Besides, you did figure out the pulse oximeter. Without that, Carl would be toast."

Joe's phone buzzed on the coffee table.

"Hey, Chuck, what did Butch Ford hear through that open window? ... Yeah, 'hi Carl.' That's what he says. Maybe it was 'high bar.'"

Chuck wasn't on speakerphone, but Eddy still heard his yell from her seat on the couch.

Later, Aubrey Ledbetter stopped by with a bottle of expensive Pinot Noir. "I thought you two might need a nice bottle to celebrate with." She had a faraway look in her eye.

Joe shot a look toward Eddy. "So, Aubrey, I appreciate the vote of confidence, but Carl is far from out of the woods."

"Oh, Joe, you're too modest. You did such an amazing job. I've just been floating ever since your closing argument." Joe was pretty sure she was floating from some sort of medication.

"Well, thank you, Aubrey. Just try to keep an even keel."

"Matt tells me the same thing. Part of it is staying upbeat for Carl, I suppose. Poor boy's anxiety is through the roof, which triggers seizures. He's had two this week."

Joe sighed. "I'm sorry to hear that. Of course, I'm happy to talk to him if you think it would help."

"That's kind, Joe, but we've got him in daily counseling sessions as it is. I will tell him you said hi, though. He'll like that. You two have fun," Aubrey said, heading for the door.

Joe hesitated then called after her. "Aubrey, wait." He'd thought about whether to tell the Ledbetters about his theory that Ford had heard "high bar" rather than "Hi, Carl." It was a painful mistake to admit, but Joe felt they deserved his honesty.

Aubrey listened as Joe shared his belated revelation. "Can't you re-open the case?" she asked. "Surely there must be a way."

Joe shook his head, knowing the chances were slim to none. Very rarely, he explained, if faced with a deadlocked jury, a judge requested further argument from the attorneys. If this were the case, Joe could make his "high bar" argument then. Barring that, the jury would never hear it.

Joe and Eddy said their goodbyes, and Aubrey Ledbetter floated home, remaining confident of her son's acquittal.

CHAPTER 80

After nine days of waiting, Joe's nerves began to fray. With Eddy back in Tallahassee, he struggled to occupy his time and rein in his anxiety. Just back from an afternoon run, his cell phone buzzed with a text from Pettigrew. — *Judge wants to meet us at 4:30 p.m. today.* Joe had a feeling his opponent already knew why but wasn't sharing.

Typically, he arrived in court to find them already chatting in Boniface's chambers with coffee mugs. In virtually every other jurisdiction in the nation, meetings with the judge without the other party present—ex parte communications—were unthinkable. He started to mention it but held his tongue.

"Afternoon," the judge grumbled. "Today, after lunch, one of the jurors passed Alvin this note," he said, pushing a folded paper across his desk toward the attorneys.

Joe picked up the note. It was written on five by eight-inch paper torn from a juror notebook.

Your Honor,

One of the jurors, Dirk Pinion, has created a hostile environment. It is the consensus among the group that his intimidating and insulting behavior makes it impossible for the group to deliberate. It is our request that he be removed from the jury.

Sincerely,
Jack Painter, Foreperson

The note was also signed by Ellen Graves, Duncan Morris, Priya Manjeer, Elston Arbett, and Sara Epstein.

Joe searched his memory. Pinion was the construction foreman. He'd been concerned about him, so this was probably good news. The first alternate, a grocery store manager, had seemed okay.

"Thoughts?" asked the judge.

Pettigrew sipped her coffee. "We should probably bring him in and get his side of the story."

"Mr. Turner?" the judge asked.

"Makes sense," Joe said casually, not wanting to tip his hand. If he suggested removing the juror, he feared the judge would do the opposite.

Boniface stared at him, studying his face. "Really, no preference?" Joe knew he was trying to read him.

"Well, six out of nine jurors have weighed in," Joe answered calmly, "so I think you would be well within your discretion to replace the juror. But Ms. Pettigrew makes a good point. The allegations may be baseless."

The judge sighed. "I'd rather not waste time on it, but okay. Let's meet with him first thing in the morning."

Back in the courtroom, out of earshot of the judge, Pettigrew wore a knowing smirk. "Playing it close to the vest, I see. You know Pinion is your worst juror."

"No idea what you're talking about," Joe deadpanned, leaving the DA behind.

CHAPTER 81

Carl
The questions have been incessant lately. "Carl, how are you feeling? Carl, why are you feeling this way? Carl. Carl. Carl." Again, this obsession with my name. I'm the only one in the room! But I dutifully answer each one as my mother has asked for my cooperation.

How am I feeling? I'm feeling pain. Why am I feeling pain? Currently, the roof of my mouth hurts because I ate a piece of pizza for lunch that was excessively hot. This happens often. That is, the pizza is often hot because of its high thermal conductivity, and I often eat it too quickly because I find pizza quite delicious. Why they need to know any of this, I'll never know.

Then there are questions about the trial. "Carl, are you concerned about the decision the jury might make?" My answer is obviously no. Right now, I am not concerned about the jury's decision because I do not know what that decision will be. Obviously, when they decide, I will either be not concerned at all or extremely concerned.

"Carl, why would you be concerned if you're found guilty?" This is a question that I prefer not to answer, so I do not. I don't tell them I would miss being away from my mother, and also my father, admittedly, to a slightly lesser extent. And the Cubs games, of course. I would certainly be concerned that my life would be significantly affected were I to live in prison. Although I have avoided learning about the specifics, the accounts of prison as portrayed in movies and books lead me to this conclusion.

Anyway, I do not wish to speak about my concerns regarding prison. I hope my mother will not see this as a lack of cooperation on my part. Some things I would simply prefer not to think about.

For example, there are a few things I haven't told my attorney, Joe Turner, about the night Justin Cassady Holt was murdered. While this might seem shocking, two things are worth noting. First, I have never been dishonest with Joe Turner. While I never told him anything that was not true, in two instances, I simply chose not to tell him about my observations. Second, in neither case did these observations have anything to do with the murder of Justin Cassady Holt.

The first involved a very unfortunate experience with a Rudy Jameson, a player on the Barton High Steelers football team. Rudy Jameson presented me with a soda that evening. Rudy has rarely spoken to me, so this gesture was met with my sincere appreciation. Then, when I opened the soda, it exploded all over me, covering much of my face and shirt. It occurred to me immediately that Rudy had intentionally orchestrated the event at my expense, although I still do not understand his motivation.

The soda pop was easily wiped from my face with the assistance of a very thoughtful girl I'd seen in physics class. The problem, however, was that my shirt was also covered in soda. This was quite upsetting to me because my mother and I had put a great deal of thought into what shirt would be most appropriate for the event. After the soda incident happened, I decided to leave the party. There seemed to be a great many football players laughing at me, and I did not wish to be the butt of any more jokes.

The other thing I didn't tell Joe Turner about the night of the murder is of very minor significance as compared to the soda event, which honestly, I still find quite upsetting. Again, I emphasize that I answered each of Mr. Joe Turner's questions honestly. When he asked me if I saw any other players around Justin Holt's bedroom when I went to say goodbye to Justin, I answered truthfully since I had not seen any other players. However, I did not reveal that as I arrived at the front door to Justin's room, I observed Karen Sarkliss walking around the corner of the building. I believe she was accompanied by the thoughtful young woman from physics class who assisted me after the soda pop incident.

I do not believe Karen Sarkliss saw me. Otherwise, she may have said hello as there were not many people around. Under normal circumstances, I would have surely approached Karen Sarkliss since she is quite a wonderful person. However, I did not for two reasons.

First, earlier in the evening, I attempted to say hello to Karen Sarkliss as her presence at the party was one of the main reasons for my attendance. However, when I said hello to her, she appeared to pretend not to notice me. I have noticed in the past, she seems reticent to interact with me socially when we are around other students. I have no idea why that would be, but as someone who does not find socializing enjoyable, I certainly did not want to subject Karen Sarkliss to unwanted interaction.

Second, the soda pop incident left me quite untidy. As I mentioned, that was especially unfortunate because it ruined the appearance of my shirt that my mother and I had chosen.

Anyway, Karen Sarkliss being quite a wonderful person, I always try to look presentable when I am in her presence. At that time, I was not and so did not attempt to say hello to her again.

As to why I did not reveal the soda pop incident or seeing Karen Sarkliss outside Justin's bedroom to Joe Turner, both were occurrences that I have forgotten, although not in the traditional sense of the word. For episodes in my life that I do not enjoy, I have the unique ability to nearly erase them from my consciousness. I say nearly because in quiet moments like this one, I can conjure their memories.

Both of these events were decidedly negative—the soda pop incident because I was the butt of a joke and seeing Karen Sarkliss because I believed she did not wish to interact with me and because of the appearance of my shirt.

CHAPTER 82

During Joe's walk to court, Chuck called. "Hey, I heard you had a juror issue. Anything I should know about?"

Joe stopped in his tracks. "Chuck, how the hell did you know about that?"

The investigator laughed. "C'mon, Joe. This is Barton. It was all over Nadine's. Something about a bully on the jury. People are taking bets it's the big burly guy in the front row."

"Unbelievable."

"Okay, see ya, Joe. I got to go place a bet."

Joe shook his head. Holler whispers. He walked back to court wondering about the leak at the courthouse. He thought the bailiff or clerk were unlikely candidates. In their own way, Barbara and Alvin took pride in their jobs. He also didn't see how the leak would benefit Pettigrew or Boniface. They both seemed in favor of a quick and tidy conviction without controversy.

A more likely scenario was one of the jurors. Probably just an innocent comment to a spouse. But in the back of Joe's mind, the prospect of jury tampering by the Ledbetters loomed.

Soon, he was back in Judge Boniface's chambers, this time crowded with the judge, the court reporter,

Pettigrew, Alvin, and the hulking presence of Dirk Pinion. After some introductory remarks on the record, the judge read the jury note aloud. "Mr. Pinion, we wanted to give you an opportunity to respond. In your response, please do not reveal how you or any other jurors are leaning in terms of the verdict."

The big man sat with his forearms crossed and resting on his belly. His face was fixed in a contemptuous smile. He wore jeans, a red and black plaid shirt, and new looking work boots. "My response is that jury is filled with the biggest passel of feeble-minded, gutless pricks I've ever seen," he said, with a sneer. "You've got a retard, a fag, a…"

"Okay, Mr. Pinion," the judge cut in. "We don't need any more of that. You're excused from jury service, sir."

Pinion stood and moved toward the door where Alvin blocked his path. The deputy stood defiantly, hands on hips. "Hold on, I'm not finished," the judge said. The big man continued to face away from the judge, looking down at the bailiff with a smirk.

"Mr. Pinion, I'm ordering you not to discuss your deliberations until the conclusion of this trial," he said, sternly. "Any violation of this order and I will hold you in contempt. Am I clear?"

"Yeah," came the gruff reply as Pinion pushed past Alvin and out of the room.

The judge shook his head. "The first alternate, Mr. Moffatt, will replace Mr. Pinion. We're off the record. We need to get the alternate down here. Alvin, you can tell the jury they have the morning off. They can start again after lunch."

Joe was parsing the juror's words in his mind as he left the courthouse. Usually, descension among jurors was good for the defense. Six jurors had signed the note, but he cautioned himself not to read too much into it. No matter which way they were leaning, Pinion's hateful speech would have been untenable for any jury.

At lunch time, Joe texted Aubrey Ledbetter. —*Hey, have you heard anything about an issue with a juror?*

The response was immediate. —*No, why?*

CHAPTER 83

Day Ten

"So, Gregory Moffatt, I suppose it's welcome to the jury," Jack announced from his seat at the head of the table. A few others nodded without enthusiasm at the new arrival, a thin, fidgety man in his late thirties.

"Well, thank y'all," Moffatt said, rubbing his hands together. "I have a feeling my take on the trial might be a tad different from yours, but we'll see." His eyes darted around the room, looking for a reaction. The jurors stared, sizing up the newcomer.

Jack continued, undaunted. "Well, Gregory, we usually start things off with a quick vote. We currently stand at three for guilty—Frank, Duncan, and Ellen—and four for not guilty—me, Sara, Priya and Elston. Quinn is, um, still unsure."

"So, any changes of heart overnight?"

"Which never happens," grumbled Sara.

"Actually," said Ellen, "I'm switching to not guilty."

"You're joking?" asked Frank with disgust. "What happened, Ellen?"

"Well, … you all know I've been very stressed about this decision. And I know I shouldn't really consider this, but last night, I got a random email. It was a link to a website for the Innocence Project. Do you all know that since 1973, 190 people have been wrongly convicted of murder?"

"Wow," said Duncan. "That's something, Ellen. How interesting."

"I just couldn't live with myself if I voted to convict and I was wrong."

"Are you serious?!" said Frank. "What does that have to do with this case? Jesus, Ellen, use your head!"

"Easy, Frank," Duncan scolded.

"Yeah, Frank," added Jack. "There's no cause to be insulting."

The former military man showed his palms. "Apologies, but most of those convictions were overturned based on DNA evidence. In our case, the DNA evidence points to the defendant!"

"Not the way I see it," said Priya. "Did you listen to the paramedic?"

"Oh, Christ, this is too much," Frank said, shaking his head. He folded his arms and stared hard at Jack. "So, Ellen, who sent you this email?"

"I'm not sure."

"Oh, I think I might have an idea," Frank said, holding his stare.

"So," Jack said, pretending not to notice, "I'd like to hear from…"

"And I suppose you're not far behind, Duncan," Frank interrupted.

"I make my own decisions," snapped the paramedic, glaring.

Jack spoke up again. "Okay people, tensions are running high. Let's hear from our new juror."

"Well, you can count me on the side of the prosecution, although not for the reasons you might think," Moffatt said with a smug smile.

"Awesome," Sara said, sarcastically, "so we're back to five to three."

Priya sighed. "I feel like this may never end."

Gregory spoke up again. "So, if anyone is curious, I have a feeling my theory of the case is something you probably haven't considered."

"You've said that twice now, and you're clearly excited to tell us," Sara grumbled. "So, let's hear it."

Moffatt leaned forward, resting his elbows on the table, fingers steepled in front of his face as if deep in thought. "What is missing from the prosecution's case?"

"Motive," Priya said.

"Precisely. Which means he must have committed the murder on behalf of someone else," Moffatt said, his eyes searching the room for approval.

Sara frowned. "Or, he didn't have a motive and someone else did it."

"Ah, that's what they want you to think," the store manager said. "Don't fall into that trap."

"You've lost me," said Duncan. "Who's they?"

"The conspirators," Moffatt said, as if the answer was obvious. "There is a massive conspiracy afoot here." Around the room, eyebrows raised as the jurors exchanged looks of concern.

"Dude, what the fuck are you talking about?" asked Sara.

Moffatt smirked. "I knew none of you saw it. It jumped out at me from the beginning, of course, but I have unique powers of perception. The Justin Holt murder is the product of a conspiracy carried out by a secret cabal that runs Daulton County. Don't you see it?" he asked, looking around the room. "Carl Ledbetter committed this murder at the direction of the conspirators."

Frank smiled wide. "Makes perfect sense to me. I'll take my guilty votes any way I can get them."

"So, Gregory," Jack said politely, "perhaps I'm missing something. By conspiracy, do you mean by people who we haven't heard about in this trial? Because that seems…"

"Of course!" Moffatt exclaimed. "This case isn't about just a murder of a high school student. It goes much deeper than that. These people control every aspect of society. The legislature, education, the judiciary."

The room fell silent as the jurors tried to make sense of Moffatt's pronouncements. Outwardly, he appeared normal, but his grasp on reality seemed tenuous. "Oh, boy," Elston said, under his breath. "Now what?"

"Greg," Priya finally said pleasantly, "please don't take this the wrong way, but by any chance are you on medication?"

Moffatt was shaking his head before Priya had finished her question. "I knew that would be the reaction. It's always about my medication. 'Gregory, you should see someone. Gregory, wouldn't medication help? Gregory, you're not making sense.' But that's what the conspirators want you to believe!" His voice now dripped with desperation. "It's classic misinformation! Why am I the only one who can see it? If you'll just listen," he said, looking around the room, "you'll hear the truth."

He prattled on about his conspiracy for thirty minutes, never mentioning a single trial witness or item of evidence until Jack called for a break. The jurors filed out in a fog, dejected with the realization that a verdict was further away than ever.

CHAPTER 84

August 26, 2025, The Night of the Murder

Justin Holt's burnout on football had made his recent fling with Sophie Montgomery all the more alluring. They'd first met when partnered together for a presentation in government class. Justin found her interesting, intelligent, and sexy, in a very non-cheerleader sort of way. With no blonde hair, pink bows, or fake smiles, she was really the anti-cheerleader. Her most attractive trait was one Justin envied. Sophie Montgomery did not care what people thought of her. She wore black lipstick because she liked it, and Justin thought that was hot—her attitude and the lipstick. She was absolutely true to herself.

As Justin showered in preparation for his latest rendezvous, guilty thoughts crept in. To be sure, he felt bad about cheating on Karen. He planned to break it off with her, but the middle of homecoming week seemed like terrible timing.

More than anything, he was excited to see Sophie. The more time they spent together, the more he liked her. With the SAT tomorrow morning, Karen had already gone home, and they wouldn't be disturbed. Out of his bedroom shower in the converted guest house, he'd just pulled on his pants when he heard a knock at the door. Justin checked his watch, his heart pounding. She was a little early. Even better.

CHAPTER 85

Day Eleven
The newly constituted jury had spent its first two days together spinning its wheels. Sara, Priya, Elston, Jack, and Ellen were firmly in the not guilty camp. Frank, Duncan, and now newcomer Greg Moffatt remained staunchly for conviction. Quinn had still yet to cast a vote.

It was Moffatt's nonsensical ramblings that had the group more discouraged than ever. It was one thing to disagree about the evidence. With Dirk Pinion around, while their discourse had been uncivilized, at least the argument had been based in reality. Moffatt's grandiose conspiracy theory seemed impossible to overcome. The group had unwittingly traded a bully for a lunatic, and now rational debate seemed impossible.

Returning after a lunch break, Jack found Moffatt alone, smoking on the side of the courthouse. Jack approached the new juror cautiously, looking around furtively, as if checking for spies. He stopped at arm's length and turned to stand with his back to Greg. "Did anyone follow you here, Greg?"

"What do you mean?"

"You can't be too careful, am I right? Listen, Greg, I'm well aware of the conspiracy. Like you said, no one can be trusted."

"Finally, someone with some sense," Moffatt said, taking a drag on his cigarette.

"One thing, though," said Jack. "Ask yourself who's behind the conspiracy and what they want?"

"I told you. It involves everyone. From our congressional representative to the mayor, the judge. Everyone."

Jack was nodding, enthusiastically. "Yes, and what do they all worship, Greg? What is this town's obsession?"

"Football?" Moffatt asked, tentatively.

"Bingo." Jack again made a show of looking secretive. "Listen, Greg, you're one hundred percent right about the conspiracy. As you put it, this entire trial is a sham. But the question is, what do they want us to believe?"

Moffatt stood silently for several seconds. "I'm not sure I follow," he whispered.

"This town needs this murder solved, Greg." Jack waited in silence, praying his gambit was working.

Finally, a flash of recognition appeared on Moffatt's face. "He's a patsy," he whispered.

"Exactly! The real killer is likely…"

"Yes!" Greg cut in. "The real killer was used by the conspirators, and now they need someone to blame."

"Now, Greg, I don't have to tell you that this conversation has to remain between us. The rest of those idiots in the jury room will never see it this way. They don't have our vision."

"You're right." Moffatt nodded. "They don't want to believe that all of their lives are being controlled."

"Exactly. So, let's just work on getting this innocent kid acquitted using language they understand. We can reference the evidence and all that crap, even though we know it's a sham."

Moffatt dropped his cigarette to the ground and stepped on it. "Sounds good. And hey, after this trial is over, I'd like to talk to you about other aspects of the conspiracy. It's nice to finally meet someone who realizes what's going on."

"I look forward to it, Greg."

CHAPTER 86

August 26, 2025, The Night of the Murder
Justin opened the door ready to see Sophie and was startled. From there, everything felt surreal and confusing. After an awkward exchange of "high bar" greetings, things got even weirder.

"You can have anything you want, can't you? You're so handsome, sexy, and smart." The sweet words did not match his guest's hateful tone.

"Listen, I really don't think…"

"Everything comes easy for you, doesn't it, Justin? Girls, grades, your golden arm. You make it look easy. Isn't that what the scouts say?" A hand extended, touching his bare chest, tracing down his stomach. Justin stood speechless, his mind racing.

"Anything you want is yours, isn't it, Justin? Any college, any girl."

The attack caught him completely unawares. Justin's hands were at his sides when a quick step closed the gap between them. He had no time to process. A flash of metal caught his eye then something cold and hard against his chest. He felt a strange reverberation as his flesh absorbed the bullet's impact, his last sensation before the back of his head hit the floor.

CHAPTER 87

Day Twelve

After returning from lunch, the usual debate among the jurors continued. For once, Greg wasn't droning on about his conspiracy theory, so the focus returned to the evidence and then to the standard of proof.

Sara stood and walked to the water cooler. "For me, the standard of proof is so high. Given all the questions about the evidence, I just don't see how you can say you don't have a reasonable doubt."

"I'll tell you how," said Frank. "Just like the DA said, it's the accumulation of the evidence. Sure, there are questions about most of the evidence, but there's just so much of it that points to Carl? Is it just a coincidence that Carl was the person whose finger was in the pulse gadget? Maybe. But is it also a coincidence that it was Carl who ran from the scene? That's stretching it. But now you tell me it was also Carl who took the victim's pulse and got gunshot residue on his hands?" The former military man shook his head. "I'm not buying it."

Ellen spoke up. "So, Frank, what changed my mind is this. Say we all vote to convict, and Carl is taken from his family and goes off to prison for the rest of his life. We'll all go home and go about living our lives again. The question is, will you wonder whether we made the right decision?"

To Ellen's left, Duncan sighed heavily. "You know, I think I agree with you. I'm changing to not guilty."

Frank snorted. "It was only a matter of time."

"What's that's supposed to mean?" Duncan snapped.

"Oh, please, Duncan. You've been hitting on Ellen since day one."

"Hey, Frank," Jack cut in as Duncan blushed, "let's not get personal."

Frank rubbed his neck and grimaced. "So, now it's just me and Greg's conspiracy theory? Great," he grumbled sarcastically.

Greg looked at Jack, who subtly nodded. "My conspiracy theory is anything but crazy," Greg countered, "but I'm for not guilty now."

The group sat in stunned silence. "Wow," Sara finally said, stifling a laugh, "I guess I don't really care why anyone votes to acquit. The fact is, it's now seven to one, with Quinn's abstention."

Frank was shaking his head. "This is unbelievable," he said, glaring at Jack. "Something's going on, and I don't like it."

"So, about this abstention," said Duncan, looking down the table at Quinn. "I mean, I don't want to insult you, buddy, but eventually, you kind of have to vote."

Quinn bowed his head and angled his body away from the group. "He will when he's ready," Sara said, patting his shoulder.

Sensing they were close to a verdict, the jurors continued through the afternoon without a break. They took turns lobbying Frank to change his vote. He was slowly losing his resolve, but at 4:00 p.m., he remained unconvinced.

"Okay," Frank said, addressing the group. "Here's where I'm at. I grant you there are different interpretations of the scientific evidence. I'm willing to concede the possibility that the DNA and gunshot residue were transferred. But there's one piece of evidence I can't get past.

"Butch Ford, the kid that was taking a piss outside Justin's bedroom. He said he heard Justin say 'Hi, Carl,' through the open window. That means that Justin was alive when Carl was in his room. If someone can explain away that evidence, I'll change my vote."

The jury room was silent for a full minute.

At the end of the table, Quinn shifted in his seat and turned to look at Sara.

"What is it?" she asked. "Do you have something to say?"

Quinn folded his arms and stared at the table, feeling the eyes of the room on him. Then he breathed deeply, cleared his throat, and spoke to the group for the first time since introducing himself two weeks ago.

"Maybe Butch Ford heard Justin say, 'High bar.'"

CHAPTER 88

As the deliberation dragged on, Joe's concern about juror tampering by the Ledbetters weighed heavily on his mind. He wanted a not guilty verdict more than in any other case. But he wasn't willing to turn a blind eye to fraud. Not only could he lose his license to practice law, but jury tampering would also cheapen Carl's justice.

He knew Aubrey had lied when she denied hearing about the juror issue. If the news was all over Nadine's, then the Ledbetters would certainly have known.

With Eddy's research in Tallahassee completed, she was back in town. On her advice, Joe met the issue head on. "Aubrey, I'll get to the point. I'm concerned that you have contacted a member of the jury in order to sway the verdict."

"I know you are, Joe," she replied, coyly.

"Well?"

"For the record," replied Aubrey, "I am absolutely unaware of any contact with a juror. There has been no jury tampering by any member of our family."

Joe paused, still suspicious. "For the record, huh? What does that mean?"

Aubrey laughed. "Oh, Joe, you're a litigator to the end," she said, kicking up her Southern drawl. "I'm sure I wouldn't know the first thing about how to influence a jury."

"Aubrey, really," Joe pressed. His tone was serious. "I need to know."

"I stand by my answer," Aubrey said, quietly. "But someday I hope you experience a mother's love."

Great, thought Joe. Her comment was basically an admission. But if the Ledbetters had managed to tamper with the jury, it hadn't exactly yielded a swift result. The deliberation had reached the twelfth day.

Each time Joe's phone buzzed over the past week, he'd cringed, desperately hoping it wasn't the court with news of a verdict. As with most trials, he'd welcome a hung jury—anything to keep Carl free, even if only in the short term.

Joe was reading on the porch when he received the call, the court's number on his screen. He held his breath. Please, not a verdict. "Hello, Mr. Turner." He recognized the clerk's voice. "The jury has reached a verdict."

He texted Aubrey, who immediately called. "What do you think?" she asked, fear in her voice. "I've been trying to stay strong for Carl," she said, her voice cracking, "but I don't know if I can face this."

"You can, Aubrey. If it's a guilty verdict, Carl will need you more than ever."

"Oh, God," she said, dissolving into tears. "Don't say that."

"Listen, Aubrey. You need to pull it together. I'll see you guys at the courthouse. Boniface wants us there before 5:00 p.m."

Eddy walked in from a run as Joe was pulling on a suit. "Oh, shit. A verdict?"

Joe nodded. "Can you drive? I'm not sure I'm up to it."

Eddy walked to him and held his face in both hands. "Joe Turner, you did your best. Remember that."

Ten minutes later, Joe greeted the Ledbetters outside the packed courtroom. Aubrey was holding her son's hand. Joe hadn't seen Carl since the closing arguments. He'd lost weight and looked exhausted.

Joe nodded to his client. "Okay, Carl, let's go in." Aubrey hugged her son, holding him in a long embrace.

Joe and Carl walked up the center aisle of the courtroom side by side, hearing the whispers of conversation as they passed. They took their familiar seats at the counsel table opposite Pettigrew, who was pretending to read something from a file. Behind Joe, Carl's parents took their usual seats in the front row.

"All rise." Alvin's voice boomed throughout the courtroom with more gusto than ever as the judge took the bench. "The Superior Court of the State of Georgia, County of Daulton, Judge Franklin Boniface presiding, is now in session. You may be seated."

"Ladies and gentlemen," the judge began, "before we begin, I want to make clear that we will have order in this courtroom throughout the proceedings. There will be no outbursts. Alvin, please bring in the jury."

A theory common among attorneys is that you can predict the verdict by looking at the jurors as they file into court. If the jurors look at the defendant, it's an acquittal. If they avoid eye contact, it's a conviction. Joe had found this to be true in nearly all his trials. This time, though, he couldn't bring himself to look in the jurors' direction.

"Mr. Painter, I understand you are the foreman."

"Yes, Your Honor," Jack said.

"And my bailiff has informed me you have a verdict. Is this true?"

"Yes, Your Honor."

"Then please give the verdict forms to the bailiff." There were two forms. One for guilty, one for not guilty. One was signed and one was not. Alvin took an envelope from Jack and handed it to Boniface. The judge opened the envelope in front of his microphone, the crackling paper echoing throughout the silent courtroom. He looked at one form then the other, remaining expressionless.

"The defendant will please rise," the judge said, as he handed one form down to his clerk.

Joe breathed deeply and looked to his left where Carl was rocking rapidly, staring straight ahead. Attorney and client then stood in unison, shoulder to shoulder. Barbara put on her reading glasses and cleared her throat. "Superior Court of Georgia, County of Daulton. In the case of The State of Georgia versus Stanley Carl Ledbetter, we, the jury, find the defendant not guilty."

"Yes!" Joe whispered. Carl collapsed in his chair, his face in his hands. Joe heard Aubrey's sobs of joy behind him. He put a hand on Carl's back and half listened to Boniface thanking the jury for their service.

"Ladies and gentlemen," Boniface said, addressing the jury, "the attorneys may or may not want to speak to you in the jury room. Often, they learn from your feedback. Feel free to talk to them about the case, but you are certainly under no obligation to do so. With that, we are adjourned." Boniface banged his gavel one final time. "Will counsel approach?" Joe shot a questioning look at Pettigrew, who shrugged.

"Ms. Pettigrew, you prosecuted a good case. And Mr. Turner, you're a fine attorney," the judge said when they'd reached the bench. "I don't expect to see you again, but you're certainly welcome in our courtroom."

Stunned, Joe mumbled a thank you. "It's been something, Judge."

"Do me a favor, though," Boniface said with a twinkle in his eye. "When you're jogging, watch out for old men on bicycles."

CHAPTER 89

Joe rarely missed an opportunity to speak to the jury after a trial. When he lost, however difficult to take, he learned from the jurors' input. When the verdict was in his client's favor, he learned less, but reveling in the victory was fun.

By the time Alvin escorted him into the small room, most of the jury had cleared out. The foreperson and the social worker remained, along with the schoolteacher and the paramedic, who appeared to be exchanging phone numbers. "You did a great job," the foreperson said, gathering his belongings. "This was quite an experience."

"I'm sure," Joe said. "Apparently, some of your deliberation was unpleasant. I'm sorry about that, but I appreciate your diligence. I don't want to keep you, but was there one piece of evidence that you thought was the key?"

"The paramedic, of course," the foreman said.

"Yes," Joe nodded. "Thank goodness for him."

"It's funny," the social worker added. "The final piece of the puzzle came from Quinn. He was the super shy guy. Maybe on the spectrum."

"Really?" asked Joe, recalling the young man who spoke in a monotone and wore the patriotic watch band. "I wouldn't have guessed that."

"Us either," Sara said. "Out of nowhere, this afternoon, after literally not speaking for two weeks, he says, 'Instead of hearing "Hi, Carl," maybe he heard, "High bar."' That hadn't occurred to anyone, but once we heard it, it seemed so obvious."

Joe smiled at his good fortune. "I know the feeling."

Outside the courthouse, Joe was greeted with a kiss from Eddy and tearful hugs from the Ledbetters.

Coach Clint Burgess approached. "High bar, y'all. The team is headed over to Skeeters for some barbecue. Carl, we'd love it if you joined us."

"What do you say, Carl?" his dad asked. "They got a few big screens at Skeeters. I'm sure we could get the Cubs game on."

"Mother, I…"

"Carl, speak directly to your coach," Aubrey said, firmly.

"Coach Burgess, thank you for your invitation, but I would rather watch the Cubs game at my home with my earbuds to prevent distraction."

The coach smiled. "Suit yourself, Carl, but the team would love to see you there."

"I would imagine the cheer squad will be there too, Carl," his dad said casually, winking at Aubrey.

"Oh, I'm sure they will," the coach agreed.

Carl thought for a moment. "Perhaps we should go then."

"Skeeters it is!" announced Aubrey.

"Hey, Audrey," said Eddy, "I'm desperate to change out of these sweaty clothes. Can Joe ride with you, and I'll meet you there later?"

"Of course!"

Joe found Luke Stuckey, who was standing nearby with his parents and other football players. "Hi, Stuckeys. Luke, I wanted to say that I apologize for putting you through that and, um…" He paused.

"Blaming me for the murder?" Luke asked with a good-natured smile. "No worries."

"Joe, we know you were just doing your best for Carl," said Coach Stuckey, "and we appreciate it."

"We surely do," Monica added with less enthusiasm.

Joe and Aubrey walked through the court parking lot to the Ledbetters' SUV. A small truck pulled up a few spaces away. "Hi there, Aubrey," the driver said. "Congrats to y'all. I just heard."

"Thanks, Liz! We're just so relieved. Honestly, I think it's still sinking in."

A young man was approaching the truck from the direction of the courthouse. Joe thought he looked familiar but couldn't place him right away.

Then it came to him.

"High bar, Mrs. Ledbetter," the young man said as he reached the truck and got in.

"Hi, Quinn."

CHAPTER 90

Inside the Ledbetter's SUV, Joe locked eyes with Aubrey. "What?" Aubrey finally said, but Joe held his stare. "Oh, Joe," she added, rolling her eyes. "Don't be paranoid. Quinn is mildly autistic. Liz and I were in a mother's group."

"And it just happened to be Quinn who came up with 'High bar?'"

Aubrey turned away and shrugged. "Holler whispers, I suppose."

Joe sighed. He recalled telling Aubrey about his "High bar, Hi Carl" revelation. "Surely, something can be done," she'd said, and Joe had heard desperation in her voice.

On the way to Skeeter's, Joe rode in silence, resolved to sort out his jury tampering concerns once and for all. Thankfully, while Aubrey had admitted to knowing Quinn and his mom, she'd stopped short of saying that Quinn knew Carl. In jury selection, Quinn had stated under oath that he didn't know any of the parties. If Joe had evidence to the contrary, he'd have to report it.

Also, while Joe strongly suspected Aubrey had passed along "high bar" to Quinn, he had no solid proof of it. Still, deep down, he knew.

Joe turned to look at Carl in the back seat. Earbuds in, he looked markedly different from the intense young man Joe had known. The tension was gone from his face. Instead of rocking in his seat, he reclined comfortably, gazing out the window, the hint of a smile on his lips.

As Aubrey's SUV rolled through the sleepy streets of Barton, Joe stared into space and considered disaster narrowly escaped. A collage of images filled his mind— Carl looking plaintively at his mother as he was led away in handcuffs, then frightened and victimized in prison, desperately covering his ears from the screams of the insane and the clangs of the metal bars.

Joe blinked away the horrors and turned to look at Carl again. Cubs cap slightly askew, his head lolled peacefully with the motion of the car. Then a subtle fist pump for the Cubs game in his ear.

At that moment, Joe settled any concerns of jury tampering in his mind. Although he loathed the term "plausible deniability," in this case, he would make an exception. He looked at Aubrey and smiled. "A mother's love," he whispered to himself.

CHAPTER 91

At Skeeters, a down-home place with picnic benches on a cement floor, Joe found Chuck sitting with a pitcher of beer and three glasses.

"So let me get this straight," the investigator said. "There was DNA, gunshot residue, an incriminating statement…"

"And an eyewitness," Joe added.

"And he walks?" Chuck asked, rhetorically. "Inconceivable!"

"The Princess Bride," Joe answered, beaming. "And I have to admit, I had my doubts about this one."

They ordered ribs and hush puppies, drank their beer, and talked about the trial.

"So, I've been thinking about this murder," Chuck said after Eddy had joined them.

"Here we go," Joe said, rolling his eyes.

Eddy looked confused. "Did I miss something."

Joe shook his head. "After every trial that ends well, Chuck feels the need to solve the crime."

"I'm sorry, but this is my hometown," the PI said, "and there's a murderer on the loose. Are we all just supposed to say, 'It's not our problem?'"

"As a matter of fact, yes," Joe said with a laugh. "That's exactly what we're supposed to say. Seriously, Chuck, I want to drink beer and eat barbecue and not think about anything."

"Oh, you're no fun," said Eddy. "I'm with Chuck. It's a fascinating mystery."

"It really is." Chuck nodded.

"Oh, Christ, okay." Joe threw up his hands. "We know it wasn't Luke Stuckey," he said, lowering his voice. "The gas station video proved that."

"Which leaves Clem Tettleton," said Chuck, refilling their glasses. "I believe he admitted to you his alibi was BS."

Eddy shook her head emphatically. "Why not?" Chuck asked. "He admitted he knew how to mess with his GPS."

"Call it woman's intuition," Eddy said. "I'm afraid I got skunk-sprayed for nothing."

"Speaking of Clem," Joe said, "his observations seemed pretty solid. I believe him when he says he saw the killer walk out of Justin's room then around the main house toward the street."

"Where he heard a car door slam," added Eddy, nodding, "then a car with a bad engine drive away, sputtering and backfiring."

"Okay, so who was it?" Chuck asked.

After a gulp of beer, Joe looked out across the restaurant filled with teenagers. The boys sat in small groups, laughing, shouting, and teeming with testosterone. Girls flitted about, steeped in drama, flashing fake smiles and emitting the occasional scream. "A lot of teenage angst out there," he said. "Probably countless motives."

Soon, their conversation turned to Eddy's harrowing skunk encounter then Chuck's football career. Finally, filled with pork and beer, they headed toward the exit where the Ledbetters were just leaving.

Joe saw Aubrey whisper something to Carl and gesture toward him. He walked to Joe with his tilted gait. "Joe, my mother says I should thank you for your representation. It occurs to me you were financially compensated for your efforts, so thanking you for completing a business transaction seems odd. However, social conventions are important to my mother, and so I honor them scrupulously."

Joe smiled. "I've heard that about you, Carl. Thanks."

Carl started to speak again but stopped then stood in awkward silence. "Was there something else, Carl?"

"Yes. I know I am not always easy to interact with. I wanted to say that I have found you to be quite a wonderful person."

Joe put his hand over his heart. "Carl, it has been my pleasure," he said, shaking his hand. "Good luck to you. And the Cubs!"

Outside Skeeters, the night was heavy and damp with tule fog. Feeling nostalgic, Joe decided to walk home. While he longed for a good bagel and Thai food, he knew part of him was going to miss Barton—the Southern manners, soft air, and Sweet Sally's rolls. More than anything, he'd miss the slow pace of the place.

Outside Skeeters, Luke Stuckey stood leaning against a street sign. "Hi, Luke. Still not driving, I see," Joe kidded, as he walked past.

"No sir, still waiting for taxi rides."

As Joe walked away, his thoughts returned to the unsolved murder of Justin Holt. Despite his protests to Chuck, it had never really left his mind. While Joe never doubted Carl's innocence, he marveled at the coincidences that nearly had him serving a life sentence.

But who had Justin greeted with "High bar" shortly before being shot? He reviewed the case in his mind—the scientific evidence then the accounts of Sinclair Lewis, Butch Ford, and Clem Tettleton. Then, three words he'd heard very recently chimed to him through the fog.

Retracing his steps, Joe returned to the restaurant, where Luke still waited outside. "Hey, Luke," he asked casually, "what car did you leave your phone in?"

"Huh?" he asked, looking confused.

"You said you left your phone in someone's car the night of the murder. I was just wondering whose car it was?" Just then, a sleek roadster from the 50's pulled up at the curb. Joe could make out the peroxided locks of Monica Stuckey behind the wheel.

"Sorry, Mr. Turner." Luke shrugged. "I don't remember."

"Hi there, Joe," Monica called from the open window, as Luke climbed in. "Congrats again on the verdict!" she said, fake smile in place.

"Thanks, Monica. That's quite a car."

"Yeah. It's my husband's expensive hobby, but he lets me take it out once in a while. Take care!"

And with that, the vintage sports car was off down Main Street, coughing and backfiring as it sputtered away.

Joe nodded. "A mother's love."

CHAPTER 92

"What a crazy, vile bitch!" Eddy said with wide eyes. "Are you sure?"

On his walk home, Joe had contemplated that very question, doing his best to put aside his intense dislike of Monica Stuckey. That wasn't easy. From her pasted-on smile to her judgy looks and haughty air, she was a living embodiment of Joe's least favorite human traits. But was she a killer?

"Pretty sure," he said, settling in next to Eddy on the porch swing with a beer.

"So, what now? Can she be prosecuted?"

Joe shook his head. "Not nearly enough proof. Especially given her status as football royalty. She had motive, I suppose, but only if you assume that she'd kill to be the most important woman in Barton, Georgia."

Eddy smiled. "Which, when you say it out loud, is absurd, but go on."

"She has a car that backfires, but without Clem Tettleton's testimony, that fact is worthless. And she may have had opportunity, but there's no way to prove Luke left his phone in her car."

Eddy groaned. "Well, that sucks. Is there really nothing that can be done?"

"No." Joe shook his head but stopped abruptly then smiled at his girlfriend. "Unless…"

CHAPTER 93

The next morning, Joe braved the line at Sweet Sally's, ordered a medium coffee, then added cream and an ungodly amount of sugar. He sat facing the entrance with the undrinkable beverage resting on the table in front of him.

He heard the obnoxious cackle before she appeared in the doorway. As usual, Monica was lapping up attention as the patrons passed her on their way out of the shop. She wore designer jeans, high heels, and another of her collection of sparkly sweatshirts. This one was navy blue with QB1 spelled out in silver sequins. A belt buckle the size of a salad plate completed the gaudy ensemble, its large turquoise "B" encrusted with rhinestones.

Joe watched as she ordered her coffee and poured in the endless stream of sugar. Shit, she ordered a large. Joe was about to approach her when, to his surprise, Monica walked toward his table, strutting across the coffee shop like a runway model.

"Good morning," Joe said, mustering a pleasant tone.

"Hello, Joe." She took a seat at the table with her back to the entrance. The smile seemed more intentionally fake than usual. "You know, honey, Luke told me about your question last night." Now she was sneering.

"Excuse me?" Joe hadn't expected her going on the offensive.

"Your question about what car he left his phone in," she said with a smirk. "I suppose you're a tad bolder with a young boy than you are with me." Now, as she glared across the table, for an instant, Joe saw the dull eyes of a killer.

Joe sensed the brief meeting was nearing its end. It was now or never. Looking past her toward the entrance to the coffee shop, he waved to an imaginary person. When Monica turned to follow his gesture, Joe deftly switched their drinks then held his breath.

She turned back to face him and, for a split second, glanced at her coffee, a fleeting thought passing at the edge of her consciousness. Desperate to distract her, Joe said the first thing that popped into his head. "I love your hair," he said, drawing a look of total confusion.

The distraction worked. "You know, Joe," Monica said, regaining her menacing focus, "here in the South, one of the rudest things you can do is overstay your welcome."

While she spoke, Joe subtly turned the cup in front of him to obscure the pink lipstick smear on its lid. "Good to know," he said, barely able to contain his glee. He knew there would be plenty of Monica Stuckey's DNA on the lid to compare it to whoever scratched Justin Holt's chest before they shot him. And now, he was also certain of the result.

As she stood to leave, Joe thought of this glittery, peroxided monster taking an innocent life then sitting by as Carl suffered through the trial. "Oh, Monica?" he said, just as she turned on her heel.

"Yes?"

"Have a wonderful day," Joe said with a syrupy smile of his own.

ABOUT THE AUTHOR

T.L. Bequette is a criminal defense attorney turned writer from Lafayette, California. His award-winning Joe Turner Mysteries have received critical acclaim: "Bequette's prose is reliably crisp and descriptive, and lots of intrigue and suspense are embedded in a thrillingly serpentine story." –*Kirkus Reviews.*

Much of Bequette's law practice involves defending young men from Oakland accused of murder, so his day job provides a trove of plotlines waiting to be written. A Georgetown Law graduate, he serves annually on the faculty of the Stanford Law School Trial Advocacy Clinic.

He enjoys playing with a tireless Border Collie mix, Russet, and is, and will remain, a lifelong fan of the Oakland A's.

Other Titles by T.L. Bequette

NOTE FROM THE AUTHOR

Word-of-mouth is crucial for any author to succeed. If you enjoyed
Holler Whispers, please leave a review online—anywhere you are
able. Even if it's just a sentence or two. It would make all the
difference and would be very much appreciated.

Thanks!
T.L. Bequette

We hope you enjoyed reading this title from:

www.blackrosewriting.com

Subscribe to our mailing list – *The Rosevine* – and receive **FREE** books, daily deals, and stay current with news about upcoming releases and our hottest authors.
Scan the QR code below to sign up.

Already a subscriber? Please accept a sincere thank you for being a fan of Black Rose Writing authors.

View other Black Rose Writing titles at
www.blackrosewriting.com/books and use promo code
PRINT to receive a **20% discount** when purchasing.